AS SHADOWS GATHER

WORLDWALKERS: BOOK 2

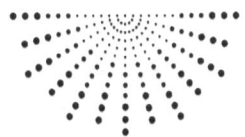

DANA ARDIS

This is a work of fiction. Names, characters, places, and incidents either are the product of author imagination or are used fictitiously, and any resemblance to actual persons, living or dead, business establishments, events, or locales, is entirely fictional.

As Shadows Gather
Copyright © 2021 Dana Ardis
All rights reserved.

This book is licensed to the original purchaser only. Duplication or distribution via any means is illegal and a violation of international copyright law, subject to criminal prosecution and upon conviction, fines, and/or imprisonment. No part of this book may be reproduced in any form or by any electronic or mechanical means, including information storage and retrieval system, without written permission from the author, except for the use of brief quotations in a book review, and where permitted by law.

PUBLISHER'S CATALOGING-IN-PUBLICATION DATA

Names: Ardis, Dana, author.

Title: As shadows gather / by Dana Ardis.

Description: First edition. | Feathered Dog Books, 2022.

Identifiers: ISBN 979-8-98-549360-3 (pbk.)

Subjects: Man-woman relationships – Fiction. | Kidnapping – Fiction. | Magic – Fiction. | Predation (Biology) – Fiction. | Ability – Fiction. | BISAC: FICTION / Fantasy / Romance.

To Andrew. I would follow you to any world.

To Mary, Shami, John, Emily, Scott, James, and Ryan, for your feedback and suggestions. Thank you.

CONTENTS

Chapter 1	1
Chapter 2	10
Chapter 3	26
Chapter 4	40
Chapter 5	44
Chapter 6	52
Chapter 7	62
Chapter 8	71
Chapter 9	78
Chapter 10	93
Chapter 11	97
Chapter 12	110
Chapter 13	115
Chapter 14	123
Chapter 15	133
Chapter 16	145
Chapter 17	161
Chapter 18	169
Chapter 19	175
Chapter 20	182
Chapter 21	195
Chapter 22	202
Chapter 23	208
Chapter 24	221
Chapter 25	227
Chapter 26	239
Chapter 27	253
Chapter 28	265
Chapter 29	273
Chapter 30	282
Glossary	289

CHAPTER ONE

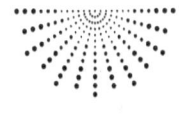

KATE

Let me take you home, I'd told Cor. It had sounded romantic when we'd both been giddy to find each other alive after our battle with the Hunters. Then we'd slipped from Kuyen, Cor's world—from the healer's rooms in the mansion that used to be Cor's home—to my low-rent, one-bedroom apartment in San Jose.

This was what he'd traded everything for when he'd defied his father to have a relationship with me. He'd given up the wealth and power he'd had as *denet*-heir, future leader of House Temarel and all his extended kin. Family was everything to a Thurei.

Well, not quite everything. A *dacha* came before blood and House.

Now Cor's *dacha* would be his only family. Me.

As soon as soon as we slipped back to my apartment on Earth, Cor wrapped his arms around me and dipped his head down for a kiss. I tilted my face up to his and leaned into his embrace, comforted by his lean strength and the steady thrum of his heartbeat. Fewer than twenty-four hours ago, he'd been ripped open by Hunters, almost killed because I hadn't mastered my skill fast enough to stop them.

He'd protected me for years and I'd almost gotten him killed the first time he'd relied on me. The Hiraches, one of Kuyen's predatory species, had almost won.

Not an auspicious start to our relationship.

I pulled back reluctantly, trying to ignore the tempting way his hands cupped my hips. I was supposed to be taking better care of him and I had specific instructions from the healer on what that meant for tonight: food and rest.

"Let me get you something to eat," I said.

Havro, a Lewrit with skills in healing, had greatly accelerated Cor's own recuperation, but Cor's body had still done the work. He needed to recover.

"I'm not hungry," he murmured against the curve of my neck, which was bared by the French twist that bound my shoulder-length, brown hair.

The warm brush of his breath on my skin swept every other thought right out of my mind.

"Coran," I whispered, using the most intimate form of his name, like a close friend or family member might in Kuyen.

Or a lover.

Not right now. I cleared my throat. "Food first, then you need to sleep."

"I'm yours to command, *dacha*." Cor dropped his hands and stepped back. He offered me a ridiculously low bow, his manner easy and charming, without the tension and worry he'd carried the last few weeks.

It was good to see him like this, even if it was only a temporary side effect of the healer's skill. I remembered that false calm from my own healing.

"My commands are pretty simple at the moment," I said.

Tugging him back to me, I gave him a chaste peck on the cheek before heading into my tiny kitchen. "Just sit down while I make some food."

He grabbed a chair from my secondhand dinette set and brought it over to the edge of the living room. Spinning it around, he folded his arms over the chair back, resting his chin on his wrist. His slit-pupiled, amber eyes shone brightly in the electric light, reflective like a cat's, and brought out the warm gold undertones in his skin. His features were too angular to be human, a narrow face with sharp cheekbones and a thin, straight mouth. Looking at him, I could only think how much I wanted to tease a grin to his lips with a kiss.

I wasn't going to get anything done if I just stood there and stared at him.

After a quick inventory of the fridge, I gathered a few ingredients and set a frying pan on the stove. I cracked a couple of eggs into a bowl, then whisked in a splash of milk, some cinnamon, sugar, and salt. Two slices of bread went in it to soak. It might have been nighttime here on Earth, but the sun rose on Kuyen when it set here, so technically, it was morning for Cor. Not that Kuyen had a traditional mealtime for French toast.

Since the question couldn't be put off forever, I asked, "So, do you think we'll have more Hiraches after us?"

"I'm not sure." The question sobered him a little. "Tharkesh, the kith's Finder, is dead, along with four of their strongest warriors. I don't know how many members are in their kith."

"Kith is the Hirach version of a Thurei House, right?" I asked.

Cor raised a bright-orange eyebrow at that. I could make a guess at his thoughts on the matter. *Hiraches aren't anything like my people.* But he just rippled his long fingers in a Thurei-style shrug.

"A similar idea, yes. They are both made up mostly of family, but Houses can number in the hundreds and kith are much smaller." He returned to my first question. "But are there too few to send more warriors after us? It matters, too, whether Tharkesh himself owed a service to the Scholars or if his kith as a whole carried the debt. Perhaps with the death of Tharkesh, the Scholars have lost their weapon."

I set the first slice of soaked bread into the hot pan. It sizzled and filled the kitchen with the satisfying aroma of something delicious and homemade. For a moment, I wished I were in a better frame of mind to enjoy it. "The Scholars tried to have us killed. Doesn't that count as breaking Truce, even if they used Hunters to do it? Can't we call the Kuyen police or something?"

Cor tilted his head, considering. I tried to imagine what I might have told him about police back when we'd been kids. It wasn't like we'd taken the time to discuss American law enforcement in the few weeks since we'd started talking to each other again.

The gap in translation only slowed him a moment, though. "Those who break Truce face justice from the leaders of their own people. I can bring an accusation against them, but…"

"But the Scholars are the leaders of the Sheverns." I slid the French toast out of the pan and onto a plate, then set two more slices into the skillet.

He nodded, human-style. "If we challenge the Hall, it's their word against the suspicions of two solitary individuals."

He'd used the term *solitary* to describe the former Scholar Issai, the Shevern who'd been exiled from the Scholars Hall because she'd defied her colleagues and refused to hide what she'd learned about humans.

Humans were unstable and dangerous, even considering Kuyen was a world with intelligent Hunters.

"We're not entirely solitary. There are two of us now."

"Ah, that's true." His gaze caught mine and he grinned, then sobered again. "But they would have listened more closely to a *denet*."

I didn't have an answer to that, and Cor lapsed into silence.

"What do we do in the meantime?" Sliding the last of the toast out of the pan, divided it between two plates, then handed Cor the taller stack. I grabbed the other plate and the butter dish and followed him over to the table.

"We stay careful. I'll bring the matter to the Sheverns." Cor cut a precise square of the French toast with his fork, as if he were at some posh Thurei function instead of safe in the home of his... someone he trusted. He popped the bite into his mouth and mumbled around it. "This is wonderful."

"Good. It's easy enough to make." I was glad to see I merited as least a little informality from him. "You're staying with Shom's *tol*, right?"

Cor had been kicked out of his House right before we'd fought the Hiraches, left scrambling to find a place to stay. As much as I would have welcomed him, he couldn't stay here. He—or anyone from Kuyen—could only visit Earth during my night, his day. Once the sun rose here, the way between worlds closed, wrenching any out-of-place worldwalkers back to their own worlds. Sometimes fatally.

"Yes, near the arena where Shom taught you your skill. Her *tol*, Pella, commands soldiers for the city of Aubello, to defend and to ensure the Truce. Pella offered me a place to stay and a chance for employment if I wish. As an instructor, not as a soldier."

He added the last with a glance up at me. I'd told him he couldn't be a soldier. He'd risked his life often enough over the years, pitting himself against the Hunters who'd come after me, attracted by the *jeira* that made me a worldwalker.

"So, you'll be someone else's Seretun?" I named his own mentor, thinking of how comfortable and satisfied Cor had seemed when he'd tutored or set up lessons for young Fosen and other cousins in his House.

Cor dropped his gaze to his plate. "Pella's troops are all trained and experienced. I'll be helping them practice, that's all."

"Oh." I'd stepped in it, reminding him of home. "Um, it sounds safe from Hunters, at least, being surrounded by all those soldiers."

"Very safe," he agreed. "And your apartment here is warded, so you'll be safe as well. The Scholars don't know where you are on Earth. You have the training now to hide the brightness of your *jeira*—you're doing well on that, Katen."

"They do know where I work, or at least Tharkesh did." I suppressed the rising memory of the Hunter lunging at me outside of After Image, the photography studio where I had a part-time job. He'd raked his claws over my back before I'd escaped through the staff door.

"The knowledge may have died with him," Cor said, but his expression had grown serious. "Be careful, Katen. Try... Try not to be alone there at night."

I nodded. Since I'd left Bayshore Psychiatric, I'd made it a habit of staying indoors at night, since that was the only time I "hallucinated." Now that I knew Kuyen—and Cor, and the Hunters—were real, I had an even better reason to stay somewhere safe.

Switching subjects, Cor lifted his last bite of toast on his fork. "Your dad used to make this."

"Yeah, he did." I hadn't thought about that in a long time. Sometimes, when I'd still been in first or second grade, he'd let me take a plate to my room for my "imaginary friends."

Back before my parents had decided I was crazy.

Cor lifted a hand, imperfectly hiding a monstrous yawn.

"This is the sleeping part the healer warned me about, right on schedule." I gathered the plates, waving him off when he tried to help. "It's my turn to play host."

"Thank you for your care." Fatigue shadowed his amber eyes, but he still managed a smile.

"No thanks are necessary, Coran." I brushed my fingers through his hair and he leaned into the caress like a cat. "I'm supposed to take good care of you, aren't I?"

"*Dacha.*" Cor tipped his head back to look up at me seriously. "You don't owe me anything."

"Of course I do," I said, shaking my head when he opened his mouth to continue. He meant his *dacha* vow, since I hadn't sworn one in return, but I owed him plenty. He'd saved my life, more than once. He'd been loyal for all the years I'd refused to see him. He had helped train me to defend myself. He loved me.

"The least I can do is make sure you're taken care of tonight." I reached for his hand and tugged him to his feet.

Cor slid his arms around my waist and warmth uncoiled inside me. I rested my forehead against his shoulder, treasuring the closeness for a moment.

"You need sleep," I told him, pulling away. Glancing at my bedroom door, I hesitated. "Should we stay here or go to your new place?"

'Whose bed?' seemed too personal to say out loud, vow or no vow.

"Ah." His gaze slid away from mine. "If you'll have me, I would prefer to stay here."

That was the first hint of misgiving I'd seen in him since he'd woken. Was the euphoria wearing off? Or was he that afraid I'd reject him?

"I want you to stay." I recaptured his hand to lace my fingers with his and led him the few steps to my bedroom.

Great, I didn't make my bed. I'd been a wreck this morning, just after leaving Cor with Havro. Before I could die of embarrassment, Cor sat heavily on the edge of the bed, like the walk across my postage-stamp-sized living room had been the final straw.

"Those clothes should do okay for pajamas," I said. He still wore the clothes Havro had given him, a loose tunic and pants.

Cor nodded, his eyes half-closed.

"I'll go change," I said. "You get in bed. I'll just be a minute."

Maybe if I were braver, I could have just changed there, but we'd only shared our first kiss a couple of days ago. Instead, I grabbed my pajamas—off the floor, jeez, I needed to be a better housekeeper now—and headed to the bathroom.

I changed quickly and unwound the elegant hairdo. For a moment, my brown hair, brown eyes made me feel too...human, but I pushed the thought away.

When I got back to my bedroom, Cor had snuggled under the rumpled covers, his head on one of my pillows. Fast asleep. His eyelids didn't even flutter when I flicked off the ceiling light.

I climbed into bed as carefully as I could, feeling downright virtuous in letting him rest.

As soon as I settled, though, he rolled over and reached for me, murmuring something in Thurei. I didn't know the words, but his meaning was clear enough. I scooted toward him until we nestled comfortably together. Cor gave a satisfied sigh before his breathing slipped back into the slow rhythm of sleep.

That made one of us, at least.

By all rational metrics, I was pretty tired, too. I'd been off of work for the last two weeks, after the Hirach had attacked me outside the shop where I worked. After Havro had healed the slash across my back, I'd trained with Cor, learning my skill so that the Hunters wouldn't be able to catch me helpless again.

It almost hadn't worked. Cor's father had given me a time limit and I hadn't been able to master my skill as well as we'd hoped.

The Hunters had gutted Cor before I could disbelieve them out of existence.

Even with all my practice disbelieving Cor and his world, I'd almost failed.

Today had been my first day back at work at the end of my medical leave. I'd spent the entire shift counting down the daylight hours, unsure if Cor had survived.

I should have been tired. I *was* tired.

Also, vibrantly, electrically awake and intensely conscious of the heat of Cor's body against mine, the subtle way he shifted with his breathing, the weight of his arm draped over my waist. His breath ruffled my hair. His heartbeat reverberated against my back, so softly I had to concentrate to feel it. With both of us in pajamas, the only place our skin touched was the curve of my instep right above his ankle.

It was by far the sexiest my foot had ever felt. No wonder Victorian ladies had had to keep their ankles hidden.

A few weeks ago, Cor's ex-fiancée had insulted us—the worst of insults, Cor had said—by offering us a guest room with a single bed in it. She'd known I was Cor's *dacha*, while Cor was my… nothing official. Nothing that could make the offer of a bed honorable.

Maybe I shouldn't have been here, thinking about…his ankles.

Cor didn't stir as I climbed carefully out of bed. I headed out into the living room to get some paper and a pen. If I was going to be awake anyway, I had some questions I needed to ask and I hoped I knew someone who could answer them. Afterward, I could get back in bed and do a better job staying on my side.

CHAPTER TWO

COR

Something tugged at me, drawing me toward wakefulness. I tried to roll over, but a warm weight pinned me in place.

I was not in bed alone.

I must be dreaming. It didn't feel like a dream. Opening my eyes, I found myself staring at the plain, white ceiling of Katen's bedroom.

My *dacha* lay snuggled against my side with her head pillowed on my shoulder. Her right arm reached across my chest and her leg hooked around mine, a warm embrace that woke me the rest of the way up.

I'd dreamed of this—or at least something like it—quite a few times, but the present moment proved my imagination inept.

Unfortunately, it wasn't Katen's presence that had woken me. The approaching dawn pulled at me, an insistent tugging in my bones that would only grow worse if I lingered. The gap between worlds would close as the sun rose on Earth and set on Kuyen. If I failed to return on my own, I would be ripped from Earth back to my world.

"Katen," I whispered, brushing my fingertips across the back of her hand.

She stirred against me, still caught in sleep, and made a little, contented sound that might as well have been a touch the way it tingled across my skin. Then she looked up at me, her dark eyes wide and full of wonder.

"Good morning, dear heart." She smiled and pressed a kiss to my shoulder, her lips soft through the thin fabric of my tunic.

"Wait," I said, shifting a little. I could take care of these clothes in a moment.

Kate drew back, putting space between us, her hands spread as wide as a wall. "Sorry! I didn't mean…"

She trailed off, leaving me baffled. *Sorry* meant so little in English.

Understanding struck too late. Kate had taken pains to say she'd been offering me a place to sleep. Sleep, and nothing else. She knew the vow I'd sworn, all that I'd offered her. It was her choice now, to accept what she wished. She owed me nothing more than that.

In fact, she had kindly, subtly turned down my advances last night, when the side effects of the healing had turned me foolish.

"There's nothing to apologize for, Katen," I said gently, and I gave her the best smile I could manage. I sat up, putting more space between us, bunching the blanket into my lap. I should get out of her bed entirely, but even that self-discipline failed me. "You gave me company and care. That's not something to be sorry for, is it?"

"No. I'm glad you stayed." Kate's lips curved in an achingly sweet smile. She sat up, sweeping her tousled waves of brown hair out of her face. Then she glanced up at the window, where the predawn glow leaked around the edges of the closed blinds.

"I should go." The tug of the coming sun grew with each passing moment. Reluctantly, I climbed out of her bed.

"Wait." Kate moved to the edge of the mattress and held out her hand.

Unsure what she wanted, I took it. With a quiet laugh, she tugged me down for a kiss.

I hate the sun, I thought as Kate leaned back and released me.

"You'd better go," she said. "Take care, dear heart."

"Until tomorrow, *dacha*," I murmured, tucking the kiss and the endearment in a corner of my heart for saving.

I pictured the room granted to me by Shom's *tol*, focused my *jeira*, and reached reluctantly across the gap between here and Kuyen. My world had never felt less like home.

My *dacha*, sitting in her bed on Earth, faded away.

A shadowy space replaced Kate's apartment, faintly lit by a skillwork lamp hanging by the bed. Tracing the etched lines on the sphere's surface, I willed it brighter, lighting up the bare wooden walls and floor. The room, roughly twice as deep as it was wide, had a paneled wooden screen dividing it into even smaller spaces. Intended for a member of Pella's unit, it had a bed a little larger than Kate's and a wardrobe at this end. The other half, beyond the screen, held a table and chairs. The whole of it would have fit comfortably into my sitting room at House Temarel.

I sighed. Temarel wasn't my House any longer. For years, I'd tried to walk a fine line between protecting Kate from Hunters when her own people would not and doing my duty to my own House. For a time, the *denet* had allowed it, honoring the loyalty I'd owed my friend. In time, he had judged that I'd overpaid and forbade me from protecting her any longer. My service belonged to my House.

When I'd sworn the vow that had made Kate my *dacha*, it had put my responsibility to her beyond his reach. I'd been young, then, and had thought myself invincible. I would best the Hunters, make Kate see me, and welcome her joyfully into the House because who wouldn't want to join House Temarel if their own family had deserted them?

Instead, the *denet* had removed me as his heir, choosing my sister to be the next *denet* in my place. He had forced Kate to choose between respecting my vow or seeing me banished. Holding my tongue through that had been one of the hardest things I'd ever done. *The* hardest, and I'd faced my first Hunter at thirteen.

Whatever answer she'd given, I would have abided by it. I'd made my vow already and my father had known the answer he'd get from me. While I'd lost my House, I'd gained Kate's...love. It had to be love, whether she had sworn a vow or not.

Kate's absence made the empty room even emptier. So much for my dreams of bringing her to the luxury of a House. I still needed to earn our place here.

The two chests I'd had sent over remained unpacked beside the empty wardrobe. My mentor, Seretun, had agreed to hold a few other things for me. In the end, a son of the House had little of his own once the doors barred themselves behind him.

I pushed those thoughts away and dug out a set of practical but presentable clothing, cut loose enough to allow for combat if the situation called for it.

As I stepped out into the hall, the door two rooms to the left opened. Perfect. I didn't know the way to Pella's offices.

"Excuse me," I began, but the words died in my throat as I saw who emerged.

The figure stood a head shorter than myself, broad-shouldered with a solid frame and shaggy, mottled gray-brown fur that covered her scalp, ran down the back of her neck, and disappeared into her shirt collar. Shorter fur covered the rest of her visible skin.

A Drammon, an ambush Hunter whose skill could send a debilitating pulse of force, like lightning, through her prey at a touch.

She turned toward me, her large, dark eyes scanning over me. Her broad mouth, twice as wide as a Thurei's, tightened when the silence stretched between us. She wore clothing tailored to her long arms, thick torso, and relatively short legs, quite different from the style I'd seen on Pella's Lan troops, but the sturdy brown cloth was the same and it had the *tol*'s insignia stitched into the right shoulder.

My hand itched for the hilt of my *zaret*, but I stopped short of summoning it. I would not break the Truce.

She's not hunting here. "I don't wish to bother you, but perhaps you could tell me where to find the *tol*?"

The Drammon folded her long arms over her chest, tapping powerful, claw-tipped fingers on her biceps. I'd fought Drammons more than once on Bayshore's grounds. A brush of those fingers could unleash agony.

"And who are you?" she asked, her voice level.

"Coraven Tem—" I bit down on the rest of it. I had a shorter name now. "Just Coraven. And your name?"

She ignored the question. "You stand in the instructors' hall, but you don't know where the *tol*'s chambers are?"

"I'm here as a guest for the moment." I offered a slight bow. "Though I hope to make instructor."

The Drammon didn't offer any friendly gesture of her own. "Are you teaching ways to kill my kind, Temarel?"

Ah. So she'd heard of me.

"I'm no longer a son of House Temarel," I said, ready to call my *zaret*. Just in case. "If you're here serving with the *tol*, those who prey on the helpless are not counted as your kind."

This hallway was narrow, designed for defense. The Drammon's reach would make a difference, if it came to that.

I doubted Pella would accept a battle with a fellow instructor as proof of my skill. I took a deep breath and then exhaled. "I'll teach whatever Pella assigns to me, but I hope to help keep the peace in Abuello. I have no quarrel with anyone but those who threaten me or mine."

The silence stretched.

"I'm Greta," the Drammon said finally, rolling the *r* into a growl. "The *tol*'s chambers are on the ground floor, off the north corridor. Early in the evening like this, she walks the practice grounds."

"My thanks," I said, offering her a bow of gratitude. As I walked down the long hall to the stairwell, the skin between my shoulder blades prickled, but she didn't follow.

When *Tol* Pella had offered me lodgings here a couple of days ago, she'd given me the full tour so I knew the route. The stone keep that housed the *tol*'s troops marked the center of the claimed land, surrounded by a tall, stone wall. In a ring around it lay skillwork studios, stables, and other necessary outbuildings, including a closed arena for sparring with skills or running skillwork experiments, and an open-air space for weapons and hand-to-hand work. A wooden palisade, manned by guards, circled the whole of it, with a stretch of cleared land separating it from the thick, lowland forest that made up the wilds here. A short road linked the outpost to the city of Abuello, close enough for easy transport, but far enough that Pella controlled the claim on the land.

Thirty fighters were working in pairs across the training yard when I arrived. I found Pella at one end.

Pella's kinship to her niece, Shom, proclaimed itself in her solid, muscular build. For a handful of years after Kate had driven Shom away, Shom had followed behind her aunt, though she had returned to studying skillwork a few years ago. I could empathize with young Shom's desire to face opponents who could be beaten by force. I'd done the same myself, after all, but I found myself glad that she'd gone back to the puzzles of *jeira* that had piqued her interest as a child.

Shom's aunt, however, was a warrior born. Despite the white strands that now threaded through her black hair, she still wore it clubbed back in a combat style. An impressive woman in her sixties, Pella looked like she could easily handle half of the fighters on the grounds. While she wore an understated but expensive tunic and breeches in the fashion of a high-ranking Lan, her long, leather vest doubled as light armor and was slit up to the hip for ease of movement.

"Coraven." She inclined her head. The Lan didn't bow as Thureis did, so I appreciated the courtesy. "Have you settled in?"

"I have, thank you. And my thanks, again, for your hospitality and patience." I bowed, offering the best of my manners. "My *dacha* and I defeated the Hunters I told you about. I would be honored to provide a demonstration of my skill if you wish."

Over much of the last six years guarding Kate, I had devoted myself to training with the *zaret*, the skill unique to Thureis.

If I had one thing I could offer in my new, upended life, I could offer this.

Pella gave me a measuring look and lifted her hand in a gesture to one of the fighters on the field. "Osha, come over here."

A Lan woman pulled back, lifting her sword up and away to disengage from her sparring partner, a Lan armed with a spear. Osha thumped her partner companionably on the shoulder and strolled over to us.

"Our guest needs a tryout," Pella said, gesturing toward me. I offered a bow of introduction. "Coraven's been recommended by my niece as a sword instructor. Let's see what he can do."

Osha spun the sword slowly in her hands, an idle movement as she looked me over. "With all due respect, I doubt we have much use for a duelist."

I suppressed a smile. "I've never had much use for dueling, myself," I said. "I'm originally from House Temarel." That and the sponsorship of Shom should have added up to something. If the Hunter in the hallway had known who I was, there was a chance that one of Pella's favored fighters would as well.

A slight widening of Osha's eyes showed me I'd guessed correctly. She looked me up and down and turned her palm up in acquiescence. "Let's get you a weapon, then."

"I have a blade," I said, bringing my hand up as I focused on my *jeira*, the energy and razor-edged intent within me that would allow me to manifest my skill. My *zaret* materialized in my palm, its hilt in my grip as familiar as breathing, clearer than glass and with a blade sharper than any weapon of honed steel.

"That might be useful at times," Pella acknowledged. "But if you're training Lan, a *zaret*'s not going to do any good. Bruises fix a lesson in place."

The Lan, the people who made up the majority of Pella's forces, would be unaffected by my blade. The skill unique to the Lan rendered them impervious to the offensive or defensive skills of other peoples. Thurei swords would not cut a Lan, and Shom had even proven herself unaffected by Kate's powerful disintegration skill. Though I would never have admitted it, the human skill had shaken even me. I'd seen the devastation a single human could do.

Osha beckoned to her sparring partner, a burly Lan man who trotted up and offered his metal sword, leather-wrapped hilt first. I took it, weighing the balance of the blade.

The *zaret* had a single edge with a slight curve to better serve a slashing motion. More importantly, a *zaret* weighed next to nothing in the hands of its wielder, though it could hit with the power of a heavier weapon.

This blade was double-edged, with a wide cross-guard and heavy pommel. The blade ran perhaps a handspan longer than a *zaret*. Made of blunted steel, it weighed my arm down just holding it motionless. Thurei students trained with wooden staves to mimic the light, springy play of the *jeira*-formed weapon. I had never fought with steel.

"Does that suit you?" Osha asked, a single black eyebrow raised in challenge.

Not so many hours ago, my *dacha* had asked me to choose between my quarters and hers, as if I still had something to offer her. I might again if I earned it by my work rather than by my name. I had trained for *one thing*.

Hefting the blade, I took a couple of practice swings. The balance sat a little forward of what I was used to, taking advantage of the greater weight. "It'll serve well enough."

I offered Osha a respectful bow, as one Thurei duelist would to another. Though I had always steered clear of such games, I knew the forms.

Osha gave a decent approximation back.

I lunged first, feinting toward Osha's chest. She parried and the blades rang off each other. My attempt to disengage with the heavy steel blade took a moment too long and I missed the chance to follow up. Osha countered with a slash, and I retreated out of her reach. My feet, at least, moved quickly enough.

Osha read the situation in a moment. She pressed the offensive, attacking again and again. I had both hands on the hilt for more leverage, holding it close to my body to mitigate the greater weight of the sword. Compared to the *zaret*, I might as well have been fighting shackled, but I could parry and return to guard without letting Osha push my point off her line of attack. In each exchange, I still lagged, too slow for a successful riposte.

With a *zaret* at full speed, I could have beaten her. With steel, she would find an opening before long. Techniques I'd mastered with a lighter, one-handed blade wouldn't serve me here and Osha knew it.

I had to turn that to my advantage.

Instead of deflecting Osha's next swing, I took the strike along the lower, strong portion of the sword, catching her blade against my guard. Unlike a *zaret*, two-handed swords had the heft and leverage to excel in a bind like this.

This was the first time I'd allowed Osha to close with me where she had the advantage. It would have been smarter for me to retreat, as I had the whole match, but my gamble surprised her enough that she hesitated. Her next move would twist her blade out of the bind and send it straight at me, while I was too close to dodge.

She didn't get the chance.

I gave way, stepping aside as Osha stumbled forward, her balance committed for a moment too long. I rotated my blade, using the cross guard to leverage her hilt out of her hands. Osha caught her balance as the steel sword clanged to the ground. She straightened and scowled down at the weapon.

I'd wanted the kind of bout that would have dazzled an audience in a House sparring circle, but I'd trained to fight Hunters and they didn't care for forms, only for survival. Though I'd beaten Osha with what others might have considered a trick, I'd still disarmed her. As the head of a band of mercenaries and peacekeepers, Pella didn't need to see an elegant play of speed and precision.

At least, I hoped not. Suppressing a sigh, I held out the practice sword, hilt first, toward its owner, who stepped forward and took it.

I offered Osha deep respect in my closing bow. She replied with a little, off-hand bob, still stiff with annoyance.

Pella grunted. She didn't seem impressed. "You can train for proper sword weight, I suppose. I'll take you on a temporary basis to see how you do. Osha can set you up with a training group tomorrow morning."

"I will endeavor for improvement, as always," I said, considering my next words. Kate would be here in the morning and I didn't want to miss that time with her. Not tomorrow. If we had to adjust after that, so be it. "Would it be acceptable to take students in the afternoon or evening? I'll need a day…at least a morning, if you can spare it."

After a measuring look, Pella turned her hand up in agreement. "Shom's told me a little about you. You'll have your first students tomorrow evening, and we'll discuss more after that."

Shom had been so angry when Kate had come back. Her rendition of my story must have been more generous than I'd thought. I offered thanks with my bow. "It's a great kindness and I thank you for it."

Pella raised one of her black eyebrows. A slim, pale gray scar ran through it. "Do as well as my niece led me to believe you will and no thanks are necessary."

"You've been generous beyond measure—"

She interrupted me. "And it's about to become 'beyond measure and this one more,' isn't it?"

I put on my best supplicant's smile. I'd had practice enough under the rule of my former *denet*. "I seek redress against a grievous wrong, under circumstances that make it difficult to get a fair hearing. It's a matter that reaches beyond the threat to an individual and cuts to the heart of one of our most valued institutions."

Pella gestured back toward the keep. "Explain as we walk, please. I have many duties to attend to."

"I have no wish to waste your time," I murmured, falling in next to her as she left the practice ground. The polite, implied apology had been drummed into me thoroughly enough that it spilled out without a second thought.

The Lan te Kos weren't Thureis, though, and Pella just snorted at my formal manners. "Shom's told me about your theories on the Scholars."

Shom had added to my "theory" with information of her own, but I bit my tongue on that. A friend of hers had looked through the Scholars' debt log and found the name of the Hirach who had Hunted Kate. "I'm not sure how much Shom has told you, but it seems the Hunter targeting Kate had owed the Scholars a debt of service. His presence at the time we visited raises my suspicions."

"I understand your concern," Pella said, steering us down a path between two buildings. "But you must admit, the idea of Scholars directing feral Hunters like knives in the dark, polluting their own memories... I understand Katherine's skill is potentially formidable, but this theory strains belief, I'm afraid."

I clasped my hands behind my back, a respectful posture that also let me clench my fists without anyone noticing. "I agree, but sometimes the truth must be believed, however unlikely it appears. If the Scholars have lied to us, where else have they played false? If they will kill to keep their secrets, what else will they do with all the secrets the people of Kuyen bring them? Supplicants share information with the Scholars in the belief that it will be safe. What else do they know and how are they willing to use it? To what ends?"

"This peacekeeper post is my portion within the greater dav

Ferrum," Pella said, naming her familial coalition. That network of families, allies, and business partners served as the closest thing the Lan te Kos had to a House, though ruled by consensus rather than a single head. "But the research laboratory where Shom creates new skillwork is another portion. Our coalition hangs together like beads on a weaving, all strung from one to another. Some of those strands rely heavily on the Scholars. Should I snip those parts out by accusing their most honored Scholars of assassination and betrayal—based on the assumptions of a hot-headed boy and an ignorant outworld girl?"

Especially when that foolish pair might as well have been strangers, but she didn't say that aloud.

"I believe this goes beyond assumptions," I said, holding my voice steady. "If you wish to stand clear of the matter, though, I understand."

"I'm not standing that far away," she said. "You have a room surrounded by trained warriors, a position that fits your skills, and an income that will serve you tolerably well, if you're prudent. If you do make accusations against the Shevern Scholars, I won't interfere."

They were all substantial gestures, every bit as generous as I'd just admitted only moments ago. If they weren't everything that I'd wanted, it was also true she didn't owe me any of it. "I appreciate your kindness. I intended no offense."

Chuckling, Pella waved the concern away. "None taken. But you're here as an instructor, not as my niece's friend."

You're no son here. Act like it.

"My thanks for the reminder," I murmured, stopping on the path as she continued up the steps and into the keep.

Gaining Pella's support had been a slender hope, unlikely from the beginning. Truly, if I'd had a *denet* to petition, he might have answered the same way. *You're striking at shadows. Stop acting like a hot-headed boy.*

My *denet* would have enjoyed that one.

I ran a hand through my hair, tilting my gaze up to look at the crescent moon. Even after the few hours of sleep I'd had at Kate's, fatigue still clung to me, a reminder that I was still cheating my body out of a full recovery.

Later.

Right now, I needed to change into more formal clothing and find the local Scholar's post in Aubello. There was so much to get done before the sun rose, making it possible to walk between worlds. I would not waste a moment of Kate's company.

Sarotrea Ambrolyn, representative of the Scholars in Aubello, regarded me impassively, her dark eyes missing nothing as I laid out my formal call for review by the Shevern council. We sat in her receiving room, its low door facing a courtyard off a sedate side street in upper Aubello.

She had not seemed pleased to be roused to her work after dinner.

"Tharkesh os Chigaf, the Finder of the Akevad, visited the Hall with a request for information over twenty days before our visit," I said, repeating the information I'd had from Shom. I shifted in the chair. Built for the short, broad Sheverns, it was a poor fit for me. "He paid his debt in service, returning the day that Katherine Kjelgaard and I visited. He threatened Kjelgaard then and ultimately met us in combat with four warriors of his kith. Endangering lives by inducing Hunters to attack is a violation of Truce and merits censure by the Shevern council."

The Shevern lifted a hand in acknowledgement, splaying her stubby fingers. "Where was this combat?"

"In Kjelgaard's world, Earth," I said.

Most of my memories of the event were clear: The moonlit sand of the beach, the gloating growl of Tharkesh, delighted to have his prey invite him to battle. The waver in Kate's voice as fear shattered her faith in her skill. The final moments, though, dissolved in a haze of chaos and pain. I would have died, had Kate not brought me to a healer.

Ambrolyn smoothed the cream fabric of her robes over her knee, perfectly at ease in her own domain. Her copper skin contrasted elegantly with the cloth. "Allow me to confirm. You say that you went to the Hall with a question and were informed of the location of a former Scholar in exile. You exchanged words with a Hirach on the grounds. When you chose to journey through the wildlands, you met with more Hunters—Gorvas, a Wogra, and Visenis. Later, your companion was attacked by the Hirach on an empty world. Following that, the two of you decided to Summon the Hirach to a duel on that same world. Do I have that correct?"

"The Scholars lied to us, honored one," I said, emphasizing the most heinous part of the situation, at least from the point of view of Sheverns. "They hid everything they knew about humans because they feared the human skill and then they lied about it."

The Scholar sat back, tilting her bald head to the side to halt my explanation. "The council will reason on these matters and the Scholars' role in them. You've made your concerns known. We focus now on the facts. Do I have the events correct?"

I forced the muscles in my jaw to relax. "The sequence you listed is correct, Scholar."

The Scholar made no notes, kept no paperwork. Sheverns' skill lay in their memories: eidetic recall that they passed along as a birthright to future generations. She would remember exactly what I had said.

Ambrolyn rose and so I rose with her, towering over her short stature. "I will bring your concerns to the council, Coraven. They will contact you if they need any further elucidation of events."

I was sure she would listen to no other arguments from me. If I could have brought a louder voice than mine to the conversation… I bowed my acceptance. "Thank you, Scholar Amrolyn, for your consideration."

I let myself out of the Scholar's quarters, closing the door quietly behind me.

If I heard back from the Shevern council about this matter, there would not be enough room on Kuyen or all the other worlds combined to hold my surprise. The choice between their own honored ones and a Houseless Thurei was no choice at all.

CHAPTER THREE

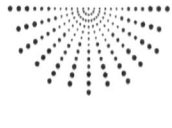

KATE

I discovered the problem with my plan to meet Cor after work as soon as the sun dipped below the horizon. With so much going on, I'd forgotten that I'd lost his token in the fight with the Hiraches. Without a token linked to him, I couldn't slip from my world right to his side. Instead, I would have to know exactly where I intended to travel—slipping across the gap with no destination in mind would land me somewhere at random.

Cor had said he was staying near the arena where our friend Shom had helped me learn my skill. I would just have to find him from there.

When the sun disappeared completely, I closed my eyes and reached within myself to focus my *jeira*. As a kid, I'd thought of it as magic, though it was more like a combination of focus and inborn ability that could be used in tandem with various trained skills, like worldwalking. Once I was ready, I visualized the training arena as I'd seen it with Shom: a large, rectangular building with high ceilings and a sandy floor. With my destination in mind, I reached across the gap between Earth and Kuyen and pulled myself across.

My apartment faded out of existence as the arena formed around me, the distant sounds of traffic replaced with shouts and the clatter of metal on metal.

I'd come across right next to one of the long, wooden walls. I stumbled back against it, trying to get my bearings.

Glowing orbs of glass that reminded me of fairy lights hung along the walls. A couple dozen figures lunged and clashed across the sandy arena floor, scattered in pairs or small groups.

Ten feet in front of me, two gray-skinned Lan te Kos with staffs and small, round shields faced a lanky figure not much taller than I was, with shaggy, mottled hair covering their head and neck, running below the collar of their tunic. The two Lan noticed me almost at the same time. One of them, a lithe woman with close-cropped black hair, leaped back on her nimble, faun-like legs. The other, an older man with a heavier build, didn't move in time.

"Who—" he began, his gaze still on me. Then their opponent lunged, reaching out with one long, thin arm. The man jerked his shield back up a moment too late and the combatant pressed their hand on the man's chest.

A boom like a bass drum thrummed through me. The two combatants stumbled apart, catching their balance. The center of the Lan's tunic bore the faded print of the other person's hand, with its splayed, long fingers.

What was that? But he was a Lan. Whatever skill that person had used wouldn't have affected him. His shirt had to fend for itself, it seemed.

"Who are you?" the Lan woman asked me in Kuyen's common tongue.

The lanky one turned, finally aware of my presence.

I recognized the person, then, from a book Cor had shown me.

A Drammon woman. Drammons were Greater Hunters, one of Kuyen's several predatory species. I pressed back against the wooden wall, my heart jumping into a higher gear.

Some of the other fighters sparring across the sandy arena floor glanced over at the disruption I'd caused, though they didn't stop their work.

"Who. Are. You?" The Lan woman stepped closer, letting her shield arm relax. "And what are you doing here uninvited?"

"Uh, I'm Katherine. Katherine Kjelgaard." I swallowed hard. The Drammon hadn't made any other moves, though the mouth that stretched twice as wide as a human's and her deep-set eyes were hard for me to read. I tried to stay focused on the Lan woman. "I'm...I'm looking for Coraven Temarel. Um, Coraven."

He wouldn't have been going by his House name anymore.

The Drammon spoke up. Behind her thin lips, she had pointed teeth. "She's looking for the Hunterslayer."

The Lan woman cocked a black eyebrow and I answered her unspoken question before the Hunter could say anything else. "He's a Thurei, with orange hair. I think he's asking Pella for a job as an instructor?"

"All right. You two get back to work." Then she turned to me. "I'm Verli. You can send a Summons for your friend and have him meet you here." She waved for me to follow her and headed toward the short side of the building closest to us. We stayed well out of the way of the other fighters as we passed, walking close to the wall. Some had weapons, but most seemed to be using different forms of skillwork, like the Drammon had. Perhaps it was safer to do so indoors.

The far wall held racks of practice weaponry: long, wooden sticks like the ones Cor's kin used for sparring in place of swords, as well as blunt-tipped spears, clubs, loops of rope weighted with smooth stones. Wooden shields.

Verli plucked a small sheet of paper and a pencil from a box on a shelf. She held them out to me, like a challenge to prove I was here for the reason I'd claimed. "Here you go."

I steadied the paper on one of the shields, for lack of another option, and wrote my note quickly, in Kuyene. The message could not be sent in English. My friend Shom had taught me to write Kuyene as a child for this exact reason. *Coran, please come meet me at the arena where Shom gave me lessons. Kate.* The awkward writing angle gave my handwriting a strange slant, but it was still legible.

I folded the square sheet of paper into a shape that reminded me of an origami bird. The combination of the Kuyene message, the proper shape of the folded paper, and my *jeira*-fueled intention for it to reach Cor would all combine to send it winging off on its way to him. I lifted the pencil to write on the wing of the Summons and stopped. I needed to use Cor's full name for this to reach him, like dialing the right phone number. But Cor's father had thrown him out of his House. Did that mean he was no longer a Temarel?

I started with the shorter option. On each wing, I wrote *Coraven*. Then I balanced the birdlike note in my hand for a moment and focused my *jeira*. The paper bird flexed its wings, then lifted into the air and flapped through the open doorway of the arena into the bright, early morning sunlight.

I couldn't see much beyond a stretch of flagstone, another windowless wooden building set back some distance, and the pale-blue sky with gauzy, golden clouds. Verli stood between me and the door and she seemed wary of me.

Verli wasn't my biggest worry right now, though. What was Cor doing, since I hadn't shown up to meet him first thing after dawn?

It only took a few minutes to find out. Cor came jogging through the arena doors and his gaze snagged on me immediately. The tension drained out of him and he closed the distance at a walk, sparing Verli a glance but otherwise looking questioningly at me.

"Thanks for coming to get me," I said as soon as he came close enough.

"Of course," he said, with a smile. For a moment, I thought he might reach for my hand, but of course not in public. I'd yet to meet a people more formal than Thureis. He turned to Verli and gave her a polite bow. "I'm Coraven, here on the hospitality of Pella tol dav Ferrum. My thanks for keeping my *dacha* company while she waited for me."

Verli widened her eyes, so she must have known how rare *dachas* were. Or perhaps she was connecting the dots between a Houseless Thurei and a *dacha* who also happened to be an outworlder.

Or maybe she just didn't like my manners. She introduced herself to Cor and then added to me, "I recommend you pick another slip anchor instead of the training arena." She gave us both a disapproving look that would have made any hospital head nurse proud.

"We'll be sure to do so," Cor assured her, his manners polished to a shine. Verli turned on her heel and strode back to where her training partners still sparred.

"Sorry for the trouble," I said quietly. "I lost your token in the fight and it sort of slipped my mind until this evening."

Cor's eyebrows went up at that. "It's lost? Are you sure?"

"When I got back to my apartment after getting healed, I had a welt across my neck like the cord had snapped." I touched the spot on my throat, though the mark had faded and there was no welt left for my fingertips to find. "I think I remember one of the Hiraches catching it with his claws. I can't believe I forgot."

"We've been a little busy," Cor said, touching my arm lightly. Nothing about his posture encouraged more affectionate contact between us in such a public place and I followed his lead. "It shouldn't matter. You defeated the Hiraches and no one on Earth knows what a token is or have the *jeira* to use one."

I hadn't thought of it from that perspective before. If a person activated a token as they slipped between worlds, the token could take any worldwalker to its anchor point, whether they knew the destination or not. It wouldn't just work to bring *me* to Cor, it would work for *anyone*. Or at least, as Cor had pointed out, anyone with the *jeira* to worldwalk.

"Your token and Shom's don't look the same," I said. "How would a person even know what it was?"

Cor moved his fingers in a little rippling gesture, the Thurei equivalent of a shrug. "It wouldn't be easy to figure out and it's unlikely most Kuyenes would be sensitive enough to detect the skillwork in it. They'd probably count it as a bauble and discard it. There's no need to worry."

That wasn't as reassuring as he might have meant it to be. He'd told me before that Hunters were especially sensitive to *jeira*, the power in a person that could be used on skills, to worldwalk, or to activate skillwork items like the token. Would they be able to sense it?

Then again, the fight and Cor's devastating injury might have made me paranoid. I decided to take his word and stop worrying about it. "In any case, the tide will have washed it off the beach by now."

I couldn't recall if we'd been above the tideline by that point or not, but Cor was right. No one on Earth would know what it was in any case, and there hadn't been any Hunters left by the time the fight had been over.

That reminded me. I kept my voice low. "There's a Drammon here. She was sparring with Verli when I showed up. I recognized her from that Hunter book in the Lore Hall."

Though he didn't look concerned, Cor did grow serious. "Most of Pella's soldiers are Lan, but there's a fair number of Hunters among them. Very few Hunters actively hunt any longer. The rest find work elsewhere. It's not a problem."

He'd mentioned before that Hunters had largely abandoned their predatory ways, at least as far as the hunting of sentient prey was concerned. Public places on Kuyen were protected by the Truce, which kept the peace. The information had gotten buried beneath the more relevant knowledge that some Kuyene Hunters did still hunt and had chosen Cor and me as their prey.

"She called you 'Hunterslayer.'"

Cor took a deep breath, then offered me another smile. "I doubt they're all standing in line to be my friends, but they don't plan to drag me off into the woods, either."

I hid a shudder, thinking of the Drammon's sharp teeth. How many hours had it been since I'd seen Cor's insides, clawed open by a Hunter? "Don't joke like that."

He tucked my hand into the crook of his elbow and changed the subject, identifying different buildings for me as we headed for the gate in the stone wall. The stout wooden doors stood open, guarded by a couple of Lan who let us pass with a cursory wave.

The general bustle grew as we reached the main building, mostly people in more casual clothing, or at least unarmored. A few acknowledged Cor as they passed. The front doors opened into an austere entry room with high ceilings and plain, smooth stone walls. Cushioned benches lined the wall beside the main doors, facing three closed doors that led deeper into the building.

Cor opened the one on the right, revealing a stairwell. He gave me a rueful look. "Now we both have apartments with stairs. At least you can slip straight to our rooms and skip these."

For some reason, that made me blush.

On the second floor, we walked down a long, windowless hall

set with wooden doors at regular intervals. Skillwork lamps kept the hallway bright.

Cor stopped at a door perhaps a third of the way down, pulled a key from his pocket, and unlocked it. He pushed the door open and waved me inside with a flourish.

Light from the hallway didn't reach far past the doorway.

"Ah, here." Cor hurried around me and fiddled with something hanging on the inner wall. A lamp bloomed into life, shining warm light over the room.

I'd seen how close the doors were spaced together, but I hadn't been guessing at the room sizes.

The overall space was maybe thirty feet deep, but only about fifteen feet or so wide. A set of painted wooden panels with a door in them divided the area into a sitting room and a bedroom. The front room held a pair of simple wooden chairs and a small but serviceable table holding a bouquet of tropical flowers. It made my one-bedroom apartment in San Jose look spacious.

"What do you think?" he asked, and I thought the question stretched beyond the rooms. He ran a hand over the painted room divider, mottled in subtle patterns in plum and charcoal. "It reminded me of the shadows in your father's forest."

My family's garden nursery, he meant. We'd met under the moonlight among the potted trees, over a decade ago.

"It's lovely." Tiny Katie, hunting for lizards among the plant pots, had had no idea where this would have all led.

"Good. I'm glad." He glanced around. "It isn't much yet, but—"

"Hey," I said softly, holding a hand out to him. "I mean it. It's lovely. Now, come here and say good morning."

A smile softened his expression and he wrapped me in his arms, ducking his head to press his lips against mine. I leaned into him, deepening the kiss, but he pulled back, a mischievous light in his amber eyes.

"Good morning, *dacha*. Did you sleep well?"

I tried to hide my smile and failed. "Yes, very well, and good morning. Thank you. I did mean the first kind of *good morning*, though." I tugged him back down to demonstrate just what I'd had in mind.

A soft, tapping sound behind me made both of us jump. I whirled around and caught the flicker of something in Cor's hand from the corner of my eye. His *zaret*, the blade there and gone in a moment. "It's just a message."

A paper Summons sat on the bare, wooden floor near my feet. It had my name written in Kuyene syllables on the wings.

Of course, the answer to my question had arrived while I stood right next to Cor. Messages couldn't reach me during Earth's day, while the way between worlds was closed. I snatched the folded paper up off the floor.

Cor lifted his brows. "Birasef?"

Well, he'd recognize his own cousin's handwriting. I nodded, trying to think of a way to explain it without saying too much. "I wrote to him yesterday, while you were sleeping."

Nice one, Kate. That doesn't sound at all suspicious.

"Ah." I thought he'd ask me why, but he only added, "It's kind of him to answer."

I frowned down at the paper. "Why wouldn't he?"

"We're strangers now." Cor's lips twitched in a faint smile. "Then again, it's Birasef we're talking about. How careful would he be?"

"I'll try not to get him in trouble," I promised, folding the Summons flat to slip into my jeans pocket. I could read it later and see if he answered my question.

A second Summons rustled discreetly at our feet just as I tucked the first away in my pocket. I bent to pick it up. I'd only written to Cor's cousin, and I'd only had the one question. This one had

Coraven's name on the wings, though, and whoever had sent it had known to leave the House name off. Either it was someone we knew, or news traveled faster than I thought.

"It's a day for messages," Cor said, frowning a little as he unfolded it.

It was hypocritical, I know, but I had to ask. Cor had the unfair advantage of recognizing people's handwriting. "Who's it from?"

"It's from House Leratom, here in Aubello. You can read it if you'd like." He tipped the paper toward me.

I bit my lip. It wasn't an offer so much as a trade. When I'd visited House Temarel, Cor and his cousin had been as edgy as alley cats around each other at first. At the time, Cor hadn't told me about his vow yet, afraid I'd send him away again. I think most of the friction had come from his worry that Birasef might blow his secret. His cousin had been genuinely distressed when Cor had been injured in the fight with the Hunters, at least.

But I wasn't ready to tell Cor why I'd written to his cousin yet.

I shrugged, playing it cool. "You can fill me in, if you want."

He pressed his lips together to hide a smile. Maybe I wasn't as subtle as I'd thought. Gesturing to our little sitting room, he said, "We can read it together."

Bir's note crinkled in my pocket as we sat down at the square table. Cor flattened the letter from House Leratom on table between us, but I didn't have much experience with Kuyene handwriting beyond Cor's and Shom's as children. Whoever had written this had a bold, angular style. I was sure I could read it, given some time, but Cor reached the end of it after a quick scan, before I'd finished the first, flowery line of greeting. It just reminded me that I was all but illiterate here.

Whatever the note said, it had made his frown deeper.

"What's wrong?" No one would start out with well-wishes if they meant to be cruel, would they? Not that I'd had the best experience with Thurei courtesy lately. Cor's House had seemed polite enough up until his *denet* had banished him.

"Nothing's wrong," Cor said, though his tone of voice didn't agree. "It's an invitation for both of us to visit the House for the noon meal. An open gather, whatever that may be."

"They couldn't be as bad as the Pareshols were for lunch, could they?" Of course, Cor had broken his engagement with House Pareshol's daughter Turavi when he'd made his vow to me. Some of them had moved on, some of them hadn't. Leratom didn't have that kind of beef with him. Probably. How many fiancées could one man have?

That pulled a laugh out of him. "I'm sure it would be a different experience. The question is: Why would they want to see me? I have no House. I'm not of any use as an ally. Either of us," he corrected diplomatically.

"That's not true," I protested. Cor was honorable, loyal, intelligent, skilled, and determined. He would be a treasure to any House. His father had been a fool to bar the doors against him. "They would be lucky to have you as an ally."

"My thanks, *dacha*." His smile deepened into something more genuine. "In truth, they haven't offered anything beyond a meal, but if we have their backing, the Scholars will have more cause to listen to our claim."

Cor shrugged, moving his shoulders in the human manner. "I think you'd like the city, *dacha*. We can see it by ourselves if you can't stomach another Thurei House so soon."

"Well, I have a fifty percent success rate so far," I said, then I bit my tongue. I'd been thinking of how uncomfortable we'd been at House Pareshol compared with the time I'd spent among Cor's cousins. I'd enjoyed the cocky banter of Birasef and Cor's other cousins, the fatherly concern of the armsmaster who'd taught Cor the skills he'd used to protect me all those years, and watching Cor tutor his little cousin Fos.

But I could hardly call it a success since I'd been the reason he'd lost everything.

Too well-mannered to comment on it, Cor folded the letter back up and stood. "Well, if we're going, I should put on something more formal than this."

He wore "casual Thurei" clothes, a buff tunic and dark green trousers. Though they lacked any elaborate embroidery or accents, the fabric was still high quality and expertly tailored. The lunch at House Pareshol had been painfully formal, with intricate hairstyles and the Thurei equivalent of black tie clothes.

Alarmed, I asked, "How formal are we talking about?"

"Not that bad." But he hesitated. "More to show that we don't lack…" He trailed off with a gesture that took in everything around us.

I didn't think he meant the room. "Maybe we should stop by my apartment so I can change."

"You're beautiful as you are and you should wear what you like," he assured me. But then he added, "We can leave from your apartment and slip back into Aubello, though. I know a spot that's near enough to House Leratom."

Yes, let's get you better clothes, is how I heard it. I'd bought some nicer clothes recently, but compared to Thurei formality… I sighed. "Do you even own clothes I would consider casual?"

He hesitated, which just piqued my curiosity. "I did have the tailor make me some clothing in the… I believe it's the style of human casual clothes."

"Really?" I asked, completely charmed by the idea. "What kind? When was this?"

"Just the general kind." Cor's golden skin flushed darker across his high cheekbones, though I couldn't guess what had made him uncomfortable. He rippled his fingers in a Thurei-style shrug. "If we go to this 'gather,' we shouldn't be late. I still need to change. I could show you the other clothes later if you'd like."

"Sure, if you want," I said. His embarrassment made me feel awkward, too. If he'd had some clothes made on a lark and now wished he hadn't, I wouldn't press him on it. And then, since Birasef's letter was burning a hole in my pocket and making me feel guilty at the same time, I added, "I'll just wait out here."

Cor stood and headed to the bedroom. Once he'd closed the bedroom door behind him, I unfolded the note.

Birasef was wordy in person and no different in a letter. Questions about our wellbeing, updates on Cor's sisters, which I guessed I was supposed to relay to Cor himself. Was his cousin truly unable to write to Cor himself?

That hurt, and I wasn't even the one who had lost family. I pushed the thought aside and kept reading.

Birasef had come through for me. He'd tidied his somewhat scrawling handwriting into precise lines for the middle paragraph. In clear Kuyene letters, he'd written a phonetic version of the Thurei words for the *dacha* vow. It could only be sworn properly in Cor's mother tongue.

I doubted that I would sound like a native speaker, but now I had the words I needed to say. All I needed to do was memorize them and find the right place and time to say them.

Birasef confirmed that the *dacha* vow could only be given in the hearing of the *denet* for one of the two Houses involved. He'd never heard of any Houseless Thurei swearing it. That made sense. The *denet* ruled the House and the *dacha* vow allowed one partner to legally put the other above their ties to the House they'd been born in. A Thurei without a House wouldn't need to bother.

While I was, legally, the most important person in the world to Cor, he was just my… I didn't have a word for it. Maybe that shouldn't have made a difference, but I thought it meant something to Cor.

The bedroom door behind me opened and I quickly folded the letter back up and stuffed it into my pocket.

Cor had changed into slim-fitting black trousers and a dark blue, formal jacket that made his orange hair nearly glow.

A question lingered in Cor's eyes as he glanced from my pocket to my face.

"Your sisters are well," I offered, glad Birasef had given me something to say. "Damoret's sat for her first House hearing, and Netari has found a suitable stud for her new *morsai*."

His younger sister had lately been obsessed with breeding and training the dog-like Kuyene riding animals. Birasef had added, too, that Cor's sisters missed him, but I thought repeating that would just make Cor sad.

Cor nodded a human-style agreement to the news. "My thanks. Take care, though, *dacha*. Birasef won't win any praise from the *denet* for keeping ties with us."

Though mild, his warning made my shoulders tense up. "Understood."

His expression softened, and he reached for my hand and kissed my knuckles as a reassurance. There didn't seem much else to say.

After that, we made a quick stop by my apartment. Cor, all politeness again, waited in the living room while I changed into a ruffled, lavender skirt and a matching flower-print skirt.

I'd left my phone on my nightstand to charge. Though it was close to midnight, I checked it by habit. Rose had sent a text hours ago to see if I wanted to get dinner. I winced. When I saw her at work tomorrow, I'd have to apologize. Leaving the phone behind on a world with cell towers, I rejoined Cor, who slipped us over to Aubello.

CHAPTER FOUR

KATE

We arrived in a small, low-walled courtyard paved with a distinctive pattern of light and dark cobblestones. It must have been a slip anchor, a memorable place that worldwalkers could use in their travels. I followed Cor out and onto the street, leaving the space for whoever might use it next.

The buildings around us stood two or three stories high, topped with curved tiles or flat roofs with what looked like container gardens on top. Rather than having sidewalks along the outside of the buildings like we did California, these buildings had archways running the length of the lower floors, providing broad walkways beneath the overhanging upper floors. The hot, midday sun beat down on the street, reflecting off the brightly painted walls, but the arcades offered cool shade. The repeated arches of the arcades reminded me of pictures I'd seen of the Roman Colosseum. Most of the archways held shop stalls or tables where customers were served food and drink.

The cobbled street thronged with a variety of pedestrians, many of them peoples I couldn't identify. Carts and single-axled buggies clattered by, drawn by *morsais*, which always reminded me of horse-sized, black German shepherds. There were slower, bulkier draft beasts, too, that resembled massive pigs.

Cor watched me closely, either worried or curious to see how I would like the city. I grinned up at him, reaching out to take his arm.

"We can explore after the lunch, right?"

"We can explore a bit now if you'd like. We ought to bring a guesting gift." Cor looked around at the packed arcades. "Would you like to help me find one?"

"I'll tag along while you tell me what a suitable guesting gift is," I said, laughing. I knew the basics of the Kuyene custom—a gesture to soften the inconvenience of admitting a stranger to one's home—but I'd learned as a child. The stakes were different now. I lifted my hand to the comb seated in my upswept hair, Cor's gift when he had returned to my life.

With a soft smile, he said, "You make it beautiful by wearing it."

Embarrassed, I chuckled. "You mean that the other way around." His English was pretty good, but still, he wasn't native.

"I mean it just like I said it," he insisted, making me blush. "Come. Let's find something for the Leratoms."

We ambled over to the closest arcade, joining a stream of pedestrians flowing between the pillars and the row of stalls up against the back wall. The street market offered a wealth of choices.

Tiny, exquisite ceramic cups that flared like opening flowers. Wirework jewelry that looped and arced in what I suspected was calligraphy of some type, though I couldn't read it. Heaps of pastries on waxed cloth, wafting a sweet, buttery smell that must have been beloved the universe over. Coils of intricately woven cords, ranging from the thickness of a straw to the size of my wrist. Cor hesitated at that one.

"What are these?" I asked.

My memory offered the match at about the same time he answered. "Wards, some of them, and other types of skillwork."

"Like the ones you've put around my apartment to keep Hunters away?"

He nodded and drifted on to the next stall. "I should bring a new set over tomorrow, just to keep them fresh."

A stall with stacks of paper, bound books, and racks of pens and inks. Another with small blocks of wood, sharp with the scent of resin, like cedar or fresh pine. I had no idea what they were meant to do.

In fact, most of this marketplace was just a little beyond my understanding. Skillwork items like the wards? Something fancy like fine stationery? I didn't even know enough to guess.

"Sounds good," I said, returning to his offer of more wards, trying to keep the thread of the conversation amidst all this distraction.

"I can come first thing in the morning," he said, glancing over from where he'd been scanning a display of painted fabrics. "I'm afraid most days will be more like this morning than this afternoon. I have lessons to take as well as to teach, by Pella's orders."

"You mean you don't know everything already?" I teased, wriggling a finger against his ribs. In the crowd, I doubted anyone would notice or care.

Cor gasped and dodged away, nearly bumping into a Lewrit man making a purchase at the next stall. Shock warred with delight on Cor's face and he didn't quite suppress a laugh. Maybe I'd offended his sense of propriety, but he'd liked it.

"Actually," he said, straightening the drape of his tunic, "there's quite a lot I don't know. You've heard Shom tease me about the failures in my studies."

I drifted closer to him, unable to tamp down on the

mischievousness entirely. "She just did it because you're easy to tease."

"Well…" He lowered his voice. "I like it when you do it."

I leaned forward until I could whisper in his ear. "Unless I do it in public."

Cor laughed and stepped back out of my reach, charmingly flustered. "Yes. Unless that." He cleared his throat and tried to give me a glare that was spoiled by his grin.

Neither of us was paying any attention to our surroundings, so when someone bumped into Cor, I thought it was no more than we'd just done by accident. A short figure wearing a brown robe bounced away from the contact, dissolving in the characteristic manner of a worldwalker slipping away.

But Cor slapped his hand to his hip. "Thief!" he shouted, lunging forward toward the disappearing shape.

Then he started to fade away, too.

CHAPTER FIVE

COR

I lunged forward, reaching for the fleeing Grejo's wrist as he began to slip across the gap to who-knew-where. Without a destination, I pushed myself away from Kuyen, hopefully close enough in his wake—

Got him. My hand closed over his wrist, both of us solid, halfway between one world and another. I willed us to stay, concentrating my *jeira* like an anchor to keep us from slipping farther from Kuyen. Worldwalking always took some energy, but this struggle drained *jeira* like water from a cracked jug. I couldn't let the thief pull me onward into a trap. He fought, both against my grip on his arm and with his *jeira*, trying to free himself.

Stupid, stupid move, Cor.

We were each halfway between one world and another, but not the same two worlds. Slipping without a chosen destination had been my only hope for following in the Grejo's wake, but I'd gone adrift instead.

The hazy landscape that overlaid my view of the Aubello

market was an icy, moonlit rockscape and the ghost of a chill wind that I could feel, still in the gap between.

The thief flung his weight to the side, jolting my focus from *jeira* to my physical balance. The stones and ice of the otherworld fouled my feet. Foggy shapes of Aubello shoppers dodged out of the way as the Grejo and I lurched to the left. A merchant's stall loomed ahead.

My attention was split between too many things, but I glimpsed a shadowy spire of stone in the otherworld and grabbed for it with my left hand to steady myself. I caught my balance at the same instant that pain bit into my palm.

It snapped my concentration and everything unraveled. The thief slipped out of my reach, escaping off Kuyen into some world beyond and taking my money with him. My own world formed back around me: heat, stone stone-paved walkways and a babbling crowd. Strain hammered behind my temples and I sagged against the nearest solid object.

"You're bleeding on my wares," a voice snapped.

A Ziddesh man glared from behind the sales table I'd tried so hard to keep from crashing into. He stood with his squat, lizard-like body drawn up to its unimpressive height. Dark-red splotches marred the pale, delicate scarf displayed at the front of the table, dripping from my left palm.

"Cor!" Kate pushed out of the crowd and took hold of my arm. "What happened?"

The fact that she asked in English betrayed her worry as much as her tight grip did.

"A coin thief, that's all," I reassured her. The ragged cut across my palm still wept blood, though it wasn't too deep. My handkerchief might suffice.

"But your hand—" Kate started.

"You'll need to pay for this," the Ziddesh merchant said, jabbing a clawed finger at the ruined cloth. His scaly skin flushed scarlet as he made a deliberate show of his anger.

"I was just robbed!" Of…nearly everything. What had I been thinking, to carry all my coin together? All in high marks, too, the largest denomination given straight from the House accounts for my parting share. I pressed the handkerchief to the wound, clenching my fingers in a fist around it. To Kate, I said, "I'll mend, don't worry."

"My merchandise was just ruined," the merchant hissed, his bright skin darkening to maroon along with his mood. "You're responsible. I'll bill your House if you won't honor it!"

Some members of the crowd muttered protests, but none loud enough to stand out.

"What do you know of honor?" I straightened up to my full height and squared my shoulders, nearly overwhelmed by the desire to draw on him as I should have done to the thief. "You self-serving—"

Kate stepped forward, squeezing my arm. She leveled a glare at the merchant. "Cor just got attacked in your market, and you're complaining that he bled on this cloth?"

"If he's done the damage, he owes the payment. I can't sell that scarf now that it's stained." The Ziddesh man spread his hands over his wares and allowed a tinge of purple condescension to suffuse his skin. A Ziddesh could hide his reactions if he wished, and he would make a poor merchant if he hadn't practiced that skill, whether Kate could read his moods or not. He shifted his beady gaze back to me. "What is your House, Thurei? If you don't have the pocket money for it."

The heat in Kate's voice surprised me. "That's not your business. I can fix the stain."

Before the Ziddesh could object again, she snatched the stained scarf up off the table and stared closely at it. The dark spots of blood disappeared, leaving the fabric pristine. She had used her skill to erase my blood from the weave as cleanly as if it had never fallen.

She'd disbelieved it out of existence.

Kate shoved the scarf back at the merchant. "There. Good as new. Satisfied?"

"You have some skill at Seeming and expect me to fall for it?" The Ziddesh narrowed his eyes, refusing to take it back.

The merchant from the next stall spoke up. "Leave off! They're not responsible for what happened. The thieves have gotten bold around here, but that's a matter for the peacekeepers, not customers."

"If I let every clumsy lackwit…" The Ziddesh must have spoken out of spite because then he waved us away, though Kate still held the scarf. "Forget it. I've never seen either of you, as far as I'm concerned."

The man was too craven to start a feud with his neighbor over the scarf and too proud to accept it back now that he'd called Kate a liar. I steered Kate away from the stall, inclining my head in an abbreviated bow for the neighboring merchant as we passed.

"What a jerk," Kate muttered, dropping into English.

"Yes." A peevish merchant was the least of my concerns. If the Leratom had offered to open their doors to us, I had no doubt they would still do so without a guesting gift. Surely, it would be no worse than they'd expect, for a Houseless pair. Not quite a pair, even.

Kate held out the scarf, now folded into a neat square. "I *did* get the blood out of this. It was no different, really, from how I cleaned my training clothes when you were helping me learn my skill. Will it do as a guesting gift?"

I smiled, pleased to see the worry lines ease from between her brows as she smiled back. "I believe it will."

It would have to. We didn't have anything else.

Kate nodded, but she still had her lips pursed. "Coran, I almost used my skill on that thief."

"Ah." Now that I was paying attention, I noticed she held her shoulders rounded in fear or uncertainty. While a *zaret* could kill, I'd grown up handling the blade and the responsibility that came with it. Kate's skill was powerful and she'd come into it so recently. "I considered it myself, but there was no need. It was only coin, Katen, nothing worth killing for."

Again, the reluctant nod. "If there had been a need, I still wouldn't have been any help. I was too slow."

So a failure if she had, a failure that she had not. That didn't seem to be a thing I could fix, but I offered my best. "We'll practice more, and next time, you'll be faster if you need to be."

"You're right. I can practice more at home, too." She straightened her spine, her determined expression familiar from the time we'd spent training together.

Good. She needed to be confident in her skill to use it properly and I had no doubt that we would need it again if the Scholars still considered us enemies.

House Leratom took up an entire urban block, three stories high, with a tower in the northeast corner that reached two floors higher. Medallions inset into the plastered walls bore the colorful knotwork of the House name and I shoved aside my memory of House Temarel's familiar gray silhouette.

The street flared out into a paved square facing the grand front doors. Though the doors were closed, a handful of guests mingled in the square—not just Thureis, but also a Lan te Kos and a Frebel, nearly Thurei in her slender build, but with natural armor that grew in tough plates along her back and limbs, left artfully bare by her bright, festive clothing.

Over the chatter in the square and the background street sounds, I caught laughter and music from above. Near one corner of the square, someone in a gantry on the roof lowered a small, railed platform down to street level. A couple of guests stepped on for a ride up. Judging by the visible greenery, House Leratom must have had a garden up there that rivaled Kate's home.

So, this was a Loratom 'open gather.' Out of preference, I would have chosen a less ambitious event for today, but here we were.

I glanced down at Kate, who took in everything with her wide, brown eyes. As a girl, she'd had this same air of delighted wonder every time she'd visited, so often over things I'd taken for granted. I'd felt like a genie from one of Earth's bedtime stories, able to grant wishes with a wave of my hand.

"House Leratom doesn't do things by half," I said.

"I guess not," she murmured, a smile teasing at the perfect curve of her lips. "That seems like a Thurei thing."

"Ha, that's fair," I said, mostly just to see that smile of hers in full. She wasn't wrong, but there were other Thurei things that I didn't look forward to facing today and I couldn't guess yet which ones the Leratoms had chosen. "Come on. Let's meet our hosts."

We garnered some curious looks from the guests as we strode into the square, but a Thurei man a couple years my senior came toward us, hands open in welcome.

Fashion here, in the strong sunlight and humidity, had dispensed with formal jackets and tailored trousers. Over his lightweight tunic and flowing pants, the man wore a bright ochre sash, a shade or two darker than his golden-yellow hair. The calligraphy stitched onto the sash proclaimed him a son of the House.

Sensible. My own jacket, devoid of House embroidery, had grown steadily heavier in the heat.

The Leratom offered a moderate bow when he reached us, the polite introduction embellished with a tilt of his hand that offered hospitality. "I'm Nabel Leratom, the *denet*'s close-kin, and it's my honor to offer you the welcome of the House."

Before he'd even heard our names? I kept the surprise off my face and bowed my respect to the House.

"I'm Coraven." Slapping more frills on the name wouldn't make it any longer. I offered Kate my hand, presenting her with a flourish that befit her proper position. "And I make known to the House my *dacha*, Katherine Kjelgaard, who stands *denet*-heir among her people. We were pleased to receive invitation from your *denet*."

There was no need for Kate to be shorted courtesy just because of me.

Though the situation didn't require anything further, Nabel offered a slight bow of respect—to both of us, not just Kate. "You would honor the *denet* if you'd join her upstairs for a moment, at least. My thanks for the grace of your names."

With that assignment given, Nabel waved us over to the lift and returned to his duties in the square.

A Leratom girl waited in the lift, a plank platform surrounded by a railing that came up to waist height. She held the small gate open as we approached, her pride in doing her House duty plain in every line of her body.

In English, I whispered, "Is this okay, Katen?"

My *dacha* glanced up at the ropes and the skillwork winch on the roof, then replied in the same language. "If she can, we can. She's, what, twelve?"

"Perhaps by next season." I suppressed a smile for the girl's sake as we stepped aboard. At that age, honor could be chancy.

When the lift lurched into motion, Kate steadied herself against me, the movement unselfconscious as she focused on the city square falling away below us. I put my arm around her shoulders, holding her securely.

The daughter of the House was old enough to survive seeing a little impropriety.

CHAPTER SIX

COR

The Leratom girl let us out at the roof, heeding her manners well enough that I couldn't tell if our display of physical affection had offended her.

I squeezed Kate's hand before letting go, but she was busy gazing around at the rooftop sanctuary in such avid interest that I wasn't sure she noticed.

Leratom's roof was utterly transformed. Rugs and carpets layered over each other across the flat rooftop, cloth stamped with leaf patterns draped over the low wall at the edge, and drifts of potted plants clustered everywhere. The effect gave the whole stretch of rooftop the look of an overgrown clearing in an aerial jungle.

"This is beautiful." Kate tilted her face up to me, brown eyes dazzled, the soft curve of her cheeks tinged a delicate pink.

"Very beautiful," I said around the sudden tightness in my chest. But Kate wanted to hear about the garden. I cleared my throat and glanced at the potted plants. "Very clever, too. They can rearrange it all or pack it up whenever they like. It would keep anyone from using the roof as an anchor point. No guest had to go inside to get here, and the lift doesn't travel past any windows. That's how they can afford to cast so wide a welcome and still keep their House safe."

Kate tipped her head to the side as if she were considering the practicality of the idea. "Do they have to worry about that kind of stuff?"

"Temarel and Pareshol both stand on their own ground. Here in the city…" I shrugged my fingers, thinking about my own lost coin purse. Here, a person needed to guard themselves more carefully or pay the expense of their foolishness. "A House has different needs."

She nodded, but her brows still pinched together. "There's still Truce, isn't there?"

"There is." I echoed the human gesture, hoping she would find comfort in it. "Come. Let's find our hosts and give a proper greeting."

The greenery had been arranged, not just to obscure the lines and details of the architecture, but to create more intimate social spaces. Some held tables of food, or clusters of chairs, or drifts of pillows where groups of guests lounged and chatted. We didn't catch everyone's eye by any means, but we found curiosity enough.

The size of the party excused me from having to bow every time, but nothing saved me from making introductions.

Coraven. Coraven. Coraven. As if all the world had the right to my personal name.

They did, as I no longer had House walls to stand around me.

Then Kate caught my eye and smiled, a reminder that my *dacha* had stayed by me and she held my honor safe. She guarded it well, handling prying questions with a polite reserve that would have done any socialite proud. I wondered where she might have learned such a skill in the places she'd grown up, but now wasn't the time to ask.

A Leratom daughter, Misora, broke the repetition with a slight smile after introductions. "Well met, both of you, and welcome to the House. How are you enjoying Aubello?"

The *denet*-heir, then, or a daughter of the *denet*, if she offered the House's welcome to strangers anywhere other than the door. Though her light, flowing, green dress bordered on informal, she held her trim, fine-boned frame with an understated authority that no doubt did her *denet* proud.

She gained an immediate measure of my respect for the kindness of not flaunting her position in front of me.

"It's a beautiful city," I said. "Though we met with some trouble on the way in."

Misora's teal brows drew together. "Trouble? What kind of trouble?"

"A coin thief in the market near here." Hopefully, I managed to keep the chagrin out of my voice.

"You must allow us to reimburse your loss," Misora said. "You came today as our guests, didn't you? As your hosts and as leaders in the city, we owe you no less."

"Your concern does you credit." I offered a slight bow of thanks, with a flick of my hand to indicate an honor declined. I didn't need debt to this House, especially not before I knew what they wanted from me.

"I wish I could say that every street in the city is equally safe for new visitors, but that is less and less the case, lately." Misora shrugged her fingers. "If you'd like to explore on foot, I can offer you tokens to places where it's safe to do so."

Beside me, Kate had grown tense, but she kept her voice level to ask, "Are there Hunters? Is that the problem?"

Misora soothed the air between them with a gesture. "Not Hunters of the kind Coraven is concerned with." She inclined her head in respect. "Thieves and lawbreakers, though—Hunters are often found among them. Lately, it seems their numbers in the city are growing. I've heard from others that Aubello isn't alone in this."

If Misora had intended to alarm Kate, I didn't think she could have improved her effect.

"But there's the Truce," Kate said before turning to me. "And peacekeepers. Though I don't know what peacekeepers could have done to keep you from getting robbed. That thief just slipped away."

"If I'd been faster, I could have caught him, or if I'd been more vigilant, I could have avoided it altogether. At the outpost, we won't even have that to worry about."

Misora raised her brows. "Have you spoken yet with my *denet*?"

"We've not been so fortunate." I looked over the artificial jungle. "There's a great deal of territory yet to explore."

"Perhaps she can put your concerns to rest, Kjelgaard," Misora said. "Allow me to guide you."

Misora led us to a wide space fringed with palms, overlooking the square below. The *denet* held court at a low table in the center, looking up when her daughter lifted a hand. She was a handsome woman of perhaps fifty, with salmon-pink hair woven into a braided cap, and a loose, layered skirt in pale blue. She murmured something to her conversational companions, a Lan captain I'd seen at the outpost but not been introduced to, and an older Thurei man with the sign of House Habilo emblazoned on his vest.

Though I'd never met the *denet*, she must have had a good enough description of us to recognize us. I introduced both of us and chose a conservative bow, conveying the gratitude of a guest. It couldn't be faulted for politeness and yet didn't touch on anything beyond today's attendance. She answered with slight welcome, just a bare inclination of her head, and a raised eyebrow that said she'd made note of my chosen greeting.

So, that was the first two game pieces moved.

"Welcome to House Leratom, Coraven, Kjelgaard. You honor me with your presence."

Surprise caught me for a moment, making my answer a beat late. There were many things Leratom could have offered before implying that I—we—could in any way bring honor to her or her House. By formal pattern, the answer should have been something about the courtesy of accepting her invitation. Well, if we were throwing out the training manual…

"Your invitation piqued my interest," I said.

Leratom turned her palm up in a gesture granting permission. "I welcome any questions you have. Come, come. Sit down, please."

She beckoned to one of her kin nearby to bring extra chairs to her table. Chairs were vacated and placed as she wished. Leratom's companions at her table took their leave, begging thirst or a desire to mingle, so that the *denet* was alone with Kate and me. She gestured to the low seats beside her.

Kate smiled as bright as dawn and sat readily, folding into the lounge chair like she chatted with *denets* every day. I followed as smoothly as I could manage, settling on a cushioned sling chair.

I had little remaining that I could lose to Leratom, no matter what game she intended to play.

"Is this your first time visiting Aubello?" Leratom asked.

"Yes, I've never before had the pleasure," I said. The agreement I had ground out at my former House had collected all my House duties to the hours between sunset and sunrise, when the way between worlds was closed. That meant no easy travel, though my *denet* had ensured I had plenty of society at the House to keep me…occupied.

"It's beautiful here," Kate said, her glance around us touching on the lush greenery of the roof garden. Her family had specialized in planted spaces, although in the style of Earth, of course. Her gaze sharpened again as she looked back at our host. "But it seems to be growing more dangerous."

That bald statement raised the *denet*'s pink brows. "Have you had trouble, Kjelgaard?"

I spoke up. "There was a coin thief in the market near the Valeflower slip anchor, a Grejo. I was not able to keep him from slipping away."

"Coraven cut his hand trying to catch the thief." Kate glanced down to my left hand. I tucked it under my right, glad the bleeding had stopped. "Does House Leratom have a healer?"

"Ah, no, it's fine," I stumbled over the words, caught off-guard by the impropriety of the request. Kate had no way of knowing and I had no wish to shame her by explaining it now.

"We do," Leratom said. Hospitality required her to take the request seriously, even if she could tell I wasn't so gravely ill or injured to honorably ask for such services as a stranger, guest or no. "Shall I call for our healer, Coraven?"

"No, with my thanks." Hiding a sigh, I turned my hand over. The wound was hardly more than a ragged scratch. "It's not serious enough to inconvenience your healer."

Leratom settled back more comfortably in her chair. "If you ever have trouble finding a merchant healer, you're welcome to call on us."

"Pella's garrison has healers in residence, but your offer is very kind." I'd grown up with Havro in House, so I'd never had to visit a healer for pay. Lewrits' unique skill allowed them to accelerate their own healing, but individuals powerful enough to heal others were rare.

"Misora Leratom told us that there have been more Hunters here," Kate said. Most of her experience with healers had followed Hunter attacks.

Denet Leratom lifted a hand in agreement. "My heir is correct. We've been seeing more disturbances from illegal activity. Hunters, among others, and more of them are moving in from the wildlands. It's possible that other criminals have taken advantage of the distraction these newcomers have caused." She shifted her focus to me. "This touches near the topic I wished to present to you both. I'm looking for an armsmaster for my House."

Out of the corner of my eye, I saw Kate brighten up at that. It didn't go unnoticed by Leratom, either, who adjusted to speak to both of us.

"Considering the increasing security concerns in the city, I can do no less for my House. I've heard nothing but the best about your fighting abilities, both of you."

"Both of us?" Kate echoed, like she might have misheard. "I'm not a fighter. Coraven is the master as far as that's concerned."

"I've heard you faced a pack of Hiraches, on a world beyond Truce." Leratom shaded her voice with approval. "The Hiraches were not just beaten, but...destroyed."

Kate shivered.

For me, the end of the fight had passed in a blur of claws and blade, Hiraches closing in until one had called out that he had caught my *dacha*. The last clear thing I remembered seeing was Katen caught in the grasp of a Hunter. Soon after, Kate had destroyed them, activating her devastating skill to wipe them out of existence, then slipping me to the safety of Havro's atrium. She'd saved us both.

Beyond the bare shape of it, we hadn't spoken of how the experience weighed on her.

Perhaps three or four people had heard the tale directly from us. Leratomm wasn't one of them. Rumor traveled faster than the feet of a worldwalker, but who would have told a House in Aubello?

"My *dacha*'s skill is formidable," I said, since deterrence had its own value. "I believe the Hiraches regret their choice of quarry."

"The Hunters deserve to regret all their hunts," Leratom said, flicking the subject aside. "But I will not have my own House regret our preparation in times of conflict. I would welcome your instruction, Coraven." She let my personal name hang there, unadorned, before turning to Kate. "Kjelgaard, your skill is unique. I would value your perspective in my House as well."

"I'm human," Kate said, as if anyone might not have noticed. "Coraven helped me learn my skill with techniques he used in his own training. I'm not sure my perspective would add much."

Though her words were reserved, Kate's voice held an excitement that surprised me. Was she proud of her skill? She ought to have been, having come so far in such a short time. Or was it Leratom's interest in her perspective as a human?

Kate had to know I valued her perspective.

Abruptly eager to bring this conversation to a close, I said, "Your offer is generous, but I have employment already. Perhaps if my duties for *Tol* Pella allow, Katherine and I can visit in the future. I may have time for occasional lessons in the evenings."

"I would hate to place further burdens on your time. The constraints of sunset must provide frustration enough." Leratom's pale gaze flicked between Kate and me. Spreading her hands, she smiled. "But you haven't given me the chance to explain how generous my offer is. If you prefer to teach in the evenings, that can be arranged. I hope you will find that your duties ride lightly on your time. My House stands ready to honor all your needs, if we have your service, and that includes how you choose to use your days."

That caught like a barbed thorn for a moment and I forced down a cough. "That is, indeed, generous. Too much, I think, for a few *zaret* lessons."

All Thureis paid House debt, giving of their service and talents in whatever manner the House asked, in order to balance the House providing for them. *Honoring all their needs*, in fact, as it would have been styled in our tongue.

At least, that was how it worked for Thureis who belonged to a House. The balance struck between *Denet* Temarel and I in years past had not come cheaply. In my life as it stood now, I had no debt but what I owed my *dacha*.

Hired help—certainly a hired armsmaster who gave lessons when he felt like it—would never balance a House providing for all of a person's needs. She wasn't offering employment, but the counterfeit of a son's place.

That would, of necessity, come at a price much higher than blade lessons.

Kate read something off my face, then asked, "What kind of needs would the House be honoring?"

"You would have rooms here or..." *Denet* Leratom hedged, her gaze flicking to me as I failed to hide a frown. "Or apartments in the city. The entertainment, care, and company of the House. You'd be welcome to draw upon funds and other such amenities as are traditional for those...within our walls."

Kin. She meant *kin* by that comment, and we would never be kin to Leratom.

I stood, shocking the *denet* and Kate both, and dropped a shallow bow—leave taking, nothing more.

"I regret I cannot accommodate you, *Denet* Leratom, but I have employment. Unfortunately, my time today grows short."

Kate stood, too, but more slowly. In English, she said, "It's a try-out position, isn't it? Your job with the *tol*?"

Switching to a private language in company was dreadfully rude but still ranked above my behavior on the scale of acceptable manners. I stuck to English, briefly. "I won't fail with Pella. She gave an honest offer and I'm equal to it. This is not the same."

Kate shot a glance at the *denet*, who had turned her face aside in a polite playact that something on a nearby rooftop might have caught her attention. "Okay. Then let's go."

Leratom heard that for the end of it, or she simply sallied into the pause. "I didn't intend to distress you with my offer, Coraven, Kjelgaard, but please believe I respect your decision." She stood and bowed a host's farewell. Pitching her voice to carry more broadly across the space and its occupants, she said, "Aubello is new to you both and I hope you will view House Leratom as an ally. Our doors stand open to you."

"My thanks," I said tightly, the etiquette too ingrained to drop. With Kate beside me, we headed back to the lift.

The Houseless did not have allies.

CHAPTER SEVEN

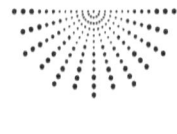

KATE

We made it from the rooftop garden all the way back down to the plaza in front of House Leratom without speaking, Cor so expressionless and distant that he might as well have been on another world.

Once we had gotten out of earshot of the guests still milling in the square, I asked, "What was that all about? I thought that *Denet* Leratom made you a good offer."

"It wasn't an honest offer," he said, his voice tight. "She hoped to get more than what she asked for. *Zaret* lessons aren't worth all of that."

I had little to compare it to, but it seemed on par with the arrangement the Temarel armsmaster had. "You're as good as Seretun. Why shouldn't she offer you the same?"

Cor stopped and turned to me, his eyes bleak. "Seretun is kin. House Temarel gives him everything he needs because he gives all he has to the House in return. He teaches his kin to use their skill because they're all his cousins." He let out a sharp breath. "I'm no kin to Leratom, nor will I give them everything I have. Whatever she wants, it must be more expensive than she's willing to ask for upfront, and that stops my feet at the threshold."

"That makes sense," I said. It did, although it didn't explain why he'd taken such offense over it. It was hard to let go of the idea of seeing Cor among his people again, even if they weren't his family. A little too formal and too much bowing for my taste, but those things were as much a part of Cor as his sense of honor or his skill. The Leratom *denet* hadn't given me the same unyielding vibe as the leaders of either Temarel or Pareshol, the only other two Thurei *denets* I'd met. She'd seemed kind. "Maybe she was just being nice."

Cor flicked the suggestion away. "She bears no responsibility for strangers. She'll be *nice* as long as it costs her kin nothing."

"All right, all right." I held up my hands in surrender. I could hardly argue these things with Cor—he was the one who would know. The *denet* had told us to consider her an ally, though, so maybe the door wasn't completely closed. I still had a favor I wanted to ask her. "Sorry I said anything about it."

"There's no reason to be sorry. You had a question, *dacha*, and it was right of you to ask it." Cor's expression softened into something wistful, and he sighed. "Today has been…unsettling. I worried when the dawn came without you, and this meeting with House Leratom was not what I expected."

"Not to mention the thief."

"Not to mention the thief," he repeated firmly. He opened his hand to check the cut on his palm but tucked it back into his pocket before I could see it.

"Will you be okay?"

"Everything's going to be fine," he said as he smiled.

Well, okay then. I stifled a yawn and rubbed my eyes. "How has it been such a long day already? It's barely the afternoon."

"Perhaps we can see the city another day," Cor said. "You have your work again, don't you?"

"Yeah, my medical leave is up, so I'm back working my regular shifts." I would have loved to see the city, but sleep made more sense. I'd be a zombie at work tomorrow otherwise. I couldn't afford to spend all of Kuyen's days awake, however much I wanted to. "Do you have time to put those new wards up at my apartment?"

"Ah. I have to make them first, but I can bring them over in the morning. It would be better to stay at the garrison for today, I think. We can use your apartment as a slip anchor on the way back and you can pick up a change of clothes if you wish. Will that do?"

"Oh, right. No problem." I hadn't meant to give him a chore, but I'd feel better once it was done. The wards deterred Hunters and made it safer for me to stay in my own apartment. Cor had a job now and I couldn't be missing from Earth every single night. Rose's text was evidence of that, though I hated the thought of missing any time with Cor.

Also, the pickpocket had made me nervous. While that incident hadn't been an attack on the scale of the Hiraches, it was still a reminder of how quickly things could get dangerous, how unsafe we were outside of Cor's House.

How unpracticed I was with my skill.

I slipped us from the street outside House Leratom to my apartment, where I gathered up a set of pajamas and some regular, everyday clothes just in case. Then Cor took us from there to his —*our*—quarters at the garrison. As soon as we stood firmly in the dark, wood-paneled room, Cor slipped his hand out of my grasp and stepped away.

"I can work on those wards while you sleep." He hesitated at the door in the wooden screen dividing the sitting room from the bedroom. "If you allow me a moment, I'll just get the supplies and you can have the room to yourself."

"Sure." I didn't know what else to say. His formality made me feel more like a guest and a guest certainly didn't belong in his bed. Vow or no vow.

Cor hurried back out carrying a box roughly the size of a shoebox and brought it over to the table. "Will you come out and say goodbye before you go home, *dacha*?"

"Of course," I said. I wanted to go kiss him goodnight, as I'd kissed him good morning—and maybe he'd just have to make the wards later—but he stood with the table between us, his hands still resting lightly on the wooden box.

Not exactly the body language of a man who wanted a kiss, even from his *dacha*.

"Good night, Coran," I said, closing the bedroom door behind me.

The next day at work, you'd have thought I'd been dead in a ditch somewhere by the way Rose flung her arms around me when I showed up. She often joked that she used her big emotions to make up for her petite size, but she had genuine concern in her dark brown eyes.

"I thought you were giving me the cold shoulder," she exclaimed, her tone only half-joking. After the Hirach had attacked me outside of After Image, she'd done her best to be there for me. Rose—along with the police and every other human who couldn't see what I did—thought I'd been attacked during an attempted robbery. I'd done enough arguing over that sort of thing as a kid, so I knew not to bother explaining about Hunters. No one would believe what they couldn't understand.

"No, no cold shoulder at all," I said, stepping back to tuck my messenger bag under the counter. As much as I appreciated her care, I still had to lie to her. I couldn't tell her I'd been with Cor last night, on another world. "I just didn't have my phone on me. It was on the charger. And then by the time I saw your message, it was pretty late."

"Were you busy?" Rose grinned suggestively and twirled a lock of her long, black hair around a dainty finger. "How's your 'friend,' Corey?"

She knew about Cor, at least the fact that he was male and that we 'had a history'—however she interpreted that. I'd told her he'd been spending some time with me since the attack, mostly to explain why I wasn't available in the evenings. I hadn't told her much about him, personally. How could I? She took that as permission to speculate freely. Rose loved gossip.

"Corey's fine," I said. I'd come up with the name because it sounded more human than Coraven or even Cor. More normal. "He did come over last night. Sorry I wasn't paying better attention to my phone."

"That's fine. So long as you don't forget your friends." Rose turned on the computer and the other machines we'd need for the day. She loaded another ream of paper into the photo printer and then gave me a stern look. "You know how some people get. Once they start dating, they pretend everyone else they ever knew doesn't exist anymore."

"I won't," I said. Rose and I hadn't known each other long. I'd only been working here for a little less than five months, but she had proven to be a good friend.

"In fact," I continued, once I'd fetched the starting cash out of the safe and brought it out to the register, "why don't we go do something after work? You don't have summer classes, do you?"

"Nope," she said, smiling. She lifted her hands high in a full-body stretch. "I'll be free all summer, thank you very much. Lots of going to the beach, lots of whatever else I want to do. Do you have something in mind?"

I hadn't thought that far. I didn't exactly have an established habit of social entertainment. Growing up in a psychiatric hospital didn't lend itself to that, and most of the social activities I'd done since getting out had been with Rose and her friends.

At least most of what I'd done on Earth.

"I was thinking of sprucing up my apartment," I said, working out the idea as I spoke. "Do you know any place with some reasonably priced home goods?" Maybe I could get something for Cor's new place to make it look more…homey.

"Sure," Rose said. "I know some places we could try. Sounds like fun."

I had a bit of cash I could use for something like this. I smiled at her. "Good."

That afternoon when we turned the store over to Frank and Evianna, I hopped into Rose's truck for some shopping. After spending half the night awake in Kuyen, I really ought to have been sleeping for a few extra hours, but this was important, too. The sun was always up somewhere.

Rose and I explored thrift shops and consignment stores and I had fun picking out and pretending to consider the most bizarre things. Eventually, I chose a mirror with a fancy, antique-looking frame—it would be a mirror all the time, unlike the skillwork version I'd seen on Kuyen—and a waist-high, brass Rococo candelabra. The last one started as a joke and then grew on me. An electric lamp would be no good on Kuyen, but Cor could put skillwork lights or actual candles on that sculptural beast. Far too elegant in my cheap apartment, but Cor's former House was filled with elegant, expensive things.

I couldn't manage any expensive presents on my income, but I thought he might like these.

We picked up a couple of other odds and ends, and I bought a new dress, just in case my future had more formal events in it than my current wardrobe could handle.

Rose seemed less concerned about our friendship as she drove me home. It wasn't too late in the day; I had about an hour and a half before sunset. Plenty of time for a power nap. We unloaded my purchases for Cor's apartment, and I gave her a hug goodbye.

Then I set my alarm and crawled into bed to catch up on some sleep.

Cor showed up in my living room just after sunset, like he'd promised—not that I'd expected him to be late.

And I *really* hadn't expected him to show up in blue jeans and a black T-shirt.

"What's this?" I asked him, my grin wide enough that I thought my face might freeze that way. "You look almost like a native."

His cheeks colored a darker gold. "That's the idea."

Like a native who had access to an excellent tailor. Though the detailing was subtly off—the shirt's neckline was a little too wide and the jeans had too many belt loops—Cor looked very, very good in the slim, dark blue jeans and the black T-shirt that emphasized his shoulders. Armsmaster, indeed. His orange hair blazed in contrast. He carried the box from last night in one hand.

I thought I might be blushing, too. "Those clothes look fantastic on you."

"My thanks." He grinned, then, and stepped forward for a kiss.

Tilting my face up to meet his lips, I wrapped my arms around him and pulled him closer. We shared so few moments like this that it seemed impossible that his arms already felt like home.

The tunics he usually wore had thicker, heavier fabric and I could almost feel his skin through the thin T-shirt material. I traced the long curve of his spine with my fingertips.

The wooden box thumped to the floor and Cor pulled back with a muttered curse.

"My clumsy hands," he said, kneeling to pick it up. It didn't escape my notice that he maneuvered himself away from me to do so. He cleared his throat as he stood, holding up the box. "I should put these wards in place."

"Okay," I said, adding a silent reminder to keep my hands to myself.

He set the box on my kitchen table, opening it to reveal coiled strips of material like thick ribbons, bright threads interwoven in the base of pale, natural-looking fibers.

"How did you make these?" I asked.

"It's skillwork, so it takes a particular pattern and type of threadwork and then the crafter's *jeira*," Cor said offhandedly as he fished one out. "A *morsai* breeder from Gettik had the kindness to teach me when he came to the House for pups some years ago."

Of course, "*morsai* breeder" would be an actual profession for someone, not just a hobby for a rich girl like Cor's sister. And naturally, that someone would be able to teach the fine art of ward making to a boy. I should have known.

Even though I believed in Kuyen, sometimes it still surprised me how Not Earth it was.

"How old were you?" I asked.

He selected four of the ribbons, leaving more tangled in the bottom of the box, and closed the lid. "Fifteen."

Fifteen, and begging some stranger to teach him wards so he

could protect me. He'd told me once before that I was the reason he'd learned. I reached out to touch his arm. "Thank you, Coran."

He smiled, pleased. "You are welcome, Katen."

Someone knocked on the door and we both jumped. I headed to answer it, Hunters on my mind. But Hunters wouldn't have knocked. Cor followed.

Rose waited on the landing, a plastic bag dangling from her hand. She held it up. "Hey, you forgot your dress. I texted you."

"Rose! Thanks. Um, my phone's on the charger." I didn't need a phone in Kuyen and, at some level, I had already mentally switched over to Kuyen time. I reached for the bag.

Rose's gaze slid from my face up over my shoulder. "Oh, sorry. I didn't realize you had your friend over."

CHAPTER EIGHT

COR

The human woman's dark eyes fixed on me, her unexpected attention as startling as a shock of cold rain. She had hair as glossy and black as a Lan's framing her face, complementing the richness of her tanned skin. She was shorter even than Kate.

"I—" Kate spun to look at me, as if she hadn't expected me to still be standing behind her. For a moment, she looked so young again, a wide-eyed girl baffled that her parents didn't see me when they came up to scold her for having her light on in the middle of the night. "I mean...yes. Of course, Cor—Corey's over here."

The woman, Rose, tilted her head and narrowed her eyes, her gaze flicking back and forth between us before settling on Kate. "Is everything okay?"

"Yes." Kate nearly sighed the word out, her shoulders sagging as if she'd set down a heavy weight. She stepped a little aside, gesturing at me. "This is Corey. Corey, this is Rose."

Corey? A child's name, like Katie? Then Kate flashed me a grin so sweet, it stole my breath away.

She could give me whatever name she wanted.

"Corey," Rose said, her own smile wide but somewhat more guarded. "Kate's told me so much about you."

I gestured agreement in the human style, with a nod of my head. "I hope I live up to it."

Because surely whatever Kate had said had to be good, didn't it? By the look Rose gave me, I grew less certain.

Well, in the absence of kin, a person of honor ought to be vigilant on behalf of her friend. It reflected well on Rose, that she looked twice before she offered welcome.

"We're not in a hurry, are we?" Kate whispered to me.

"Not at all." I had lessons to teach in the afternoon, but that was half a day away.

Kate held the door open wide. "Do you want to come in?"

"Can't. I'm about to meet the rest of the crew for dinner," Rose said.

She was a sailor? Kate did live close to the ocean. Living in a world where everyone could worldwalk, I'd always been fascinated with the variety of ways humans traveled. "What is the name of your ship?"

Rose gave me an odd look. "Jakeward, I guess. You?"

I shook my head, taking care with the human gesture. "I don't sail."

"O-kay." She shook her head, too, then she brightened. "Anyway, have you guys eaten yet?"

"Um…" Kate trailed off and looked at me.

"I have not eaten," I answered, puzzled for a moment until I realized she'd been giving me the chance to decline an offer that hadn't yet been made.

"Great!" Rose said. "You guys should come. Then you can meet everyone, Corey."

My empty stomach curled around itself. From the moment I'd contacted Kate here in her new city, she had been ruthlessly clear about the consequences should I threaten her new life. Her *normal* life among the rest of humans who were blind to everything beyond the single, limited world they knew.

Could Rose be a worldwalker? Or could she "see" me in the way Kate's parents had, sometimes looking at me and calling me by the name of a neighbor child or school companion of Kate's?

What if this crew of hers couldn't see me at all? What if all they saw was Kate talking to empty air?

Kate rested her fingertips on my arm, the slight touch warm on my bare skin. "Rose, give us a minute, okay?"

Rose frowned but nodded.

Kate closed the door and looked up at me. "What do you think? Do you want to go?"

I could have fought Hunters, had they appeared on her doorstep, but if there was anything I could do to make a human see me when they were already blinded by their disbelief, I had never found it in all these years. If any of these humans questioned Kate's eyes—or her mind—I would not be able to help prove her claims.

Kate wanted to go. I couldn't ignore the longing on her face.

I took a deep breath, willing myself to confidence. "We should go."

Kate's smile woke some warmth back inside me, though that would be a small consolation if things went poorly.

"Katen," I said quickly as she reached for the doorknob. "They might not…be like Rose."

She hesitated, worry shadowing her brown eyes before she squared her shoulders. "I know. If they don't see you, it's okay. We'll just leave, and I'll deal with it later. But Coran, Rose can see you."

I gave her my most optimistic smile.

When Kate opened the door again, Rose was peering at a small, shiny phone that she immediately slid back into the purse that hung over her shoulder.

"We'd love to go," Kate told her.

Again, Rose made a quick glance between us, as if she expected me to disagree. I kept my expression politely neutral and Rose shrugged her shoulders very slightly, directing her next question at Kate. "You guys want to ride in the truck with me? It's the taqueria on Mesa."

"That would be great," Kate replied, indicating that the string of words had made sense to her.

We followed Rose back down to the ground level, where she led us to a vehicle somewhat larger than the average, with a long bed like a wagon. *The truck.*

I'd seen human cars. The vehicles were everywhere, ubiquitous, constantly streaming across the flat, straight roads, lining the road edges like gutter stones or packed into their own special gathering spaces like biddable livestock in tiny fields.

Kate brought me to the side of the vehicle. "You sit up front. You're tall."

When Rose went around to the other side, Kate dropped her voice to a whisper. "You haven't ever ridden in a car, have you? There will be a strap on the inside of the truck with a metal tab that goes into a slot on the left side of the seat." She mimed it all, speaking quickly, then reached out and pulled on a recessed flap on the vehicle door. The door popped open. "It's perfectly safe. Stare out of the windshield if you start to feel sick. You'll be fine."

I believed she meant to be reassuring.

Rose was already in the vehicle. Kate sat herself in the row of seating behind me.

I found the strap and buckle as Kate had described, notched the two together after a couple of tries, securing myself to the upholstered chair. Rose strapped herself in as well. Kate, too, judging by the zip and click behind me.

Rose twisted something and the vehicle snarled, then quieted to the barest growl that vibrated the whole structure, like a *morsai* suspicious of its surroundings. It rolled forward, finding a gap in the flow of traffic on the road, and picked up speed until the buildings and resting vehicles slid past us, dizzyingly fast.

The merciful artisan who'd crafted this truck had included a handhold on the inside of the door. I made use of it.

"So, Corey," Rose said, shooting me a glance, heedless of all the activity on display beyond the wide front window. "What do you do?"

I had not expected philosophy under the present conditions, but I was game. "The best I can, given the circumstances. Same as anyone."

"He teaches martial arts," Kate said, her words tripping over the heels of mine.

That had even less in common with the question than my answer had.

Rose gave me another sideways look. Her hands rested casually on the rudder wheel. Another vehicle slid into a gap in front of us and ours slowed, just a little, granting it more space.

"Your dad runs a martial arts studio?" Rose asked. "That's cool."

"My...dad?" As I recalled, humans had a Thurei-like, formal ranking of terms for their parents. My *denet* had never been 'my dad.'

"Oh, sorry, I thought Kate said you worked for him."

"Ah. I don't work for my father anymore," I said, guarding my words more closely. "I have a new position with Shom's aunt."

"Shom?" Rose asked. A little mirror on the front window let her and Kate share a look, but the angle did not permit me the same privilege.

"One of our old friends," Kate supplied.

So, she had told her friend about me, but not Shom. It occurred to me that Kate had invented a story of me to tell Rose, as she had sometimes done with her parents when they'd refused to believe the truth. I had no way of knowing what the shape of that story was to be able to tell it the same way.

Instead, I switched us to a different course. "Rose, I would like to give you my thanks. Kate told me that you were there when she woke at the hospital after the attack. I'm glad she was not alone."

Another look in the little mirror. "Katherine was covering my shift. Of course I'd be there for her."

I bit my tongue at the correction. Humans didn't follow Thurei naming customs. Why did she feel the need to school me on address?

"It's not your fault," Kate told her friend, taking something entirely different from the statement than I had. "It could have been so much worse, Rose. Really."

I suppressed a shiver. In the days after Kate had sent me away—when I'd failed to find her a teacher, failed to convince her to believe me—I couldn't close my eyes but for seeing the image of her dead at the feet of some Hunter.

The worst had almost happened, except that the Hunter had found Kate at the door of her workplace. The metal door had stood firm against his claws.

I hadn't been there to protect her. She'd sent me away, still afraid I'd been a sign of illness.

The truck slowed and turned off the street into a car yard. Buildings in the standard, blocky Earth style surrounded the rectangular yard, though most of the businesses had darkened windows. One, the liveliest, had a glowing sign proclaiming 'Fiesta

Fajita' in human—no, English—over the front windows. I could read the letters but didn't recognize the words.

After we left the truck behind, Kate stationed herself beside me, lacing her fingers in mine.

"How are you doing?" she asked, tilting her face up to study me. In the nighttime dimness, her round pupils were wide.

"I'm well," I said, the tightness around my chest easing. *She's never going to send me away again, whether other humans can see me or not. She promised.* I squeezed her fingers before drawing my hand away, too conscious of her friend who called her *Katherine* waiting for us to finish our chat and follow her.

CHAPTER NINE

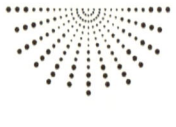

COR

Inside, the restaurant was redolent of spices and cooking oil. Patrons filled most of the small tables, chatting and laughing. The kitchen, visible behind a small service counter, was full of steel machines and sizzling metal surfaces tended by a pair of cooks.

Rose scanned the dining room, finding what she sought near the back of the space. She lifted her hand to acknowledge a group of men and women sitting at several small tables all shoved end to end in a line. Their tables were full, but a couple of the men hopped up and corralled another empty table, tacking it on the end of their makeshift banquet board.

They were all roughly the same age, perhaps twenty or so, like myself, with an obvious, easy camaraderie that reminded me forcefully of Birasef's mark. Among the Houses, that closeness in a group of age mates was common, but I hadn't expected it in humans, who all lived apart and left each other so readily.

One of the men, unusually tall for a human, with curly, dark hair, pulled Rose to him in a close hug. I glanced away to give them privacy.

"Finally, Rosie," he chided her, though his deep voice sounded more teasing than serious. "I thought we'd be done by the time you got here."

Rose grinned up at him and then stepped back, waving her hand at Kate and me. "I had to pick up these two. That takes time."

"Hi, Troy," Kate said, her voice a touch nervous. I could sympathize with that. But Rose had said *these two*. Kate slid her hand back into mine. "This is my boyfriend, Corey."

"Hey, nice meeting you." Troy tilted his head up, a nod in reverse.

"It's nice to meet you as well." I didn't attempt to copy the nod, settling instead for the broad smile that humans gave to strangers. An adequate enough response, for Corey the *nochel*. But there, how had I expected her to introduce me? I hadn't considered *nochel* an option, but it fit as well as any other. No language I knew had a word for me.

Rose gestured at the full tables, gathering everyone's attention. "Katherine, you know almost everyone here, I think. There's Logan, Chloe, Harvey, Eric, Charley, and Clara. Everybody, you know Katherine." Then, with a pause that might not have existed anywhere but in my anxious imagination, she added, "And this is her boyfriend, Corey."

Kate lifted her hand in a brief wave, though her grin bordered on giddy. "We'll be back in a minute. We need to go order."

On our way to the service counter, Kate whispered, "They saw you! Coran, everyone saw you!"

"They did." Seeing so many human eyes trained on me had been unusual, to say the least. Hearing her use my close-name reminded me of something else. "They call you Katherine."

Kate shrugged and looked away. "Most people do. It's not like Thurei names. It doesn't really matter."

But I was Thurei, and the pattern of it sounded so much like our custom of using the forms of a person's name to indicate the closeness of a relationship, that I had a hard time thinking of it in other terms. *Katherine* for acquaintances, *Kate* for friends, and *Katie, Rosie,* and *Corey* for...Kate had gone by Katie when she'd been a girl. For children?

Perhaps Corey the boyfriend needed to simply keep his ears open and try to mind his steps. I could ask questions later if I had the need.

We stood in line behind an older woman with a child of eight or so. I couldn't tell what name *he* went by, but the woman was trying to select a menu option for him without anything "too hot."

I looked up at the lit menu behind the counter. As with the sign out front, I could read the letters but few of the words. "What do you recommend, *dacha*?"

She grinned up at me, seeing through my ploy in a moment. "It's so rare to find something that you don't know. How about tacos? You've had tacos before, I think."

I nodded, trying to recall. Half the fun of eating with Kate had always been the feeling of sneaking around her house and her parents. Every visit to Earth had felt a little like a game, as if we had all merely agreed to pretend no one but Kate could see Shom and me. The fact that every now and then I would catch someone's eyes as we played in the yard or among her father's grove of trees only made it seem more like play.

It had been a fun game, until it had ruined everything.

Kate ordered for us both, pulling her wallet out of her purse. I knew too little of the currency here for the numbers to make sense, but it still nagged at me. My funds as an instructor would be thin. Especially now that I'd lost so much to the coin thief.

I'd dreamed of one day bringing Kate to my House as my *dacha*, to provide for her needs in truth, as Leratom had claimed to offer.

Perhaps Kate had dreamed of such things, too, for Leratom's proposal to have appealed so much to her.

But I'd lost both Houses and now here I was eating out of her wallet.

Kate handed me a little plastic tent with a number on it. She kept two empty plastic glasses. "They'll bring us the food. Come on."

Once she'd filled the glasses from another one of the ingenious human machines, we returned to the tables. Kate took the chair next to Rose, so I sat across from her, to the left of Troy.

Rose fixed me with her lively, dark eyes. "So, you were telling us about your work. How'd your dad take it when you switched jobs?"

Kate shot her a glare, but I had weathered more than a single uncomfortable meal in my life. Her questions had been bold but not unkind. If Kate had had cousins, they might have been the ones testing my forms instead. I took a sip of water, wishing it were wine, and tried to remember how Kate had spoken of her father's business and whether or not she would continue it. We'd been too young for such things as children and it had never come up again. Everything was different now. Wasn't it?

"He hasn't given me his opinion of my work," I offered. "But I imagine he will scarcely miss me. The family is secure in his care."

"'Secure in his care'?" Rose echoed, with a grin that didn't reach her eyes. "Are you from *Downton Abbey* or something?"

"Yes," I said, my mouth gone too dry. I didn't know how I was supposed to answer, or what Kate might have said.

Rose's expression sharpened at that, eager as a High House daughter to twitch back the curtain, but before she could follow up, Kate stepped in.

"Nothing wrong with having manners. So, do you two have any

fun summer plans yet?" Kate directed her question between Rose and her *nochel*, drawing him into the conversation.

"I have a summer internship with Inveria," Troy said, moving his bulky shoulders in a shrug. "It's just product testing, so it's not that exciting, but that's going to be taking up most of my time. Sorry, babe."

That last comment, I thought, was offered to Rose, not Kate.

"That's okay." Rose grinned sympathetically, then turned back to me. "The rest of us are all liberal arts types, so we have to prepare for our careers differently."

As if on cue, the next closest members of Rose's mark—Eric and Charley, I thought—chorused, "Would you like fries with that?"

Everyone laughed and raised glasses of whatever they were drinking, clinking them together.

Lost again, I chuckled along. I thought I might have tapped out of the ring with a tolerable showing as the conversation moved down the table to an employment offer Clara was pursuing.

"I think that's our food," said Kate. One of the servants approached with a pair of large plates on a tray, his eyes alighting on the little plastic number I had placed at the edge of our table. He set our dishes before us with a quick, "Careful, it's hot."

The human had counted me as a body at the table, at least, though he hadn't met my eye any more than the proprietress at the counter had.

Kate distracted Rose with a question about a painting she was working on, which left me free to contemplate my food. These were not the same tacos that had come wrapped in waxy paper and tucked into a plastic bag on nights Kate had been free to eat in her room "alone." These tacos were very thin circles of flatbread topped with spiced meat, a pungent diced vegetable, crumbly fresh cheese and a drizzle of thin, red sauce.

The tacos I recalled were eaten with one's fingers—or at least, children did so when no adults were around.

I glanced over at the others, but they had all ordered different dishes and most were using utensils. My *dacha* had a plate of sliced meat and vegetables stewed in a thick sauce with a different style of flatbread in a covered dish alongside, but conversation had kept her from eating.

Rose was using fork and knife. *Always follow the host.*

I sliced the neatest piece of the taco I could manage, though the toppings threatened to spill everywhere. The first bite was a potent blend of acid and heat, delicious but surprising. I reached for my water and found Troy watching me like I'd brought a *morsai* to the table.

Kate glanced over at my plate and pressed her lips together like she was suppressing a smile. One eyebrow slightly raised, Kate fished a flatbread out of the holding dish and topped it with a generous scoop of the spiced stew. She folded the whole thing in half, holding it daintily from the top, somewhat more the method I remembered for tacos.

I tilted my head in the smallest of bows, both in thanks and an acknowledgment of her amusement, and then applied her lesson to my meal.

But that little exchange reminded Rose that I existed. Rose, who could see me without any prompting from Kate, though she didn't have any *jeira* that I could sense. Perhaps she knew how to hide it.

"So, Corey, you grew up in Oregon, too?" she asked, settling back into her role as interrogator.

"Yes," I agreed. This one seemed straightforward, despite her earlier comment about my origins. Kate had grown up in Oregon and we were childhood friends, so I must have as well. "Katherine and I met when we were young."

I was contemplating some approaches to the impossible task of subtly asking Rose if she had ever met anyone from another world, when her *nochel* leaned forward. He placed his elbows on the table and regarded me from under bushy, black brows.

"You know, any time the busybody routine gets to be too much, you can just say so."

Rose spread her hands. "I'm just being friendly."

I nodded, which lacked the nuance of an ironic bow. "I'm glad Katherine has such a careful friend at her side."

"Babe, he noticed," Troy said. "Cut him some slack."

Kate was trying to hide a smile, her cheeks flushed a charming pink. In a moment of the other couple's distraction, she mouthed, *They see you.*

I grinned in response because it delighted her, but I couldn't shake the tension in my shoulders, poised for all this to go wrong. Seeing me was only one part of the problem. I wanted them to *like* what they saw, not find me strange and take that strangeness out on Kate. I wanted to know that this wasn't a momentary lapse in the rules all the other humans had agreed to live by, that they would see me tomorrow.

What would my *dacha* do when they didn't? What would she do when it caused too many problems for it to be funny any longer?

Rose's *nochel* took over the host's duties. "Did you see the Giants game?"

"No." That alone was insufficient, so I guessed blindly. "Was it a good one?"

"One-oh shutout. Great pitching duel." He nodded in satisfaction. "Not a single Dodger got past second. That was as good as it gets."

It was the menu board all over again. I understood the English but still had no idea what he was talking about. "I'm glad to hear it."

Troy grinned at me. "Not a ball fan, huh? What do you watch?"

These were hardly probing questions; they were just to pass the time. Social duty, the type that any civilized person might fulfill. At least a human guest on Kuyen had the luxury of being an obvious offworlder, with customs that a good host must forgive.

I shuffled through my mind for something to offer. My *denet* had very nearly made small talk at House functions my particular duty. Failing here would be ridiculous. "Movies. I enjoy watching movies."

We'd watched them often as children, the volume low in the otherwise sleeping house, and there had always been something on the TV in the incomprehensibly named Rec Room at Bayshore Psychiatric.

Troy waggled his eyebrows, suggestive of something I couldn't fathom. "Don't tell me you let Katherine talk you into chick flicks."

"Ah, no." I couldn't recall any movies with chickens, but fortunately, he'd made the appropriate answer obvious. I reached years back to retrieve my favorite titles. "*The Last Samurai. Kill Bill. The Princess Bride. The Three Musketeers.*"

All for one and one for all. It had been profound, then, as things often were to young ones on the edge of adolescence. The sweetness of the memory with Shom and Kate had been salted with a heavy hand by what had come later.

"Sword fighting movies," Troy said with approval.

I shrugged my shoulders in the human manner, finally on firmer ground. "They were far too flashy. Most of those moves would never work against a real opponent."

"You like fencing? I took a couple of semesters. It impressed the hell out of Rose."

"They teach the sword at your schools?" I'd only seen humans use swords in movies, exaggerated and dramatic, on par with the big explosions and fake magic. Troy didn't hold himself like a fighter.

"'Teach the sword'?" Troy repeated. "Do you play D and D or something?"

"No." I had clearly misspoken again, my English too clumsy to ignore. Now that I'd set my feet on this path, though, I'd have to walk my way out of it. I took the opening he'd given me, choosing my words with care. "I was just surprised. I can imagine a woman being impressed with a competent swordsman."

I glanced at Kate, deep in a conversation with her friend about a gallery of some sort, just in case my comment was too subtle.

Troy grinned again and stopped looking at me so strangely. "You should take a class. A couple hours a week for a few months, you'd be surprised how fast you pick it up. In fencing, it doesn't matter if you're skinny."

I looked at him sharply. *This man does not mean any offense.* "I have had practice, actually."

My voice came out more stiffly than I'd intended.

That only broadened Troy's grin. "Good. We should spar sometime. It'd be fun."

And there was the price for pride. With his 'couple of hours a week for a few months' classes, he'd be at the mercy of the House's children. Still, he had enthusiasm and I'd taught more than a few students. Never a human. Would he even see me, without Kate and Rose here to assure him I existed? I was considering that one when Rose weighed in.

She looked back and forth between us, eyebrows well up. "Sparring? What kind of martial arts do you teach, Corey?"

At least I knew better than to say *the sword*. "Fencing."

Troy tossed back his head and laughed, a sound that rolled over the restaurant chatter like thunder. When he caught his breath, he shook his head at me. "Dude, you should have just said so, instead of letting me sound like a blowhard."

Humans didn't duel, but I had no wish to trigger whatever they did in its place. These people were Kate's friends.

"No offense was intended," I said quickly. "You didn't sound like a blowhard."

Kate made a sound like she'd tried to suppress a sneeze. I wasn't fooled, but at least if she was laughing, I hadn't done anything too dire.

Troy tilted his head back and forth in a broad gesture of indecision before grinning at me. "Maybe I'm the one who should be coming for lessons."

"My schedule is unsettled at the moment, but perhaps we can work something out later." There were a hundred ways for this to slip and cut me later, but Kate had done everything she could to fit her life to mine since she'd come back. Maybe it wasn't as impossible to make a place for myself among her friends as I'd imagined.

"I'll hold you to it," he said, chuckling. He turned to Eric, on his other side, who apparently knew who the Giants were and what kinds of games they played.

I finished my meal, hoping that these humans would recall how late their night was growing and let me get back to ward Kate's apartment and whatever else we might do after that. Corey the boyfriend had little time left before he had to tutor mercenaries in something less flashy than fencing.

Luck was with me. Everyone seemed to be finishing up their meals and a dessert course did not appear to be forthcoming.

Troy tossed his crumpled paper napkin onto his empty plate and stood, prompting the rest of us to follow. "We're going to head over to the Lucky Eight and play some pool. Wanna come along?"

I deferred to my *dacha*. "Katherine?"

She wavered. Clearly, the unfamiliar game held an attraction, but she shook her head. "Rose, you go ahead. We'll get a ride home. Maybe we can catch the next game."

Troy looked back at me, lifting an eyebrow in challenge. "You do play, don't you?"

He would get along well with Birasef. "No, but I'm a quick learner."

Troy grinned. "Consider the gauntlet thrown, then."

Instantly on my guard, I glanced around for any possible projectile. *Not throwing things in an eatery, surely? No, they named another location.* I gave myself a stern mental shake and fumbled for a reply. The two humans had that uncertain look in their eyes again.

"Understood," I brazenly lied before forcing a chuckle. "Perhaps we can swap lessons someday."

"Now who's the busybody?" Rose teased Troy, stretching up onto her toes to throw her arms around his neck. She tugged him down for a kiss.

I glanced away, then nearly jumped as Kate slipped her arm around my waist and leaned against me. She met my startled gaze with a smile that tilted the ground beneath my feet. I took her cue and curled my arm around her shoulders, conscious of all the people around us.

They were humans, though, and none of them seemed to mind.

"I'm just being friendly," Troy said, still grinning down at his *nochel*. It took me a moment to run the conversation back through my head. Surely, they were being more than friendly, even on Earth.

"Well," she said tartly. "Friendly is okay. We have to make sure he likes us, or we'll never see Katherine again." Rose shot me a look as she said it, and I didn't think it was entirely a joke.

Perhaps I'd been thinking too much about those movies and the way humans liked to make things so dramatic, or perhaps I'd done too much imagining how Birasef and his mark would find their footing here, but I played for the laugh instead of the deflection.

Reaching for my best High House manner, I slid my arm from Kate's shoulders and swept Rose and Troy a formal bow of gratitude. As I straightened, I said, "Your company has been a joy."

It worked. They both laughed—Kate, too—and after, Rose had lost some of her vigilance.

"Renn Faire," Troy said, shaking his head. "It all makes sense now."

The group dispersed, heading for the restaurant's exit. Kate kept our hands linked, winding us like a needle and thread through the busy tables. We lagged a little behind the others, the space granting us a whisper of privacy.

"What's a Renn Faire?" I asked as we stepped outside. The evening air had cooled, but I refused to miss my House coat. I'd have it back soon enough, the 'Temarel' embroidery plucked out by a patient tailor.

Kate pressed her face against my shoulder, smothering a laugh. "I've never been, but I think you'd either love them or hate them."

"So, I made either a great impression or a terrible one."

"You made a great one, don't worry." She lifted my hand to press a kiss on my knuckles.

Rose's friends had gathered again around their vehicles, chatting and laughing in a circle of electric light from one of the tall pole lamps. Rose and Troy leaned together against the side of her truck, the intimate and easy manner of *nochels* a little less startling outside among their mark than it had been in the public space of the restaurant.

"I'm glad," I said. Regretting the words even as I said them, I added, "Things must be easier if your friends approve of your *nochel*."

"Coran, they *saw* you." That giddiness lifted her voice again. "I don't know why, but they did."

I took a deep breath and refocused my wandering attention. That was, by far, the most important part of the evening. "They can't all be worldwalkers. It's too unlikely."

Kate shook her head. "It's just like it used to be at school or at home. Rose saw the hair comb you gave me, but she thought it was made of something else. If I asked her to draw you, I don't think you'd look like…you. The real you."

Like a Thurei. Dress him up in human clothes, though, and he might be worth seeing. Worth kissing. *Don't say it*, I warned myself. Then I opened my mouth anyway. "That's good enough for a *nochel*, isn't it?"

A *nochel* was perfect for a night like tonight, a bit of entertainment and company, and then everyone would walk away. Rose and her mark would scarcely need to remember my face. What did it matter if they saw me?

Kate looked up at me, her expression sharp. "Good enough for a *nochel*?"

Tonight, I was having all my words echoed back at me. I didn't have a charitable answer. Though she was my *dacha*, Kate owed me nothing. My vow hadn't been her choice, nor had she reciprocated. "If they see me differently next time, they won't be surprised. Tomorrow, you may have a new *nochel* if you wish."

"You're angry with me because I introduced you as my boyfriend?" Kate frowned.

"No." Not angry, precisely. It was too snarled an emotion to tease apart. "That was a kindness. I'm not even so much as your boyfriend."

She would not have pulled away from me the morning we'd woken together in her bed if she had borne me the affection one might share with a *nochel*.

"I promised I wouldn't send you away, Coran. What else can I do? You don't want to be my *nochel*." Kate held up empty hands. "I can't make you my *dacha*—you don't have a House and you don't want anything to do with one."

"What?" I held no guard against her, so her words slid neatly between my ribs to my heart with no resistance, sharp as any *zaret*. "My House? You don't want me because I have no House?"

"Without a *denet*, I can't swear a *dacha* vow," Kate went on. "Even here on Earth, you can't just say you're married and be married. There's a ceremony and you have to have a minister, or a judge, or I think maybe—"

Kate wanted to swear a vow to me? I didn't wait to find out how it worked on Earth. I gathered her in my arms and kissed her, and I didn't care who saw it. She curled her fingers around the nape of my neck and smiled against my lips, deepening the kiss. There was no hesitation or reluctance, nothing but welcoming warmth in her embrace.

"I thought..." I whispered, the words barely audible, but of course she would feel them.

She leaned back just far enough to look up at me, her round pupils wide in the darkness. A smile tugged at her mouth, tempting. "What did you think?"

I owed her honesty, however discomfiting it might be. "When we woke together and you moved away from me, I thought you didn't want me." Even now, the possibility prickled uneasily beneath my skin. She could pull away. Nothing kept her here with me. She had only promised not to send me away.

Kate tucked her head beneath my chin for a moment, hugging me tightly. "You said it was an insult for us to share a bed, since you'd sworn a vow and I hadn't."

It took me a moment to collect my thoughts from where they'd scattered down a different trail. *Shatter that Pareshol*. Turavi

Pareshol, betrothed to me in childhood, had been the one to wield that circumstance as an insult. Not that she'd been entirely wrong. Enough gossip had circled my name to wear a path.

"But we're not on Kuyen," I murmured against my *dacha*'s hair. "There's no one to whisper news of what we do."

Kate reached up to lay her hands on my cheeks. "I hold your honor, dear heart. I want to take good care of it, no matter what world we're on."

No one would say such a thing to a *nochel*, whose life would continue on unchanged, once they parted.

"If you wish a *denet* to hear you, Katen, I'll find one," I promised. I'd never heard of a *denet* witnessing the vows of someone Houseless, much less someone from another world, but that was the smallest obstacle on this road so far.

I was already running possibilities through my head when Kate's friend called her name. Kate turned in my arms to look back toward where Rose and her *nochel* stood in the pool of electric light. Her body tensed against mine, as if she expected censure. Then she relaxed and grinned, relief in every line of her body.

Because they'd seen me tonight.

"Go see what she wants," I urged, loosening my arms from around her.

"You don't want to come?" Her eyebrows drew down over earnest, brown eyes.

"She called for you," I said. "I'll wait."

Kate's fellow humans had seen me, and Kate wanted me, and she held her vow ready on her tongue, awaiting only the proper ears to hear it. If tonight kept escalating wonders at such a pace, I might need this chance to catch my breath.

CHAPTER TEN

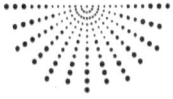

KATE

If Cor didn't want to brave another potential minefield of manners on a foreign planet at the moment, I wasn't going to make him. He'd been charming and exquisitely careful all through dinner, but I knew how exhausting it was to have to pretend to fit in.

Right now, he looked half-dazzled with the news that I meant to make him my *dacha* and I didn't want to see that expression replaced with a polite-for-company smile just yet.

"I'll be right back," I said, hurrying over to Rose's truck.

Halfway there, I heard a rustle behind me, then a growl. I whipped around, but the bright light in the parking lot had ruined my night vision. There, a swirl of motion tightened around the paler shape of Cor's vibrant hair. Just like at the beach, Hunters closing in on Cor—I reached for my *jeira*, focusing my skill, but I was too slow. He yelled, short and sharp, then all of it was gone like it had never been. I blinked, but the edge of the parking lot remained a muddle of shadows, with no figures I could discern. No movement anywhere.

"Cor!" I shouted, my voice gone high-pitched with fear. I sprinted back to where I'd left him.

Nothing there. I fumbled through my bag, hunting for my phone. When I found it, I turned on the flashlight function. It lit up an empty stretch of sidewalk, flanked by a rectangular bed of bayberry shrubs and bark mulch. Some bark pieces were scattered across the cement.

What had just happened? I closed my eyes, trying to remember more details out of the shadowy shapes. How many had there been? And that growl—

"Kate? What are you doing?"

Rose's voice beside me made me jump.

"Cor's gone," I said, before my brain kicked in.

She nodded, confused. "Corey went home?"

For a moment, I thought she meant worldwalking. Of course not. "Rose, we were right here a moment ago. You heard him yell, didn't you? Did you see anything?"

She'd seen Cor, all evening. She'd been facing this direction when she'd called my name, with the bright light at her back. She had to have seen what had happened.

"He went home," she repeated. It wasn't a question this time. She waved vaguely at the parking lot as if Cor had gotten into his own car and left.

"We drove here with you," I said, wanting to shake her. Wanting to shake myself and rattle loose better sight, or faster reactions with my skill. *What just happened?* "Rose, this is important. What did you see just now, while I was walking over here?"

"You said he went home," Rose said, the confusion on her face shifting into something sharper, more suspicious. "Are you okay? You walked over here to…to take a phone call. Nothing happened. What are you talking about?"

I took a step back. This, I'd seen countless times. I could

almost see the events of the evening rearrange themselves in Rose's head to make a story she found easier to believe. She'd driven us to the restaurant, and she'd seen Cor and I both walk over to this spot while she and Troy had headed for their vehicles just a minute ago. Now Cor was gone, not into one of the closed shops or back into the taqueria, and he didn't have a car to drive away in.

People didn't just vanish into thin air and monsters didn't exist.

Maybe she'd seen what had happened and maybe she hadn't, but in the former case, her mind wouldn't let her believe it, so she believed something else.

I'd been through this often enough as a kid. I could argue all evening and not change her mind, and I didn't have time for that right now. I had to find Cor.

"I'm fine." My voice wasn't steady, but it didn't matter. She could explain it to herself however she wanted. I'd deal with it later. "But I have to go."

"Sure." Rose hooked a thumb over her shoulder. "I can drop you off." She frowned, looking around us like she couldn't remember why we were standing here at the edge of the parking lot.

"Don't worry about it. I already scheduled a ride." I held up my phone, belatedly realizing I still had the flashlight on. I was too busy trying to figure out what had just happened and what I needed to do about it.

If it had been Hunters I'd glimpsed, Cor might have led them away from us. I couldn't hear any sounds of fighting over the background sounds of traffic. Every moment, I expected Cor and some Hunter to burst out from between a couple of the nearby buildings like fighters in an action movie. Or just Cor, coming back victorious. Maybe injured. How would I explain that?

Where was he?

Rose pursed her lips and stared at me for a long moment, but then she nodded. "All right. See you at work tomorrow."

"Okay."

The growl and Cor's yell, cut off so abruptly... He wasn't here on Earth at all. He'd said Hunters could follow worldwalkers across the gap between worlds. Maybe he'd lured something away. I didn't know how to tell where he might have gone, but I had a decent idea of where he'd go once the fight was over.

As soon as Rose climbed into her truck, I slipped away to Kuyen.

CHAPTER ELEVEN

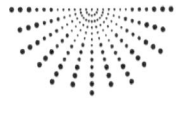

KATE

The dark, wood-paneled walls of Cor's room at the garrison replaced the shadows of the parking lot. The skillwork lamp by the door glowed with a warm, dim light.

But the narrow room was empty.

I forced myself to take a deep breath, then another. Cor was a dangerous individual, a master of the *zaret*, survivor of dozens—maybe scores—of battles with Hunters. I knew all that, but the image of him crumpling to the sand when we'd fought the Hiraches refused to leave my mind.

Had his shout sounded more angry or surprised? A warning?

I tried to push my growing worry away. Cor was fine. I was sure he was fine. Any moment now, he'd be back. I just needed to wait. Refusing to let myself pace, I sat down at the table.

I wished fervently that I still had Cor's token. If I hadn't lost it on the beach during the fight with Tharkesh, it would have allowed me to worldwalk right to Cor's side. Not if we were on the same world, of course, because worldwalking didn't work between two places on the same world, only between worlds. What I wouldn't give at the moment to have a way to show up beside him.

My heart kicked into a higher gear. If someone else had Cor's token…that shout, startled and then cut off, like Cor had been pulled away. Maybe he hadn't slipped away by choice.

When worldwalkers traveled together, as Cor and I had done so often, one directed them to the destination and the other had to allow it, relaxing into the pull. Two worldwalkers in opposition to each other would create something like a tug-of-war, pulling in separate directions in a battle that had nothing to do with physical strength. Cor was a practiced worldwalker and it was hard to imagine someone pulling him away against his will. But if someone had surprised him…

Waiting here could be wasting valuable time. Cor might need help and I wouldn't be able to find him alone.

He must have had paper around here, somewhere. Since the sitting room held only the small table and chairs, I went to the bedroom on the other side of the divider screen. A wardrobe stood beside the bed, with a couple of clothes chests next to it. The wardrobe provided a stack of small, square sheets and I brought a few out to the table. I pulled a pen from my purse and tapped it on the tabletop.

If Cor was fighting, a Summons flapping up to him would distract him. Afterward—after he won—he might return to my apartment to wait for me, or even go back to the restaurant. I wrote him a quick note, telling him to come to his apartment at Pella's, folded it up, and stuck it in my purse for later.

Then I wrote to Shom, trying to slow my racing thoughts and compose something reasonably persuasive. She hadn't exactly been a big fan of mine since I'd driven her away all those years ago, but she'd still been willing to help when I needed her. And she still cared about Cor. I wasn't sure what she could do to help, but at the very least, she could tell me how to beg for aid from her aunt. I didn't even know Pella's full name, to be able to address a Summons to her.

I described the situation as concisely as I could, folded the square sheet into the bird-like Summons shape, and concentrated my *jeira* to send it on its way. The paper lifted from my hands and flapped a foot or so away before disappearing the way Summons did on their way to their recipients.

I wrote to Birasef next. If Cor were hurt or in danger and had to make a snap decision on a safe place to escape to, he might return to the House where he'd grown up and the healer who had treated him so many times. Maybe he and Birasef weren't cousins anymore, but I thought it wouldn't break any rules to explain the situation and ask him to tell me if Cor showed up there. Just in case. And, as a personal favor, if he or Seretun had any suggestions as to what I could do next…

I sent that one off, too.

Cor had mentioned that there were healers here at the garrison, though I'd never visited them. I didn't recall him pointing out their location on our short tour of the compound. If I went looking for them, though, I wouldn't be here if someone showed up.

I'd always thought that worldwalking and Summons were so convenient and efficient. *This world needs cell phones.*

Usually, I left my phone on the charger when I went to Kuyen. After all, it was useless here in a world without electricity, much less cell towers.

Now, I had mine with me in my bag. That just allowed me to check the time every other second. A fight would be over by now, wouldn't it? When we'd fought the Hiraches, it had seemed to take forever and, simultaneously, no time at all.

I got up and started to pace the smooth, hardwood floors. I

wanted to be doing something, but there was nothing useful I could think to do.

I checked my phone again.

An eternity and eleven minutes later, a knock at the door made me jump. I pulled it open to find Shom standing in the hallway.

"Shom," I said, my voice far from smooth. "How do we find him?"

She knew where the garrison's healers were, of course. Although Lan te Kos were immune to the unique skills of other Kuyene inhabitants and couldn't be healed, the peacekeeper outpost had healers on staff for the non-Lan among Pella's forces. I left a note on the table for Cor saying we would be right back, just in case, and followed Shom to the top floor of the keep. On the way, she asked me to explain it all in better detail.

"They saw him?" She sounded as surprised by that as Cor had been when Rose had looked up at him.

"Yes, all through dinner," I said. "But when Cor and whoever it was disappeared, it was like Rose had her mind made up that something else had happened already." I'd admitted to Shom that I hadn't gotten a good enough look to say how many Hunters there had been or even what kind.

"This friend of yours was blind to it, just like your parents." Shom pursed her lips closed over that for a moment but then switched back to something closer to the problem at hand. "You said Cor made you a token linked to himself, personally? Not to his sitting room at the House?"

"Yeah, to himself. When we were looking for Issai out in the wildlands, Cor had to stay behind to keep us on track. With the token, I could meet him each day and travel with him." The wildlands shifted unpredictably, unlike claimed lands that were held static by the *jeira* and intentions of the people who lived there or visited often. The wildlands held many dangers, but their changeable nature was one of the main reasons that people seldom traveled beyond well-established, well-anchored routes.

"And you lost it among Hunters," Shom summarized. "The Hiraches, right?"

I nodded. "But they all died. I...I destroyed them with my skill." Another detail occurred to me. "But I had to focus on Cor to use the token. He said I had to think about him as I activated it. If someone else picked it up without knowing it was his, they wouldn't know to do that."

Shom stopped before another door down a long hallway and looked at me. "You don't need to do all that for a token. That's the whole point. It will take you to wherever it's linked."

"Then why..." I began, but the slightly pitying expression on Shom's face stopped me.

"Thureis don't play short on strategy," Shom said, pushing open the door.

Cor had just wanted me to think of him and found a way to make me, when I'd been doing my best to do the opposite. I swallowed down an ache in my throat and followed Shom into the healers' rooms.

Cor was not here, though the Lewrits in Pella's employ promised to send for me immediately if he showed up.

Then we went all the way back down to Cor's quarters, my skin prickling with cold sweat. *If Coran was fighting, it would be over by now...*

We stepped into the hallway to find a knot of people standing around Cor's door. My eyes caught on a tall, slender form in a familiar black coat.

I started forward, Cor's name on my lips, but the Thurei had an emerald-green braid. Birasef, not Cor at all. He'd come, in spite of everything. Beside him stood a Lan woman and the Drammon I'd met in the arena.

"Bira—I mean, Temarel." I stumbled over the words, unsure how I should address someone who had once been kin to…to whatever official position Cor held in relation to me. Cor had been clear that they weren't cousins any longer. Whatever I called him, though, I needed to switch to Kuyen's common tongue, since he didn't know any English. "Did he…Did he go back to House Temarel?"

Birasef swept a brief bow, his face stern. He looked both severe and official in his long, leather coat, with the embroidered knotwork design of his House name in Thurei writing along the hems. Cor had stopped wearing his when he'd been kicked out.

"I have not seen him, Kjelgaard." His amber eyes flicked from me to Shom and back. "I hoped you might have more news."

Through a tight throat, I managed, "No news yet."

I kept remembering the way Birasef had looked at me after Cor and I had fought the Hiraches and Cor had almost died. I had a responsibility, as Cor's *dacha*, to keep him well. Especially since it was my fault that his kin couldn't do it.

And Cor had been stolen away right in front of me.

"Then I'm here at your disposal," Birasef said.

With permission from your denet? But I didn't want to ask. Cor's father had known Hunters pursued us when he'd banished his son. He would never have sent kin to Cor's aid.

The Lan woman stepped forward. "I'll tell Coraven's students he won't be coming, then."

Shom spoke up before the woman could walk past. "Kate, were you able to send a Summons to him?"

"I was afraid it would distract him if he was fighting," I said. I pulled the Summons out of my bag. Things had gone beyond worrying about distraction by this point. I sent the simple skillwork letter on its way, watching as it flapped toward the hallway wall and then disappeared. Gesturing in the direction it had gone, I asked Shom, "Does that mean he's still on Earth, since it slipped away?"

"That's not how it works," Shom said. "Yes, the Summons use the gaps between worlds to travel, but it's not a straight line and the direction they fly doesn't reflect the location of the receiver, merely the anchor points that serve the skillwork."

"If the Summons can find him, can't we use the same thing?" I persisted. There must have been some component of the skillwork that could search for him, some compass that could lead us to him.

Shom flicked her fingers, using the Thurei gesture to make the denial clear. "No. If names could be used for tracking in the same way they're used to send Summons, none of us would be safe. I'm sorry, Kate. At least we know he's alive. We'll find him." She turned toward the waiting Lan. "Coraven may have been taken on a hunt. Osha, please gather some searchers. I'll speak with my aunt."

Hearing the words out loud made it worse. I hugged my arms around myself and took a deep breath, trying to coax my heart rate back down.

"I don't know of any hunt that ends with the prey alive," the Drammon said.

That didn't help.

Shom asked, "If it's not a hunt, do you know what it might be?"

The Hunter lifted her hand, fingers curled, but I didn't recognize the gesture. "I think that's the question to ask."

"Greta, will you come help us search?" Shom asked.

"Yes," the Hunter said, without pausing to consider. "He seemed...decent."

"He is," I said, insisting on the present tense.

"Kate, wait here." Shom touched my shoulder lightly. "I'll be back soon with a search party, and you can take us to the last place you saw him."

Birasef cleared his throat. "If you would permit, Kjelgaard, I hope you will do me the honor of admitting me to your home."

I frowned, confused, and Birasef smoothed the air between us with an elegant motion of his long-fingered hand. "If it runs counter to your wishes, I'll bow to it, but I don't know how to find you on your world if there is need. I'm sure Shom is more than capable, but why scrap a card from your hand if you don't need to?"

"He's got a point." It almost sounded like that had surprised Shom and I wondered how well she knew him. "I remember your apartment well enough to slip there, but another acquaintance would be smart."

I nodded. "Of course, no problem. That's a good idea."

"Good," she said. "I'll speak with my aunt and get some volunteers. I can send for you to come back and meet us when everything is ready." Shom gathered Greta with a glance and the two of them strode off down the hall.

I turned to Birasef and held out my hand. "Thank you for coming. Are you ready?"

He made no move to take it. Instead, he slanted a glance at the solid wooden door to Cor's room. In keeping with the rest of the fort, it gave the impression that it could survive a siege. "If you think Cor wouldn't mind, may I see inside? I can't imagine I'll need to step inside by any means other than the door in the future, but one never knows."

Hearing him call Cor by the friendlier, short version of his name loosened some of the tension in my chest. On Earth, anyone could use a nickname, but here on Kuyen, names meant more. Birasef would never call someone he now classified as a stranger by so familiar a name. Of course, he cared enough about Cor to show up here, but it reassured me anyway.

"Sure." I leaned past him to open the door, the iron doorknob cold in my hand. I hadn't locked it when we'd checked with the healers. I didn't even have a key. We hadn't been here long enough for me to get one of my own.

Birasef followed me inside, taking a long look around the space. Apparently confident he could slip back here if he needed to, he held out his hand to me. I took it. He didn't have quite the same callouses as Cor did from his years of training with his blade, but Birasef's hand wasn't as soft as I might have expected, and his grip was firm and confident as he closed his eyes. I pulled us both across to my apartment.

Cor wasn't waiting for us in my living room. The cramped room was empty except for my secondhand table and chairs, a shelf of battered paperbacks and thrift store jigsaw puzzles. The box of wards Cor had brought sat on the table where he'd left them.

"Perhaps you should show me your door."

It took me a second to realize Birasef wasn't volunteering to get kicked out. He wanted to see the literal door so he could use it as an anchor point for worldwalking instead of showing up in the middle of my tiny apartment.

"Sure, sure." I led him the few steps to the front door and let us both out onto the third-floor landing.

He gazed, wide-eyed, over the railing. The apartment building's narrow parking lot stretched below us with its row of mismatched vehicles. An overflowing dumpster crouched at the far side, spilling a drift of stuffed plastic bags. Down the street, a figure bundled in far too many layers huddled on the bus stop bench. One letter on a bright red-and-yellow minimart sign flickered on and off. More electric streetlights shone like stars on a chain, highlighting glass and metal and all the wires strung across the sky.

It was usually quiet this late at night, but a motorcyclist gunned his bike coming off a stoplight, loud enough to set off a car alarm a block or so down. Birasef's shoulders twitched.

I hadn't been to any other worlds besides Kuyen. Earth might not have *jeira*, but I didn't think technology was common in other places, either.

"We shouldn't stay here long," I said.

Birasef blinked a couple of times and turned his back on the view. "You make a fine point."

I hadn't made much of a point, but I could sympathize with the feeling that a world entirely foreign to your experience could be overwhelming. I had something I wanted to take care of first. I gestured back through the open door at the box on the table. "Cor brought some wards. He said the ones he'd left here before were getting weaker, but he didn't get to replace them with these new ones."

"Ah, of course," Birasef said. "There's no Truce here. Your home shouldn't be left unprotected."

Like I didn't know that. But Birasef wasn't saying it like a scolding, or as if he were trying to tell me what to do. Instead, he looked more than a little intimidated himself, like Hunters might appear out of nowhere.

They could. Hunters didn't bother with "blind" humans who had no *jeira*. They were counted as no more challenging than shooting fish in a barrel, but other worldwalkers made worthy prey. Earth, like every other place beyond the Truce, might as well have been considered a hunting ground.

But fear wouldn't get us anywhere.

"Do you spend much time outside of the Truce?" I asked him.

He looked at me for a moment and then laughed, once. His shoulders sagged a little, like he was forcing himself to relax. He bobbed a little self-mocking bow, more in the style I associated with him. "No. No, I have never had the need." He tilted his head in the direction of the box. "I'm not adept at wards. I know that there are some ways better than others to set them, but even if we did nothing else besides put them in the right place, fresh ones will work better than weakening ones."

"How do we know the right places?" I ushered him back inside and closed the door behind us.

Birasef shrugged, a quick ripple of his fingers, and suggested, "We can look for the old ones."

That was better than any plan I had, so we went with that. It was as good a way as any to kill the time, since we were waiting for Shom's Summons anyway. I took a handful of the ribbon-like wards, each of them about three-quarters of an inch wide and sturdy as the nylon webbing of a seatbelt, and stuffed them in my pocket.

"I think Cor put one out here last time." I went to the window leading out to the fire escape, raised the blinds out of the way, and pushed it open.

A ward ribbon fluttered on the metal railing, and I tied the new one in its place. Though I'd untied the knot carefully, I couldn't quite replicate it with the new ribbon and who knew what additional skillwork Cor had done originally. I hoped Birasef was right about the ward.

"I'm sure there are more." Birasef had clambered out the window behind me and stood looking disapprovingly around the tiny metal landing barely large enough for the two of us.

I pointed up, where the ladder continued up to the roof. "Probably up there."

He sighed—quietly, but I was close enough to hear it. "All right," he said then started climbing.

I followed, envying his cat-like pupils and keener night vision, but these were wards for my house, so I ought to be up there, too.

We found three more on the roof, tied in odd, unobtrusive places: a loop of cable wiring, a brace for the rain gutter, and the slim chimney of a roofing vent. If any normal human saw them, they would probably look like bits of trash.

Birasef pointed in the general direction of the wards, more or less a square shape. "They make a complete barrier, these four. I think they'll hold well enough, and you can ask Cor to show you how to adjust them once we find him."

He shared as much as he knew—any worldwalker who wasn't welcomed to my home would have a difficult time noticing the building at all. Strangers' eyes would tend to slide away from it, the subtle thoughts in the back of their minds would nudge them away from this place without them knowing why. The wards couldn't make the structure invisible, but it would function as the next best thing, prompting worldwalkers to ignore it and move on.

It sounded a lot like the human tendency to talk themselves into blindness when faced with things from other worlds, really. I wondered if the skillwork tapped into the same mechanism.

Shom's Summons appeared right as we returned to the fire escape ladder, flapping toward us. I caught the folded, bird-like shape out of the air, tearing the paper open to reveal the simple message she'd promised. *We're ready. Come back.* Birasef brushed grime off his elegant hands and straightened the lapels of his coat.

"Thank you for your help, Birasef."

His eyes gleamed like a cat's in the dim glow from the streetlights, but I couldn't see much of his expression in the shadows. "Oh, good. I was afraid we were keeping to House names, even in private. You might go as far as 'Bir' if you can stomach it."

That threw me for a second. Close-names were for friends, for kin. I wasn't even his cousin's *dacha* anymore, since Cor had been banished. I thought Birasef meant it as a kindness, but I didn't even deserve that much. I blinked back the sting of tears.

"You're the one who told me it's my job to keep him safe. It's my fault he's gone. I wasn't fast enough. I lost him."

Birasef took a deep breath and looked out over the nighttime glow of San Jose. "It is a *dacha*'s work, to hold their partner safe, that's true. Cor has something of a reputation for not making that easy, however. If you wish to do your duty, let's find him." He held out his hand to me. "I would be pleased if you would call me Bir."

I nodded and put my hand in his. "Thank you, Bir."

He slipped us back to the garrison.

CHAPTER TWELVE

KATE

Shom's search party consisted of five Lan and Greta, the Drammon. The Lan all wore weapons on their belts. Greta bore a sword as well, though I recalled from the arena that the Drammon skill made her just as dangerous with her bare hands.

Not one to waste words, Shom simply said, "Ready?"

"Yes," I said, though nine people was far more than I'd ever worldwalked with before.

We clustered together, everyone linked together hand to hand. I pictured the strip mall parking lot in my mind. Pulling us all there was more of a struggle than I'd expected, as if I were hauling them all there on my back. I stumbled as San Jose formed around us and Birasef caught my elbow. It was so similar to what Cor would have done that I had to bite my cheek against tears.

We'd arrived at the edge of the empty parking lot, at the spot where I'd last seen Cor. Though the taqueria still had its lights on, the neon open sign was dark, and I couldn't see anyone inside. A silver SUV cruised past on the street, bringing the bass thrum of its music with it. More than a few Kuyene heads turned to watch the vehicle go.

Shom cleared her throat, capturing their attention again.

One of the Lan pulled out an etched sphere of glass and ran his fingers over the lines to light it, then cradled the glowing skillwork lamp in the palm of his hand. The soft light shone on the sidewalk, where a dark scattering of bark mulch had been kicked up out of the sad, strip mall landscaping onto the cement.

"All right," I said in the common tongue, trying to project a calm and confidence I didn't feel in the slightest. "Coraven was here when I last saw him. I walked over that way." I pointed to the circle of light in the empty parking lot. Fog wreathed the bulb on this damp night. I tried not to shiver. "Then I heard what sounded like a growl and Cor yelled, but I never got another glimpse of him."

"Split up," Shom said, taking on an easy, no-nonsense air of command. Before she'd settled on a career in skillwork research, she'd trained to be a soldier and it showed. She pointed at various gaps between the buildings. "I want as big a sweep as we can make before dawn. Avoid the locals if you see any, but they shouldn't bother you. Bounce back to the garrison if you hit something you can't handle, but report in as soon as you can."

"Be careful crossing the streets," I added. "The vehicles are fast and the drivers might not see you."

With their gray skin and beige clothing, the soldiers quickly disappeared in the darkness.

The Hunter stayed with us, her large eyes fixed on the random spray of bark pieces across the pale cement. She squatted down and reached a long arm out to one of the dark shapes. It smeared and she lifted her fingertip to sniff it.

I knew what it was before she could say it. Blood.

"This is Coraven's," she said, tilting her face up to us. Her eyes caught the light and gleamed, like Cor's would have. "He's injured, somewhere."

Bir shifted slightly beside me but held his tongue.

"Can you tell where they went?" Shom asked. "Or who else was here?"

The Drammon wrinkled her nose and leaned closer to the ground for a few seconds. Then she stood, pulling a cloth from her pocket to clean her hands meticulously. She looked at me. "Your world smells foul."

"Sorry." There wasn't much else to say to that.

"It's been too long," Greta continued. "There's no trace of a slipwake to follow. I can't smell any others over the stink in the air. There's no more blood here, but I'll keep looking."

"Thank you," I said.

She only blinked at me and turned away.

Shom motioned Bir and me toward the street. "We can take this direction. You'll know better than the rest of us what's out of place, Kate. Your world is...distracting."

"Sure," I said quietly. As a child, Shom had only visited me at my house outside the town of Eugene, on the edge of rural Oregon. A few times, at the end, she'd slipped inside the mental hospital when I'd been a resident patient. A city street in the middle of San Jose was probably as disorienting to her as it was to Bir. I led them along the empty sidewalk. "Cor's alive, though, right? Even if he's injured?"

"You were able to send your Summons," Shom said, careful with her words.

He was alive then, she meant. But the clock had kept ticking since.

"It wasn't much blood," Bir said. He used the same determinedly optimistic tone I had. "He could still fight with a wound like that."

I didn't know if he was trying to reassure me or himself. Maybe both of us.

"I don't want to spill wine on the rug here," Shom said, "but if someone does have him, there aren't many ways to hold a worldwalker." She turned off the sidewalk to peer through the plate glass window of a closed pharmacy.

There wasn't anything useful to see in there, but maybe she just didn't want to look at us while she brought that point up.

"What ways?" I asked, my voice tight. "Is there some kind of skillwork that can keep a person from slipping away?"

"Some skillwork can keep a person out, though it's complicated and expensive." Shom gave up on the pharmacy and we resumed our sweep down the block. "I don't know of any that will keep someone in place. Only sunrise or sunset can do that, depending on the world. If someone's keeping Cor in place, he's unconscious or otherwise unable to focus his *jeira*."

I didn't want to think about that. I scanned the street and buildings around us, hoping for some sign that Cor was still here, somewhere. *Hurt* would be preferable to *taken*. If Cor had simply gotten hurt, that could be solved with a quick trip to a healer.

"If Cor is somewhere around here, unconscious, he'll be ripped back to Kuyen when the sun rises," I said. "Where would he end up?"

"Anywhere." Birasef shrugged his fingers, a quick ripple of movement in the thin light from the streetlamp. "It's no different than crossing without a token or a destination in mind."

Potentially lethal under normal circumstances, but if Cor were already injured?

"Watch out!" Bir called just as a familiar sound tickled my ears.

I spun, registering the gleam of his drawn *zaret* at the same time as the approaching bicycle. I grabbed his arm. "Don't!"

Shom's hands hesitated over the hilts of two belt knives.

The bicyclist swerved smoothly off the curb, curving around us as he continued on his way.

He'd seen us, at least enough to change course, but there'd been no hint of the alarm he might show over Bir's glass-like blade or Shom's strange, faun-like physiology.

"It's just a guy on a bike." I had to drop into English for that last word, but no one questioned me over it.

Bir's sword disappeared, vanishing as he released his focus. He dropped his gaze to my hand on his sleeve. "My thanks. It seems my nerves are all standing on end."

"No problem." I pulled my hand back, embarrassed. At least one of us had fast enough reflexes.

We resumed our search.

Shom, Bir, and I combed the San Jose neighborhood around Fajita Fiesta for blocks in every direction, but the only outworlders we saw were other Lan searchers. Greta caught up with us as predawn began to lighten the sky, but only to say that she'd found no other hint or trail.

No Cor.

Bir eyed the sky and then gave me a quick, shallow bow. "I must return to the House. Please tell me if there is news."

"Of course, and thank you," I said as I watched him disappear.

Shom promised me she'd send any news from her aunt as soon as the way opened again at sunset.

I slipped back to the garrison with Shom, just long enough to then return to my apartment on Earth before the approaching dawn closed the way between worlds.

Until sunset, I was stuck here.

CHAPTER THIRTEEN

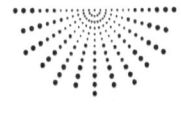

COR

My head throbbed. Everything hurt and my mouth tasted foul.

Hangover? I didn't drink. *How late did the dancing go last night?*

Moments smeared together. Proper House bowing. Bright clothes. Making nice with someone else's mark at the dinner table, all of them laughing and I had nothing safe to say.

Why was I sitting up in bed?

I'm going to be late.

I dragged my eyes open, just a crack. Good. Still dark. I had some time before the sun rose. I'd be on time to guard Kate.

The world spun, making me queasy. My eyelids sank closed.

My hands wouldn't move.

I need my hands. I don't have anything else.

My shoulders hurt. I opened my eyes, blinking through a blurry haze. Dark trees and moonlight. Boulders. No. Were they huts?

I was sitting on the ground in the wildlands, my back to a wall. My arms were tied to a wooden bar above my head.

Long, leather strips bound my fingers around the wood.

I pulled, ignoring the ache in my shoulders. A sharp pain flared in my side. The bindings held firm.

No *zaret*. Without hands to wield it, I couldn't call the blade.

My stomach twisted, lurched. Everything slid sideways, back into darkness.

When I opened my eyes again, light glowed around the edge of the nearest hut. It flickered. So, firelight, not lamplight.

With my head a little clearer, I took stock of my position: sitting against a rough wall, still dressed in the human clothes I'd worn on Earth, legs straight out before me, tied at the ankles. My arms reached straight up, hands curled around a wooden pole fixed horizontally above my head. A thorough wrapping of leather straps bound my fingers and palms in place.

My head pounded, my stomach protested, and everything else hurt, though my shoulders and side were the worst. A chill in the air tightened my cramped muscles even further.

Huts crouched among the trees, hard to pick out in the dimness as my vision wavered. I blinked, hard. Shadowy shapes moved around the fire. They spoke in growls, like thunderclouds.

Memory flickered through my mind. A pack of Hiraches appearing between Kate and me outside the restaurant. Claws and darkness. It blurred into the attack on the beach, where Kate and I had confronted Tharkesh and his packmates to end the hunt.

Katen! I straightened as much as I could, peering through the forest around me, willing my eyes to clear, as if I could have seen her. *Put your addled wits together, Cor.*

She'd been walking away, toward her friends. The Hunters' attention had been all on me and the brief fight I'd managed before one of them had caught me in the back of the head—or so I guessed from the throbbing pain.

It would be day on Earth now, the way between worlds closed. Kate was safe.

And if she wasn't safe, I couldn't help her right now.

Dawn, and the ability to slip away from all this, was more than half the night away. They couldn't hold a worldwalker once the sun rose, so whatever they planned to do would be done before then.

I couldn't use my *zaret* if I couldn't use my hands.

How do you disarm a Thurei? You dis-arm him. Funny little Lan joke I'd learned among the peacekeepers.

I still *had* my hands. I needed to keep my wits.

I took a deep breath. Pain pulled at my side. I craned my head to check, but between the black cloth of the shirt and the forest's shadows, I couldn't see any details. I remembered the short struggle back on Earth, and the rake of claws as they'd wrenched me across the gap.

So, injured and bound.

Perhaps I could move the stick if I could get some leverage behind it. If I could stand... I bent my knees to draw my feet under me. The movement set off the bright, cheerful jingle of an unseen bell. I stifled a groan.

A moment later, one of the Hiraches approached, silent but for a bare whisper of her cloak. I took a deep breath, reaching for my *zaret* on instinct, but my hands were already full. My gathered *jeira* dissipated, accomplishing nothing.

"You are awake," she said in the common tongue, though her voice still carried gravel and sharper things around the edges of the words.

There didn't seem to be much point in denying it. Either I could admit to being awake now, they would expect me to wake up later, or they would ensure I never woke again.

"Yes." My voice rasped nearly as much as the Hunter's had. I coughed against the burn in my throat and my gut twisted again.

The Hunter tilted her head aside. "Bring water."

A smaller shape I hadn't noticed detached itself from the Hunter's shadow and disappeared behind the hut.

"There's food," she said. "If you're not too sick to eat."

I was nauseated, my stomach knotted like a ward ribbon. Concussion? The world had begun to spin again. I closed my eyes for a moment. That bitter taste lingered in my mouth, burned in my throat. Something more than a knock on the head. "Why feed me? Trophies don't need food."

A rumbling, jagged sound. Laughter. "You're not a trophy."

I squinted up at the Hirach. The tree canopy filtered the brightness out of the moonlight, but my eyes should have been keen enough regardless. Fuzziness kept stealing over my vision like clouds, smearing gray and black together. I saw little of her face beyond her long jaw and the gleam of teeth.

Of course I was a trophy. The Hunterslayer. They should be hanging my severed head on a pole somewhere, not offering me water. What other value did I have to a Hirach kith?

Kate.

Kate was the trophy—the rare and dangerous human with *jeira*. She'd walked away a moment too soon or they would have taken her instead.

I wasn't a trophy. I was bait.

"I am Coraven the Hunterslayer," I said, trying to project the confidence I'd won with years of training and battle, but it came less easily while I was disarmed and bound. "Give me your name and let me loose to fight. You do your Hunt dishonor."

I had pricked her pride and she hissed.

"I'm Serkot of the Akevad and there's no Hunt." She leaned forward, putting her teeth closer to my face. "You would be dead if not for your cowardice. You fell in battle. It was your portion to die."

The Akevad? That was Tharkesh's kith. Someone had survived to see Kate ferry me away to a healer, anathema to a Hunter.

They couldn't use me as bait if I could goad her into killing me.

I grinned, tilting my own teeth up to the moonlight. "Yet here I am, alive, and your Finder's pack was wiped off the face of an empty world. What does it make you, if you're so afraid you keep a coward tied?"

Serkot snarled.

A rustle announced the arrival of water. Serkot stepped back, falling silent.

My vision was clearing, or adjusting belatedly to the scant light, and I picked out the shape of a small Hirach, lugging a bucket in stubby, clawed hands. The child set the bucket down beside my leg and held up a dipper.

"Here," he growled in a fierce but high-pitched tone.

"Drink," Serkot ordered. "Or I'll pour it down your throat myself for you to drown on."

Despite her threat, she'd mastered herself and my chance to goad her to fury had passed.

I leaned forward until my lips touched the smooth wood. The boy tilted the dipper—too much. Most of the water splashed into my lap and I flinched at the shock of cold. The water I did manage to drink slid down my throat like ice and hit my stomach, which rebelled. I clenched my jaw against it, swallowing hard. A shiver tore through me, as much a muscle spasm as a reaction to the cold. A thin T-shirt and wet jeans would not serve me well if the temperature kept falling.

Apparently satisfied by this obedience, Serkot stalked off.

The boy stayed. He lifted the dipper again. "More?"

"No." Then, because I might buy with charm what I couldn't

win with challenge, "Thank you. What's your name?" After a moment of silence, I added, "You're very fierce, but a Hunter with honor offers his quarry his name."

At least it was so among Hiraches, if I could believe what I'd studied.

"Grathki." He dropped the dipper back into the bucket. Water sloshed over the side, dripping onto my leg.

I drew my knees up to hoard what little warmth I had. The bell tied to my boot jingled.

"That's mine," said the little Hunter, peering down at it. "Smart, yes?"

My hands ached, curled around the unyielding pole above me, leather straps wound so tightly around my fingers that they couldn't twitch. I tilted my head back against the hut to examine the bindings. "Yes. Very smart."

Two adult Hiraches strode around the corner of the hut, blotting out the firelight. Serkot and a man with a limp. Little Grathki lugged the bucket away.

I made the same attempt to learn the name of the limping Hirach, but he ignored me. The Hiraches each went to an end of the horizontal pole where it had been lashed to some supports on the wall. The vibration of their movements thrummed through my chilled joints as they worked at the knots.

With my knees pulled up like this, I might have a chance, however slim.

"Where are you taking me?" I asked, more for the sake of distraction than hope for an answer.

They ignored me.

The Hunter with the limp stopped his work, resting his thick, clawed fingers on the wood, waiting. A moment later, Serkot finished untying her end.

I launched myself upward and away from the wall, throwing

my weight behind the pole. It pushed the man back and off his balance. He snarled as he staggered away on his weaker leg. I tried to swing the pole toward his face, but Serkot caught her end and wrenched it aside.

With my feet tied together, there was nowhere to go but down. I went down hard, driving the air from my lungs.

A clawed foot came down on the back of my neck, grinding my face in the leaf litter.

"Scavenger," I wheezed. I didn't have breath for anything better.

The claws dug in. *Do it, Hunter.*

"Vercho, he's no use to us dead." Serkot walked around to crouch down in front of me. "You are frail prey and a coward. I should leave you here in the dirt to freeze, but that won't help my kith."

The pair of them lifted the pole and dragged me through the trees and huts toward the fire, the tiny bell jingling all the way.

The fire was larger than I expected, with a mound of coals banked to one side of a blackened ring in the middle of a small clearing. Two forked, metal posts stood nearby. Supports for a spit.

Trussed like plucked fowl, I fought as best I could, yanking on the long, wooden pole that would fit perfectly between them. It didn't slow the Hiraches in the least.

The man—Vercho, perhaps—laughed. Speaking in the common tongue so I could understand him, he said, "Frightened meat tastes the sweetest."

But they stopped short of the fire, pulling me toward a tree whose low branches seemed to reach toward the embers. It took only a moment to lash the ends of the pole into place on the limbs, ignoring my attempts to struggle.

I faced the fire, close enough to benefit from the warmth. The pole rested securely just above my eyes. Too high for me to worry at the knots with my teeth, I supposed, though perhaps they didn't realize how blunt a Thurei's teeth were. The rope around my ankles made standing awkward, but I could use the pole to keep my balance.

Then, without a word, they walked away.

Given my preference, I would have chosen escape instead of death by Hirach anger—or hunger—though either of those came before luring Kate to her capture.

I studied the bindings on my hands, the leather straps looping over my fingers and circling my wrists. Leather straps wouldn't hold long against a *zaret*. I just needed a way to wield it with no hands.

I had half the night left before the sun rose. They couldn't hold me longer than that, so whatever plan they'd made would be in motion before then.

Plenty of time to figure something out.

CHAPTER FOURTEEN

COR

Though Serkot and her companion had left after setting me in place, they'd hardly left me alone. From what I could tell, the fire lay at the center of the tiny Hirach village and any members of the kith who moved within it would have needed to walk past my position or at least in sight of it. The tree might have obscured my outline somewhat, but otherwise, I must have made an obvious silhouette against the glow.

From my vantage point, the bright flames and embers ruined my night vision, making my eyes as ineffectual as a human's.

The thought of Kate's warm, brown eyes looking up at me stole away my pretense of calm. *Dear heart*, she'd called me, a human love-name, holding my face in her gentle hands. I'd thought she counted me as less than a *nochel*, but she'd been trying to find a way to give me her vow with honor.

I leaned my forehead against my wrists. *Please,* dacha, *don't look for me.* I had protected her from Hunters for years. Now, barely moments after she had mentioned pairing her life with mine, I'd become the bait to bring her right into their waiting claws. Some protector I'd turned out to be. I should have contented myself with guarding her from the shadows.

A quiet rustle jerked me back to alertness. I straightened up to find Serkot standing beside me. She reached out with her claws toward my injured side and I flinched. She chuckled as if she enjoyed my fear, but all she did was pull up the hem of my shirt.

Cloth bandages wrapped my lower ribs where someone had struck me during the brief fight. The strips were spotted in places where blood soaked through. Worrying about infection was a luxury for someone with a longer life expectancy. She wrinkled her nose and let the shirt hem fall, covering the bandage again.

"I've never known Hunters to keep prey on hand," I said, trying for the antagonistic boredom so common in the sharply edged conversations that filled Thurei sitting rooms. "Have Hiraches fallen all the way to farming, that you're here tending livestock?"

Her hand whipped out to clamp around my throat. Claws needled my skin. "You rejoice to see us fall, Hunterslayer, and so do the rest of your soft kind, cowering under the Truce. It is just, that you will help us rise again."

I pulled back against her hold, hoping to force her hand. This time, she released me.

I had only intended to insult her by calling her people farmers. Even Hunters who had left killing behind and agreed to the Truce disdained farming. What fall did this kith need to rise from? Hunting sapient prey was a dangerous business. All manner of things could go wrong, but I made the best guess I could.

"I can't bring back your Finder or his pack." Kate and I had killed the Hunters from this kith who had come after us. Normally, a kith should have been able to absorb the loss of a handful of warriors, even if the fallen were among their best. That was the gamble they made. "Neither can Kate. We fought with honor and

Tharkesh lost the lives he wagered. Where's the honor in hunting with a baited trap?"

"You bleat like a *kittu* tied for slaughter," the Hirach woman spat, then stalked away.

As well I should. The *kittu* and I had much in common.

With Serkot's words in mind, I saw the village with new eyes. Even for an encampment this small, this late in the evening, I would have expected more movement, more noise. Especially with a prisoner.

Possibly, the others could be out completing whatever plan they'd put in motion. If there had been a representative of the kith who'd seen the end of our battle with Tharkesh on Earth, would they have gone down to the beach after we'd slipped back to Kuyen? Kate had lost the token I'd given her during the fight. That token would bring its bearer directly to me, once they figured out its purpose. I hoped that was how they had found me—they couldn't duplicate that maneuver on Kate. The eatery where they'd captured me was tolerably far from her home, but if they could put enough Hiraches on the streets of Kate's city…

That might keep the members of a kith busy.

I forced that terrible image from my mind. I could neither warn Kate nor stop the Hunters in my current position. I had to get out of here first.

They'd tied me up, but I had a blade sharper than any material weapon. All I had to do was manage the impossible.

I shifted my hobbled feet on the soft ground, trying for the best approximation of a steady, comfortable stance that would allow me to concentrate. My headache had eased to a dull throb and my stomach's protests had dropped to a grumble. The rest of my aches would have to wait on my escape and perhaps a healer.

I closed my eyes, settling back into the first lessons I'd had as a boy. I didn't want to call my blade to my hand this time. I just wanted to call it to me. I concentrated on my *jeira*, the vibrant energy that would power my skill. It answered readily and I gathered it, shaping it into the smooth, sharp edge that had become second nature.

My *zaret*. Perfectly balanced, an extension of my will and power crafted for my hand alone…

The *jeira* unraveled, my intent shattering against the solid reality of the wooden rod bound into my hands. My knuckles ached from being locked in place. The slash on my palm I'd gotten attempting to stop the coin thief stung from pressing on the rough wood. The sensation of my bound hands, stacked atop half a lifetime's practice of calling the hilt to hand, worked like the child's challenge to not picture a green *morsai*. Try as I might, they were all I could think of.

I started over, this time imagining the transparent, single-edged sword appearing before me, hanging in the air. The moment I called for it, the gathered *jeira* dissipated, with no hand to hold it. I muttered a curse.

"What are you doing?" The Hirach boy's voice startled me out of my next attempt.

He stood off to the side, where the waning firelight limned his features. It was somewhat unsettling to see the characteristics of a Hunter altered in the familiar, chubby way of all children: a rounder muzzle, shorter limbs, stubby claws on daintier fingers.

"I'm cursing," I said. "It's a Thurei phrase for shattering your enemies' blades."

"But it doesn't work." It sounded like a guess on Grathki's part. "Cursing isn't the Thurei skill and we don't use blades."

"It hasn't worked yet. You should be asleep," I added, not that it ever worked well with the youngers in my House. Former House.

"It's the middle of the night," he said, in a manner of protest rather than agreement.

It was hardly the middle of the night anymore. Dawn had crept much closer while I'd tried to circumvent years of training in my skill.

"You don't sleep at the night?"

"No." Clearly, any fool would have known this. But if the kith should have all been awake, that made their small numbers even stranger.

"Where is everyone?" I asked.

"They're busy."

So, they were most likely hunting Kate. The confirmation sent ice creeping down my spine. I pitched my voice as best I could to appeal to a bored child. "Busy doing what?"

"I don't know," Grathki growled.

A bored *Hunter* child. Whatever occupied the adults, I could do nothing about it from here. Better to make use of the tools I had.

"All right," I said. "But they left you to guard me?"

Perhaps it kept a curious boy out from under the adults' feet, but it said much about their distraction that they risked leaving a child in the company of their prisoner. Then again, what threat could a Thurei be without his blade?

"Yes." The boy's teeth glinted in the firelight, though I couldn't guess whether it was a threat or a grin.

"Not many people live here," I said, unsure how far I could fish for information from a child. "What happened?"

"We moved." He had the same disinterested tone as any Thurei child who didn't understand the doings of the adults around him.

Hiraches typically moved from time to time, but had this group split from a larger one? A Hirach kith could have up to a hundred members, though the average was seventy or so. If this Akevad kith had numbered half so many, I would have been surprised.

"Why did you move?" I asked. "Did you leave people behind?"

Grathki looked at me for a long moment. "I'm not supposed to talk to you."

The classic answer of the uninformed. He went and selected a short length of branch from the woodpile and threw it in the middle of the embers, scattering sparks everywhere.

"Thank you," I said. Adult courtesy might gain traction with a child. "I was getting cold." Though my clothing had dried by now, it wasn't designed for warmth and the temperature continued to creep downward. My proximity to the fire helped, but the hour reminded me unpleasantly of chilly Earth nights spent on the roof of Kate's hospital.

"That's because you're prey," he said simply, poking at the embers with a stick.

"It's true," I agreed. I twisted my feet against the rope knotted around my ankles. It hadn't loosened since the last time I'd tried. It gave me enough play to adjust my footing, but I wouldn't be slipping these knots over my leather boots anytime soon. "I'm almost too weak to stand. It would help if I could sit down."

The boy was too short to reach the bindings on either my hands or the tree branches, but perhaps if I bent my knees, he could climb—

"I won't untie you," he said with all the affronted pride of a favored child. "Serkot told me not to."

I wouldn't argue that one, for fear that he'd go get the woman to adjudicate.

"Well, if you won't help, I'll have to go back to what I was doing," I said.

"Using your *jeira*?"

I hid a sigh. Hunters were very sensitive to *jeira*. It helped them find their prey. This boy could sense my failed attempts to summon my *zaret*, but either no one else could perceive it from farther away, or a Thurei who couldn't hold his blade was judged too small a threat.

If I managed to manifest the *zaret*, that might change, but it wasn't worth worrying about until it happened. What I didn't want was for him to run and tell them I was trying.

If they wanted, they could come up with more permanent solutions than tying my hands.

"I thought we might play a game," I offered. "You have good eyes if you noticed that I was using *jeira*. That's why you were sent to watch me, isn't it?"

"Yes," he said proudly. "I even saw one of the Ayuras and they don't have *jeira* at all."

I had never heard of an Ayura, but I let it go. I was running out of night, and I didn't want to know what the Hiraches had planned to keep me here at dawn. My head still ached from their last offer of hospitality.

"How far away can you be and still sense it?" I nodded my head toward the far edge of the village. "Go over and watch from there."

He seemed to mull it over as he nudged embers around with his stick. Flame bloomed at the end of the branch. "I like it here."

I didn't hide my sigh this time. I aimed for the tone of a disappointed elder. "If you stay here, it won't be good practice."

The boy ignored me in favor of the fire.

Ah, well. I closed my eyes and focused again, imagining the *zaret* hanging in space above the wooden bar. I ignored my hands. I wouldn't have to hold it, I wouldn't have to wield it, I only needed it to appear. Point down, its edge just above the bindings. *Right there.*

Then it would fall, and perhaps a very sharp blade could slice through thin leather on its way down, even without much weight behind it.

If I did it exactly right, I might even keep my fingers.

I reforged the *zaret* in my mind, step by step, as if it were a thing apart from me and not an integral piece. When I had the *jeira* collected, sharp and perfect, I reached with my will—

"You're doing it again!" Grathki's triumphant voice startled me out of my concentration. My hand twitched, an instinctive grab for a hilt that wasn't there. Gone.

"If you won't practice from a distance," I said, trying to keep my voice patient, "how about you practice with stealth? Try to count how many times I use *jeira* between now and sunrise, but you must be quiet enough that I don't see you or hear you. A good Hunter doesn't let his prey know where he is."

That appealed to Grathki more, at least for the moment. He tossed the branch into the fire and scampered away into the shadows.

I could feel dawn in my bones, some way off still but creeping closer. I closed my eyes again.

The quiet I'd bought myself went to waste. Again and again, my training took over, insisting that without a hand, I couldn't wield a blade. I could have juggled the shattered thing in and out of existence half the night—had done, more than once, because the roof of a hospital at night did not always provide its own amusements—but by the time Serkot and Vercho came stalking up, I had nothing to show for my efforts.

The sky still held the full black of true night, but it seemed dawn had come close enough. I was out of time.

"Eleven!" Grathki bounded out from the underbrush behind me.

"What are you doing over here?" Serkot asked him, lips curled over her sharp teeth.

Set to guard me, little Hunterling? Tell me one for my other ear.

Then she added, "Eleven what?"

Shatter it.

"Showing his *jeira* and then hiding it again." The boy scuffed his clawed feet. I didn't know if that was a gesture or just a child's fidget. "Just a little flicker. He's fast."

Vercho growled and stepped forward, limping on his right leg.

As I hadn't made good my escape, I had one chance to make good on the other option.

Using the pole for leverage, I lashed out with my bound feet. The Hunter's cloak obscured my target, but I still caught him in a glancing blow to his weaker leg. He roared and stumbled, grabbing for my calves. Claws scraped down my shins before I could pull back and he caught the rope binding my ankles. He pulled, yanking me down until my weight caught on my tied hands. Pain lanced through my wrists and I ground my teeth together so I wouldn't cry out.

Keeping hold of my ankles so I couldn't kick again, Vercho got his feet back under him and stood up. Serkot checked the leather bindings around my hands with quick, sure fingers, then looked me over, head to heel. Her hard gaze came back to my face.

My arms were on fire and keeping the pain from my voice took effort. "If Kjelgaard comes here, she will destroy you all. Loose me and give up this hunt and we will leave you alone."

"The human won't find us." She held a hand out to her companion, who slid his free hand into his cloak and retrieved a small, stoppered bottle to give her. She opened it and brought it near my face. "Let's see how fast you are after this."

The sharp, acrid smell sent a twinge through my stomach. It matched the taste on my lips when I'd woken. I turned my face away, but she merely took my jaw in her hand and turned me back, claws gouging into my skin.

"Drink," Serkot said. She added her favorite threat, "Or I will pour it down your throat."

Hanging like a hammock from my hands and my ankles in Vercho's grip, I couldn't fight much. In the end, she poured it down my throat.

My defiance left me coughing and pain flared in my wounded side with each spasm.

The concoction burned all the way down to my belly, spreading a warmth that made me suspect liquor as one of its components. Not just liquor, though. A tingling numbness followed the warmth.

Vercho dropped my feet and I struggled to get them under me, anything to take my weight off my hands and arms. That was important, though they had stopped hurting so much. The trees tilted around me and my feet wouldn't do what I told them to.

"Come on," Serkot grumbled. "Let's get him taken care of before he passes out completely."

The other Hirach approached and strong fingers worked at the knots in the leather.

"Wait." The word slurred across my numb lips. *If I'm bait, why don't they want Katen to find them?*

I reached for my *jeira*, but my focus blurred and slid away. By the time I had my hands free, it didn't matter.

CHAPTER FIFTEEN

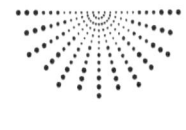

KATE

I would have loved to burrow into bed and try to sleep as soon as I left the search party, the only escape I could imagine from my fear and grief, but Earth didn't work that way. I had a shift at After Image along with Rose, who might have seen what had happened to Cor but couldn't remember it because she wasn't a worldwalker. I let habit carry me through my morning routine, as numb as a zombie.

I found Rose's truck in the parking lot when I rode up on my bicycle. I chained the bike up and hurried inside.

"Hey, Rose." I scooped up the pile of restock items and carried them out to where she counted the day's starting cash for the till.

"Good morning." She flashed me a smile that turned quickly to concern. "Oh, um, late night?"

If I had to guess, she'd edited that question from a first draft along the lines of, *You look like crap.*

I felt much worse than I looked, so it would have been a fair assessment.

"Yeah. Yeah, it was a late night." I did my best to sound normal.

I didn't want her worrying over something I couldn't explain. Not yet. I doubted I could keep my emotions a secret if it turned out Cor was—*No. Don't even think about it.* "I overslept a bit this morning. Sorry for being late."

"No worries." Rose's grin tipped back to cheerful. "Everyone missed you guys at pool. It's too bad you couldn't come."

If we'd left immediately after dinner… If we'd agreed to follow the rest of Rose's friends back to campus to play pool, would Cor have been taken?

I couldn't let myself stumble down that maze of what-ifs. Maybe the difference would have been a bunch of Hunters showing up in the middle of a crowd of college students.

"We'll have to hang out some other time," Rose continued. "Troy insists, now that he knows Corey teaches martial arts. You have no idea how excited he is."

"Absolutely. Um, although…you know, sometimes it's hard to get our schedules to line up for something like that." My voice started to wobble and I took a deep breath. *You won't know until you try.* "It's just quite a drive for him to visit, honestly, but wouldn't it be weird if…you know, it was something really strange? What if it was hard for Corey and me to see each other because…because we lived on different worlds?"

Good one. I am the absolute worst at this.

The cash register drawer clicked closed and then the silence stretched in the shop.

I looked up to find Rose staring at me, one of her black eyebrows raised. I shivered, too full of memories of being regarded as the crazy kid on the playground.

"Katherine, I don't follow you," she said, though she didn't seem inclined to go full what's-wrong-with-you mode quite yet.

"I mean…" I floundered. I'd heard there were other worlds where not everyone could worldwalk and use *jeira*, but the people who couldn't still knew it was possible. They could still see visitors from other worlds. Maybe humans could, too, if they could just... be open to the idea. Rose had seen Cor. She might have seen what had happened.

If I could just make her believe it.

"Remember when Troy was so interested in that multi-world theory they talked about in his physics class?" I attempted a laugh and forced some nonchalance into my voice. *It's all hypothetical here. Don't worry about the crazy girl.* "That's how it would work in the movies, right? Star-crossed lovers separated by some really weird circumstances."

Rose moved among the shop's printers, turning each one on, checking to make sure they had enough paper. "Then you and Corey could be a science fiction version of Romeo and Juliet? That would be cute but tragic."

My heart stuttered. I managed to say, "Our story will have a happy ending."

It will. It has to, I thought. *Thank you for humoring me.*

"Well, sure," Rose said. "Don't get offended or anything, but Corey's got the kind of quirky vibe that would make him perfect for that kind of movie. Get some gel and spike that Day-Glo hair."

When I stood there with my heart pounding in my ears for a moment too long, she turned to me, eyes wide. "In a charming way, I mean. Charming quirky. He seems like a nice guy, just a bit... Sheldon, you know? I didn't mean anything by it."

"No, no, it's fine." I scooped up a stack of product brochures and straightened them up so I'd have something to do with my hands. "I agree with you. He's very quirky. The good kind."

The conversation lagged and I should have left it there. Rose wasn't any closer to believing Cor came from another world than she was to believing I'd been born on the moon. I didn't need to have anyone thinking I was crazy.

But Cor had disappeared, and one question for Rose took up all the space in my thoughts. If I opened my mouth, I had to ask.

"Rose, you saw Corey leave last night, didn't you? What happened? Where did he go?"

I knew the look that crossed her face. I knew what she was going to say before she opened her mouth.

"What do you mean? Katherine, what's the matter?"

The next question would be *What's wrong with you?* I pressed the heels of my hands over my eyes for a moment, trying to get a grip on myself again. "Nothing. Sorry, nothing's wrong. I'm just tired. I…had some weird dreams, that's all. Everything's fine."

Rose nodded, though not like she believed me. "Okay. Are you and Corey getting along all right? Did he ditch you last night or something?"

"No, everything's fine." I couldn't handle a stretch of *Katherine's crazy* at the same time as *Cor's missing*. I should have stayed well clear of this can of worms. "I just need a better night's sleep, that's all. Um, how'd the rest of the night go? Did Chloe beat everyone at pool again?"

Terrible segue, but Rose rolled with it. We chatted in fits and starts for the rest of our shift, but we both avoided the subject of Cor.

As if he didn't exist.

The moment the sun went down on Earth, I slipped over to Cor's apartment at the garrison. As I pictured the room in order to worldwalk there, I imagined Cor waiting for me, his sharp, handsome features ready to blossom into a delighted smile.

But he wasn't.

My breath caught on a sob and I took a moment to try to calm myself. *We'll find him.* I lifted the Summons I'd prepared, almost afraid to reach for my *jeira* and have the letter go nowhere. As soon as I channeled the energy and intention into it, though, the Summons flexed its paper wings, lifted, and flew away toward its goal, disappearing as it slipped away.

Cor was alive.

Some of the tension unwound from my shoulders. *I don't know where you are, dear heart, but I'll find you.*

A Summons materialized in front of me, right where the other had disappeared, making my heart beat faster. I snatched it out of the air and unfolded it so fast, I nearly tore the paper.

Not Cor's writing. I could tell that at a glance. In my hurry, the Kuyene words read like nonsense sounds as I scanned to the bottom of the message. It was signed *Pella tol dav Ferrum*, Shom's aunt and the commander of the outpost. I forced myself to slow down and concentrate on the formal words. Pella had set up a hearing with the Shevern council, later this morning.

Good thing I'd worn the new dress I'd bought with Rose. I'd also brought a set of my regular clothes, since I'd had no idea how today would go.

The letter didn't mention that the Scholars admitted to having Cor, but I didn't doubt for a moment that they were behind it. Even if the Scholars weren't holding Cor directly, they were the reason he'd been captured.

On the other hand, when Cor and I had originally gone to the Scholars Hall, they'd set a Hirach on our trail. When we'd crossed paths with the Hunter in the shadowy colonnade outside the Hall, I'd been frightened enough that it had been a comfort to repeat what the doctors had drilled into me: It was all just a hallucination. If the Scholars had arranged to have Cor captured by force, what would they do to me if I walked right into their grasp?

Last time I'd been to the Hall, I hadn't taken anything I'd seen or heard seriously. Cor had managed to talk me into returning to his world, but I'd still clung to my schizophrenia diagnosis. I'd been ignorant of everything but what I remembered from my childhood visits to Kuyen, and I'd been powerless, both physically and in regard to my skill.

None of those things were true any longer. Now, I had a powerful skill. I was dangerous enough that the Scholars were afraid of me. I had to keep reminding myself of that.

Also, it was painfully clear that I needed to get better at my skill. I hadn't been good enough to save Cor.

I wrote a quick note to Birasef, letting him know that Pella and I were going to speak with the Scholars, and sent it off. Hopefully, the rustling paper wouldn't wake him. This early in the morning on Kuyen, he was probably still asleep.

Well, if I needed to practice my skill, I couldn't find a better place for it than the garrison. Pella had instructors for physical fighting and for using skills. Maybe I could find someone to help train me or, at the very least, a corner of space out of the way so I could practice by myself.

I wished Cor were here to help me instead. He'd proved to be a patient and kind teacher as I'd been learning the basics of my skill. But sitting around wishing I had Cor back wouldn't improve my abilities any.

I changed into my jeans and T-shirt and returned to the arena. Clangs, thumps, and shouts filtered out through the doors as I approached. I remembered the scolding I'd gotten when I'd shown up here uninvited, looking for Cor. This time, though, when I stepped into the cavernous space full of soldiers, one of the Lan men caught sight of me and beckoned me over to him.

On the tall side for a Lan, nearly as tall as Cor, he had a physique that Troy would have taken as a challenge, his corded muscle obvious beneath his pale gray skin. He looked like an instructor—at least, he'd been watching a pair of fighters spar and when he held up a fist, they stopped.

One looked almost Thurei, tall and slender, but covered with a patchwork suit of leather armor. Some of the pieces were thin and flexible, but other portions were thick and sturdy. On a closer look, some of it was leather armor and other sections were a part of the man's skin, like the thick, leathery plates on an armadillo. The other fighter was a Lan woman who held a long, wooden staff. It seemed odd that they would be training in the arena, but then I noticed the geometric lines of dark metal inlaid around the length of the staff. It must have been some kind of skillwork. I had no idea what it might do or how dangerous it would be, but it merited practice here in the arena rather than out in the open air.

The instructor walked up and gave me a nod that might have been the distant cousin to a bow. He wiped sweat from his brow and ran a hand quickly over his black hair, tied back in a ponytail. "Kjelgaard—is that proper? If you're looking for Shom, she's not here."

"Oh, uh, you can call me Kjelgaard or Kate, whatever you prefer. Humans aren't very formal. Um, I was hoping to practice my skill if you know somewhere that's out of the way. I don't want to bother anyone, but practicing in Coraven's room seemed like a bad idea."

"You found the right place," the man said, gesturing at the busy arena around us. "What's your skill?"

"I can...disintegrate things. Or people." Quickly, I added, "But my control is pretty good." It didn't sound very convincing, even to me, but the Lan man just lifted a hand and tilted it back and forth.

Lan weren't affected by the skills of others, so my skill might not have worried him at all.

"That's a skill that deserves care," he agreed. "Let me set something up for you. I'm Eld, by the way." He paused for a moment, then said more quietly, "Coraven has helped me with my sword work. He's a good man. Pella will find him soon. She's fierce for her troops, don't you worry."

Of course, Cor had made a good impression with everyone, even in the short time he'd been here.

Eld turned his students over to another instructor and took me aside. He asked me more about my skill, the techniques Cor had been using to help me learn it, and what aspects I felt I needed to work on. I showed him how it worked by making some of the loose sand on the arena floor disappear.

"If you want to improve your speed and reflexes, I've got some ideas." He seemed genuinely intrigued by the challenge. "Come on. Follow me."

He found me a place near the wall and brought over a heavy crate that he thumped to the ground about fifteen feet away from me.

"Is that a box of rocks?" I couldn't help but ask.

Eld reached in and lifted a handful of small river stones, not exactly round but rounded smooth, about the size of ping pong balls. "I'm going to throw these at you—gently!" he amended when I opened my mouth to protest. He revised. "I'm going to toss these in your direction. Not at your head. We'll start slow, just one at a time, but I expect you to get faster. Even if you miss one, it won't really hurt. Worst you'll get is a bruise."

I sighed. Shom had helped me learn my skill at first and for the most part, she'd done it by hitting me with a stick. From what I could tell, the Lan were keen on training techniques that left bruises.

I had to admit, it was motivational.

Cor had had me practice with a method like this—a bruise-free version. He'd hung small pouches on strings from the ceiling, then set them swinging like pendulums. The targets were full of purple powder that would leave marks on my training clothes if I didn't dodge them or disintegrate them with my skill. Trying to make my way through a maze of such moving targets had helped me learn to use my skill at the same time I'd dodged and maneuvered between them. I liked to think I'd gotten a little faster on my feet, too, though I'd only had a couple of weeks to train.

However, the swinging targets moved predictably, rather slowly, and when they'd hit me, they'd been soft. The worst I'd risked had been purple clothes and a bit of teasing from Cor.

The memory of Cor's narrow face lighting up with a laugh made me close my eyes for a moment.

"All right," I said, trying to ready my concentration for the task at hand. "Let's go."

"We'll try a couple of practice ones first," Eld said. He waited for my acknowledgement, then tossed one of the stones at me.

Toward me, like he'd promised. I could tell by the arc that it was going to land a couple of feet shy. I reached out with my skill and the rock crumbled apart, as if it had been nothing but a dirt clod all along. Sand thinned to dust, moving along the same trajectory for a moment before even that disintegrated to nothing.

"Very impressive," Eld said, his eyebrows up near his hairline. "I think you can handle a little more speed, what do you think?"

"Sure," I said. I didn't know why I'd been so intimidated at first. This was easier than I'd expected.

Eld tossed the next rock with a flick of his wrist, like skipping a stone across a pond. It spun toward me, quick and direct...

Better practice. I focused on my skill. *I could have saved Cor if I'd been faster.*

The rock evaporated. So did a chunk of the sandy floor, leaving a curving dish of empty soil beneath the point where the rock had disappeared. It wasn't hard to visualize the sphere of space my skill had affected. Erased.

"I'm sorry," I said reflexively. And in English. I repeated myself in stuttering Kuyene. Fortunately, there hadn't been anything but the rock and the ground within reach of my destruction. I hadn't messed up that badly since I'd started learning my skill. My control should have been better by now. "Forgive me, I was distracted."

Eld studied the shallow pit in the floor, then looked up at me, holding on to his composure better than I had. "We'll try a slower toss again."

"All right," I agreed, though I was tempted to call the session off. I needed the practice, clearly, but I also needed not to ruin Pella's property at the same time. In the end, I just needed to get better.

"Keep your eyes on the stone," Eld suggested, holding one up between his thick, gray fingers. "Imagine its arc through the air. Watch its approach, allow that to sharpen your focus. Wait until it's close before you destroy it. That way, you'll practice speed, but at a slower pace." He smiled a little at his phrasing, but then his expression froze, like something had just occurred to him. "Are you likely to hurt yourself?"

"No," I said, trying to match his calm, matter-of-fact tone. Then again, he had a lot of practice helping soldiers use their dangerous skills. Maybe this was a walk in the park for him. That idiom just made me think of Cor—he'd used it when we'd been training, too. *Stop that. Focus.* Everything made me think of Cor. I took a deep breath. "No, I can't affect myself or anything from my world with my skill. Just things from another world."

"Interesting." Eld rubbed his chin with a knuckle. "From any other world? Or just Kuyen?"

"I...don't know." I shook my head before I remembered he wouldn't know the human gesture. The question had never occurred to me. "I haven't tried things from anywhere else."

He waved the speculation away. "That's a task to practice on another day. This here is a plain, honest Kuyene river stone from the near side of Aubello. It's always dreamed of being a breeze. Help it out."

He soft-tossed the rock in my direction and I did as he asked. The rock dissolved into the air.

We took it more slowly for a few tosses. So long as I focused, it wasn't hard—even Cor would have pushed me harder if he'd been here. That realization snuck past my concentration and short-circuited it. A rock hit me in the thigh as I flinched away too late.

Eld may have thrown it softly, but it was still a rock.

"Do you need to take a break for a moment?" he asked, more courteous than concerned.

"No, I'm fine," I said. I doubted he was worried about my leg. If I couldn't even concentrate enough to handle my skill—how was I going handle speaking with the Scholars? The worst I could do here was damage the floor or Eld's uniform or embarrass myself.

The Scholars at the Hall had set a Hunter on my trail because they thought humans were unstable and dangerous. A misstep there could have fatal consequences for Cor.

Eld kept on with the lessons gamely for about another hour. I got hit three more times and put two more holes in the floor when distraction got in the way of controlling my skill. My mind wasn't on my work—it was on Cor, on the Scholars, on my failure to stop the Hunters.

On my growing frustration that I didn't know how to fix any of it.

When Eld called the training to a halt, I scrubbed the heels of my hands over my eyes. In addition to everything else, it was nearing the middle of the night on Earth. I'd napped—if you could call it that, tossing and turning for a couple of hours before giving up—but fatigue gnawed at the edges of my thoughts.

"I'm sorry about the floor," I said. The trio of craters mocked me. The last one was almost two feet deep. That represented a big sphere of accidental destruction. I noticed that the other sparring soldiers had moved farther away from our end of the arena over the course of my practice session.

"Dirt's easy to fix," Eld said, cheerfully unconcerned with the damage. "You could use regular practice. I'm sure you'll see quick improvement if you put your mind to it. Come back tomorrow?"

I sighed. "I don't know what's happening tomorrow, but I'd appreciate the chance for more practice if I can get it. Thank you for your help, Eld. I… Normally, I do have it more under control."

"Good." Eld grinned. "I can't wait to see it."

CHAPTER SIXTEEN

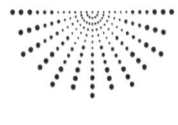

KATE

When I met Shom and her aunt in the commander's chambers, I was glad I'd brought the dress. Pella wore a formal outfit that left no doubt she was a commander of soldiers. She had a high-collared, burgundy jacket sewn over with small, gleaming squares of metal like it was armor, worn over a darker red tunic and slim-fitting, black pants that buckled above the knees of her faun-like legs. A pair of long daggers hung from her belt. Formal though it was, the outfit allowed her to make use of her long stride and maneuverability if she needed it. Her black hair, streaked with white, was braided tightly back, then doubled in on itself to make a sturdy tail that fell to the middle of her back.

She didn't look like the kind of person the Scholars would want to mess with. Then again, Cor had been son of a *denet* as well as a renowned swordsman when Tharkesh had prowled around us the first time. His position and his skill hadn't stopped the Scholars from setting the Hirach in our path and it hadn't intimidated Tharkesh, either.

"The Scholars sent Hunters after us last time," I said, hating the hesitation in my voice. "Do you think they'll try something this time, too?"

"You're accompanying me, under my protection." Pella dropped her hand to the hilt of her dagger. "Any strike made against you is a strike against the peacekeepers of Aubello. If you'd rather remain here, I can speak in your stead."

I couldn't leave this in someone else's hands. I needed to be there.

"No, I'll go." I tried to project confidence. "Are you coming, too, Shom?"

Her outfit didn't have the same military cast as Pella's, but Shom's golden, long-sleeved shirt, paired with a black vest and pants matched the formality in an understated way.

She gave me half a smile and murmured, in English, "Search and rescue."

A game we'd played as kids. Shom and I had usually taken turns as the victim, since Cor had the keenest eyes in the search party. I blinked away tears. "Thank you, Shom."

"Kjelgaard," Pella said. "You're aware they've only agreed to a small hearing, correct? Good. We need the full council in order to exert enough pressure against Scholars—how many did you say you met with originally?"

"Four," I said.

"Not many," she said thoughtfully. "That's a good sign. What were their names?"

"Um, I don't remember." My cheeks heated with shame. I hadn't taken the meeting seriously at the time and now, when Cor needed me, I didn't know the information that might help us get him back.

"Well, they do have names more or less impossible for us fallible ones to remember," Shom said. "I think they do it on purpose."

Pella pursed her lips. "If you recognize any of them, let me know. It will make a difference, whether this small council is just the Scholars to whom you spoke or not."

"You don't think they're all involved?" I asked.

Pella chuckled, but there was no humor in the sound. "I doubt it. If it was just Coraven...but a kidnapping is far less an offense for Sheverns than falsehood. Lying is the worst of their crimes. It can drive them mad. They remember everything, and all their memories pass to their children. The memory of the lie is as real as the truth, so lying means they'll carry two contradictory realities in their head at the same time. If we can convince the rest of the council that some of the Scholars are lying, that's what will get Coraven released."

No pressure.

Getting to the Scholars Hall meant worldwalking from the garrison to a slip anchor on another world, then back across the gap between worlds to the Scholars Hall on Kuyen. Shom slipped the three of us to a place I'd never been, the bank of a perfectly circular pond with evenly spaced brick squares along the edge of the water. A full moon cast its reflection on the water, but the pond itself had a bluish glow that lit the area for dozens of yards past the shore.

"Where is this?" I asked.

"Mochet. I come here all the time." Shom nodded toward the far side of the pond. "There's a market over there, on the other side of the hedges. They make alloys useful for skillwork and they have excellent smiths."

I'd never given much thought to the other worlds beyond Kuyen and Earth, but of course each one would have its own unique resources and specialties. While Earth was considered empty, with its lack of *jeira* and a population "blind" to worldwalkers, Mochet had a place like this, a collection of anchor points devoted to travel between worlds. Almost an airport terminal for worldwalkers. Some of the other squares around the pond were occupied, worldwalkers fading in and out of place like actors in old sci-fi television shows.

Pella cleared her throat and Shom and I met each other's gazes like guilty children before closing our eyes so Pella could worldwalk us back across the gap to Scholars Hall.

We arrived within the Hall itself, not at the entry gate at the base of the hill. I recognized the long colonnade, the white stone lit by the late morning sun slanting through windows high under the vaulted ceiling. Low walls divided the spaces between the columns into discrete units almost like cubicles. Most held chairs and tables, as well as shelves loaded with boxes, scrolls, and other items I couldn't name at a glance. Several of the small rooms had occupants—the bulky forms of bald-headed, copper-skinned Sheverns. The low murmur of their voices echoed through the cavernous space, multiplying until it seemed there might have been a hundred Sheverns hiding in the shadows, whispering around us.

I shivered, releasing the other women's hands. *Get it together, Kate.*

Our little room was empty, the chest-high walls plain, intended as a slip anchor instead of a place for study or discussion like the others.

"You can worldwalk straight inside the Hall?" I asked, surprised that the Scholars allowed it. "I thought everyone had to take the stairs."

Scholars Hall sat at the top of a tall, steep hill, at the end of a long flight of stone steps. Cor and I had spent hours climbing them on our visit, my first time back in Kuyen since my parents had sent me to Bayshore Psychiatric. I hadn't been pleased. Also, at the time, I hadn't thought it was real. I'd thought I'd spent the whole night walking around my neighborhood by myself and I'd given a lot of thought to calling the whole thing off and telling Cor that I'd never wanted to see him again.

Now, the possibility that I might never see Cor again filled me with dread.

"Petitioners take the stairs," Pella said. She held up a small, oval stone, the same speckled gray as the pavers beneath our feet, not the white stone of the rest of the construction. "We're here on council business and for that, they offer tokens. This is one of the few spaces in the Hall where worldwalking is allowed. Excuse me." Pella peered over the low walls as if she were looking for someone.

Shom shrugged, human-style, and lowered her voice like we were in a library back home. "Even the Scholars wouldn't push other leaders to take the stairs. Skillwork crafted into the building and courtyard paving stones keeps everyone else out, unless they have a token."

"There's skillwork that can block worldwalking? Why don't more people use it?" The Leratoms, at least, went to a lot of trouble to keep their House secure if it could simply be done with skillwork.

"It's extremely costly," Shom said. "Both to make and to maintain."

A Shevern finally approached our small chamber, smoothing her gray robes for a moment before lifting her broad palms, blunt fingers spread wide. Her dark gaze swept over us, settled on Pella. Like all Sheverns, she was short, the smooth crown of her head barely even with my chin.

She hadn't been among the Scholars I'd met with Cor.

"I am Scholar Zonji res Arrespa Melnavora evat Sestallo, Primary of the line for Unaligned *Jeira* Survey, Tertiary of the line for Outworld Cultural Adaptation..." Her introduction continued for another three long titles. I couldn't keep track of it all. She finished up with, "You may call me Zonji. Allow me to escort you to the minor council."

We followed the Scholar to a fully enclosed room, a tall, windowless chamber lit a brilliant white with skillwork lamps. My heart rate jumped. *They're just Sheverns. Their skill is memory, not any combat ability.* A ring of gilded chairs stood on a raised section of the floor around the edge of the room, making the center of the space feel like a pit. Two robed Scholars waited in their chairs already, looking down at us when we entered.

These two, I recognized from my first visit. If Pella didn't manage to get the full council gathered to hear us, these two wouldn't help at all.

"Scholar Zonji!" I whirled around, stopping the startled Shevern in the act of closing the door behind her. *Great, now what? What did she say her areas of study were?* I didn't even know what unaligned *jeira* was. Outworld cultures, though... "As an outworlder myself, I beg your attention on this matter. I would be honored if a Scholar of your esteem would observe and remember our exchange. Surely, there is little knowledge at the Hall of Earth cultures? I would hate for you to miss a rare opportunity to gather more."

I knew of only one other human worldwalker and Issai had said the Scholars suppressed any other information about humans from the Kuyen public. Something being forbidden to the public, though, didn't mean that other Scholars lost their curiosity. In a culture that revolved around information, perhaps it caused the opposite to be true.

Beside me, Shom gave me a subtle thumbs-up, a gesture no one else in the room would recognize.

"This isn't necessary," one of the seated Scholars snapped, his broad, hairless brow wrinkling. "The two of us are sufficient for this hearing."

But Zonji pushed the door open again and took a step back into the room.

Shom tapped her chin as if she were deep in thought. "In fact, perhaps the Secondary of the line for Outworld Cultural Adaptation should be summoned. It could be quite the opportunity for advancement."

Zonji held up an imperious hand, marching her way to the waiting chairs. "I will listen for the line. I insist."

"Earth culture doesn't factor into *Tol* Pella's request," the other seated Scholar said.

Clearing her throat, Pella stepped forward. "I would be honored by the Scholar's presence and attention, in pursuit of her studies. Though Earth culture has no bearing on my concern, Scholar Zonji is welcome to observe a human amidst Kuyenes. Undoubtedly, as Kjelgaard has suggested, this is a rare event. I would not put my concerns above a Scholar's obligation to pursue her studies as diligently as she can. Isn't that the mandate of Scholars?"

While the seated Scholars' expressions soured further, Zonji didn't hesitate in her course.

"That is so, *Tol* Pella." Zonji made her way to the steps leading to the raised chairs. "True, as well, that more ears improve the hearing."

The woman Scholar I recognized failed to hide a sigh. "Very well, Zonji. This hearing will be quick. I fear you'll be disappointed."

Zonji got herself settled beside the other two Sheverns while they made their introductions. If anything, the names and lists of titles for these two Scholars were even longer than Zonji's, but they offered the three of us, with our imperfect memories, the abbreviated versions Anderlis and Breshia. I remembered Anderlis as the most outspoken of the Scholars from before, the one most adamant that I didn't belong on Kuyen.

I inclined my head toward them in a little not-quite-bow. "We've met before, Scholars."

"I remember," Anderlis said.

"Pella, *Tol* of dav Ferrum." Scholar Breshia curled her fingers in a beckoning gesture toward the Lan. "You've asked for our attention and you have it. Please, proceed."

Pella let her gaze pan around the room, as if she'd only now realized that only three out of fifteen seats were filled. "I have a formal matter for the council, Scholars. Summon the full council. We are in haste and we need to make the best use of our time."

Anderlis leaned forward, elbows on his stocky knees. "I apologize, *Tol*. We of the small council will carry your concerns to our colleagues, if we judge the matter is appropriate. However, as Kjelgaard has noted herself, she is an offworlder, and thus not eligible for council rulings. If your concern relates to her… Forgive me, *Tol*, but the Shevern council has no solution for you."

Pella's stern features grew even stonier as she straightened, using her height to effect, raised chairs or no. "I bring my own concern before the council. Kjelgaard and Shom merely attend me. Understand, honored Scholars, that this is no inquiry to the Scholars of the Hall. I am here to make an accusation against Sheverns under the Truce, in my position as the contracted protector of Aubello. My call must be answered."

The three Sheverns studied her for a long moment, then Anderlis said, "Does your accusation touch upon the security of Aubello?"

Pella seemed in no hurry to answer, either. I couldn't tell anything from her stoic expression and Shom wouldn't even meet my eye. I followed the Lans' lead as best I could, trying to stay calm and still.

"No," Pella said finally. "The safety of Aubello is not affected. This speaks rather to the safety of my troops at the garrison."

Anderlis shifted in his chair and laced his blunt fingers together in his lap. Even as a human, I could feel the shift in the atmosphere. The Sheverns had won a point.

"I have taken into my garrison a new instructor." Pella's voice rang hard and clear. While I might have been scarcely able to keep my heart steady, she'd faced enemies far more intimidating than a trio of researchers. "This man has brought an accusation against your council for events that occurred before he joined my troops. I don't know what the ruling was, but yesterday, he was taken by an unidentified party. Due to the nature of his accusation, suspicion gathers on your doorstep. I ask you, Scholars…truthtellers, do you know the whereabouts of Coraven, formerly Temarel, who visited your Hall not long ago?"

"We do not," Anderlis answered immediately. "Nor is it a matter that has anything to do with us."

"Correct me if I'm wrong, *Tol*," Breshia said. "We were told that Coraven entered your employ recently. We have had no dealings at all with him since then."

"That's true." Pella lifted her palms, making a gesture of balancing scales. "But I don't see how it's relevant."

"How much a part of your garrison could he be?" Anderlis asked. "He's Thurei. Let his own people speak for him if they wish."

They knew he'd been banned from House Temarel. Pella had mentioned it, even if they hadn't heard of it on their own. If the Scholars refused to speak to Pella about Coraven's abduction, I was certain *Denet* Temarel wouldn't pursue an accusation against them. Pella was my only hope.

I thought it surprised us all when Zonji raised a finger to catch our attention.

"Let's hear it fully," Zonji said. "Tell us first what happened and then we can decide whether or not your reasons are sufficient."

"That's not necessary," Anderlis began, but Breshia contradicted him in almost the same breath.

"Lay out for us what happened," she said, throwing her considerable weight into her words. "As accurately as you can."

Anderlis pressed his broad lips together, like he'd taken a bite of something he couldn't spit out now. "Excuse my unseemly haste, *Tol* Pella. Please, continue."

Pella turned the floor over to me. Shom gave me a sidelong glance and lifted her chin slightly.

I squared my shoulders and tried to channel the key witness gravitas of courtroom dramas. "Coraven and I visited your Hall to ask about the human skill—"

Breshia interrupted me. "We're asking after his disappearance, Kjelgaard. If you have nothing to say about that, please maintain your patience through this hearing."

I shared a glance with Pella. I had no direct evidence of the Scholars' connection to Cor's disappearance. Scholar Zonji would need context in order to come to the same conclusion for herself. It wasn't as if a Scholar would simply take my word over that of her colleagues.

"Kjelgaard was there, Scholars," Pella said, pushing me to speak. "She can relate it best."

I gave them the basic version of events, stopping every couple of sentences to answer their questions. No, I hadn't been able to tell who or how many had attacked Cor. Yes, he had been injured. There'd been blood, all of it Cor's. No, not much of it. No, no signs or scents from whoever had taken him. It could not have been Tharkesh. He and the warriors of his pack had died during their failed attempt to kill us.

No Summons or other communications had reached me from Cor or those holding him.

"Earth is not a world with Hunters, isn't that correct?" Anderlis waited for my agreement. "Then I assume you are less familiar with their nature. They are predators. They seek out new prey for themselves; they don't need anyone to set them on that path. The prohibition on their practices embodied by the Truce comprises merely the latest few pages of their history, after volumes upon volumes of violence. Hunters wish to kill, even if most of them conceal that impulse in these peaceful days. This attack on Coraven needs no further explanation than that."

On our first visit to the Hall, the Scholars had done the same thing, drowning the points we'd raised beneath a deluge of facts and theories.

"The next logical step, *Tol*," Zonji said, "is to contact the Hunter councils. Your accusation does not belong with us."

"I disagree, Scholar." Pella tucked her hands behind her back—far from her daggers, but somehow, it felt like a threat. "Call the full council and let your fellow Sheverns decide for themselves."

Pella was running out of ways to force their hand. Anderlis wouldn't even listen to what we had to say right now, much less call a full council for us, and Breshia followed his lead. Zonji was our only hope for exposing the Scholars' actions to the rest of the Sheverns.

"Tharkesh chose to hunt Cor and me at the direction of your own Hall," I said, interrupting whatever refusal the Scholars were about to make. My words tripped over each other in my haste to get it all out before Anderlis could shut us down again. "He came here with a question and you took his payment in service. What service? You called him back to the Hall when Cor and I came to ask about my skill."

"It's no business of yours what service another petitioner renders," Breshia began, but I kept talking.

"You lied to us about my skill." I aimed my words at the two Scholars who had been there that day, but I kept my attention on

Zonji, who watched me with wide, dark eyes. I couldn't tell what she thought, but she was listening. "You told us that humans had no *jeira* skill, that Issai knew nothing about it. Then you sent us out of your doors to Tharkesh, a Hunter, waiting in the colonnade. Shom, tell them about—"

Anderlis pushed himself to his feet, a thunderous expression on his large features. "Enough! You are stringing together nonsense. We've permitted your presence out of courtesy, but your people are not bound by the Truce. You deserve no voice before any council, outworlder. I will not tolerate slander from your lips."

He shook his sleeve sharply, dropping a small, square stone into his hand. He pressed it between his palms, staring at it intently. I shook my head, unwilling to let him distract me from what I needed to say.

"It's written in your own visitor logs! You called Tharkesh back to kill us. Me because I'm human and Coraven for bringing me here." My voice sounded muffled and distant, as if my ears had gotten blocked and I could only hear my words thrumming through my bones.

Pella glared at the Scholar. "That was unnecessary."

Shom lifted her hands, palms up. "Records of visits and service exist, don't they? Let's look at the ledgers together and see whether Kjelgaard's statement is slander or truth."

She knew perfectly well such ledgers existed. Shom had been the one to tell Cor and me the information they held.

Breshia narrowed her eyes. "We welcome petitioners from many peoples. This outworlder has made accusations that have nothing to do with records of payment. Scholars cannot lie."

"Enough," Amberlis said, his tone severe. "In light of your baseless accusations, I almost hesitate to offer you anything, but our duty as Scholars is to share what we know." He enunciated those last words with care, as if that alone might convince Pella of his sincerity.

I wasn't interested. "What did you do to my ears?"

Shom put a steadying hand on my shoulder and shook her head, a human gesture as good as a secret language. The Scholars and Pella ignored me, engaged in their own conversation. I might as well have disappeared.

I could still hear them speak, so Anderlis hadn't done anything to my ears. No, he'd used that bit of skillwork in his hand to silence my voice.

The Scholar continued, dispensing his information as duty demanded. "I have been told that the Akevad kith holds the Thurei known as Hunterslayer. As it often turns out, the most logical of possibilities is also the true one."

"What?" Of course, no sound came out. Talked over, silenced, brushed aside. I had resources now that I hadn't the first time I'd come here. I focused my *jeira* and concentrated on that bit of stone or tile in the Scholar's hand. *His hand is empty. There's nothing there.*

Anderlis flinched in his chair when the skillwork item disintegrated.

"If you already knew who had him, why didn't you just tell us in the first place?" I snapped, glad to hear my voice ring out like normal. "What is this Akevad whatever? Where is Cor?"

"Kjelgaard." Pella made my name a cold warning. "Scholar, the question is valid. How do you know this? Who told you?"

Anderlis had recovered himself. "*Tol* Pella, remove this human from the Hall. She is no longer welcome here. If you have official business with the Scholars or the Shevern council in the future, commander of peacekeepers, send someone else from your coalition."

"As you say." Pella inclined her head.

"No! You know where Cor is," I began, but Shom took hold of my arm, startling me.

"Kate," she whispered. "We're done here."

"I'm not done. You know they—"

"Enough." Her fingers tightened on my forearm. "We lost this one. We're leaving."

The three Sheverns watched from above us, their round faces impassive. If I'd hoped for sympathy from Zonji, I'd lost my chance. I turned my back on them and followed Shom and her aunt out of the room.

I ground my teeth together the rest of the way back to the stone cubicle.

Pella held out her hand to her niece. "Shom, if you please."

As I took Shom's hand, I tried to banish the shivers of leftover adrenaline running through me. She pulled us across the gap to one of those brick squares next to the glowing pond. Cool, nighttime air chilled the nervous perspiration on my skin.

Even if Anderlis had told the truth and the Hiraches held Cor on their own motivations, the Scholars had still been the ones to put them on our trail. After today, I had no reason to think they meant us less harm. That would just have to be dealt with later. It was painfully clear that there was nothing I could do about it now.

"How do we find Cor?" I asked as soon as the gritty surface solidified beneath my shoes. "What is this kith they were talking about?"

"The Akevad kith," Shom said. "It's the group of Hiraches that Tharkesh belonged to. A village, almost, though they move from time to time."

That was why it had sounded familiar. Cor had used Tharkesh's full name to challenge him to fight us.

"The Hiraches have a council, same as any other people." Pella's expression wasn't quite as severe as it had been at the Hall, but she hadn't softened much. The blue glow from the pond lent her a coldness I hoped I was just imagining. "I will speak with them. They have the authority to find the kith and see that Coraven is returned."

"Can we go meet them now?" I asked.

"You won't be going at all," Pella said, the tone of her voice final. "I recommend you remain at the garrison. It will be safer for you. Shom, please accompany her. I have other matters that need my attention, so I'll part with you here."

I kept my hands balled at my sides. "Of course I'm going with you."

"You just used your skill—a deadly skill—to intimidate a member of the Shevern council, in a space governed by the Truce." Pella flicked her fingers, using a Thurei gesture for refusal, as if I might have been too dense to understand anything more subtle. "You shamed me and discredited yourself. If the logbook would have proven any suspicions, I doubt those pages will remain."

"He acted first." I stumbled over my justification, shocked that I had to make one. "My voice just stopped working and—"

Shom interjected. "Kate's never seen that kind of skillwork before."

"Troubling as I'm sure that was," Pella said severely, "it was no excuse. I understand your world doesn't have the Truce and your experience here has been limited, but you would be a liability walking into the Hirach council. You're not going with me. Exercising some patience and self-control is your best contribution to Coraven's return."

"I'm sorry." I bowed my head, trying to convey respect. I was well aware that she didn't have to help me. She'd offered Cor a job as a favor to Shom. What responsibility did she feel for us?

"I'll let you know what happens with the Hiraches," Pella said, then she faded away, leaving Shom and me alone.

Holding out her hand, Shom gave me a sympathetic, human-style shrug. "We should go to my workshop so you'll know how to find it with your feet."

"All right," I agreed, out of any useful options. If my only goal was to hang around and stay out of people's way, I might as well learn the route between Shom's workshop and Cor's apartment. I fit my hand to hers and slipped the two of us back to Kuyen.

CHAPTER SEVENTEEN

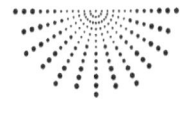

KATE

The alcove that Shom kept as a slip anchor to her workshop was just as I remembered it: plain, serviceable gray stone. The room beyond it, with a long, wooden table and floor-to-ceiling cabinets and shelves stocked with all manner of books and bins of materials. It reminded me of nothing more than a stereotypical wizard's workshop, except that it was tidier than I imagined Merlin's would have been.

At least, everything was tidy except for a large table in the center of the room. It was covered with spools of wire and twine, stacks of different types of paper, bowls full of powder or pebbles or bits of wood and shells. Materials for skillwork, I guessed. Shom worked as the equivalent of an inventor. Small hand tools were scattered amongst the rest, and a page of notes sat near the small, cleared space in front of one of the chairs.

Sliding aside a pile of components, Shom made room for me at the table and motioned to one of the chairs.

She sat down with a sigh. "I've been trying to come up with

modification of the Summons mechanism to make something useful for finding Cor."

"I thought you said that wouldn't work."

"It doesn't work," she said, her voice bitter. She poked through the materials on the table and fished out a pair of pale green shells. They had the petal-like shape of clam shells, about half the size of my palm, clearly two halves of the same original creature. Natural ridges ran along the outside curve, but the insides of each shell had been plated with silver.

"I can manage this…" Shom set one half in front of me, where it rocked gently on its curve, then traced her finger around the edge of the shell, where the silver plating ended and the original material began. The shell half in front of me spun a quarter turn, reorienting itself so that the point of the shell faced the shell in Shom's hand. When she moved her half back and forth, the other half rotated to follow, like a compass tracking a magnet.

"I can tie like to like," she said, setting her shell down. She must have released the skillwork as well, since the apparent connection between the two disappeared. "At the most basic level, that's the way Summons work. A person's name is a part of them, in a sense. The two halves of this river clam will track each other, but you didn't happen to cut Cor in half before he was taken, so the concept isn't really going to do us any good."

The mental image put me off for a moment, but then the implications clicked. "What about some of his hair?"

If I scoured my apartment, I was sure I could find a strand or two of his bright orange hair somewhere.

"No, not with skillwork," Shom said. She rubbed her chin and her gaze slid past me. "Although Nesbons have a hunting skill that lets them track living prey with…well, they need to have fresh material."

Judging by her hesitation, I didn't want to think what 'fresh material' might include. "It was just a shot in the dark."

"Shooting in the dark with your human eyes?" Shom gave me a forced grin. Cor had always teased us about how bad our eyes worked in the dark. Rubbing a hand over her face, Shom leaned back in her chair. "Speaking of hair, does his hair help him look more human?"

"More human?" I asked, lifting my eyebrows. Cor's hair had the same unnatural orange hue of a traffic cone. No one would ever mistake it for human, unless they factored in some fantastic hair dye. "His hair doesn't look human at all."

"That's too bad," Shom mused. "You would not have believed the clash he had with his *denet* over cutting his braid off. I never understood it. It's just hair."

To a human or a Lan, maybe. All the other Thureis I'd seen had grown their colorful hair long, usually worn in formal styles that showed it off. As a kid, Cor had had a long, brilliant braid and been rightfully proud of it.

I'd asked Cor once why he wore his hair short and he'd never answered me. I squeezed my eyes shut for a moment, trying to hold back tears, but thinking of him reminded me of another detail.

"He was wearing human-style clothes, too, when Rose saw him. Do you think that helped? If he'd been wearing his regular, Thurei-style clothes, maybe she wouldn't have seen him." I could hear the pitch of my voice climbing as my throat tightened. I swallowed hard. It was easy to slip into thinking he wouldn't have been taken if we hadn't gone out to dinner. If someone had managed to track him to Earth, though, they could have tracked him to Kuyen just as easily.

"I'm sure it helped." Shom turned her hand up in a Lan version of a shrug. "You humans are very good at not seeing what's in front of your faces unless it fits with your expectations."

"Hey," I said, but there wasn't any heat behind it.

"Were we not just talking about Cor cutting off his hair for you and you barely noticed?"

My cheeks flushed with embarrassment. "I asked him about it, but he wouldn't say anything."

"For a stupidly brave man, he can still be a coward." Shom rolled her eyes, but her voice held genuine affection. "Did this human friend of yours know that you and Cor are…whatever it is you two are?"

"Um, more or less." Rose knew I was spending a lot of time with Cor. Maybe she'd half-expected him to be there when I'd opened the door. "I don't think she was surprised to see him."

"Unlike your parents, who never expected to find other children up in your room in the middle of the night. And they never saw a gray girl who had legs that bent differently from theirs, no matter when I was there." Shom gestured at herself and for a moment, I saw her as my parents might have: her skin a rich gray that made her look sculpted from stone, with darker lips and irises nearly black. Her legs had proportions closer to those of a deer or mythological faun, making it seem like her knees bent backward, at least compared to human expectations.

Unbelievable, in other words. Shom was something their minds had no way to explain, so they had refused to see something they couldn't understand. They'd edited her out.

Just like the human skill could do in truth, if a human only had the *jeira* to make it work.

"When Cor comes back," Shom continued, her tone as certain as if he'd merely stepped out to run errands, "you'll have to run some experiments. See how far these human friends can believe."

"Maybe so." I suppressed a shiver. My insistence that the 'imaginary world' of Kuyen was real had gotten me labeled disruptive at first and eventually diagnosed as schizophrenic. As much as I might have wished that Rose and her friends—and everyone else on Earth—could see what I did, heading down that road might be more trouble than it was worth.

Trust Shom, though, to see it in terms of experiments.

I spun the shell with my fingertip. It twirled, rocking slightly on its curved surface. Its mate, resting on the table in front of Shom, didn't so much as twitch. Without some *jeira* to power it, the two halves of the shell were as lost to each other as if they were on different worlds.

I picked up my piece. "Do you have a use for these?"

"Nothing in particular," Shom said, pushing the other half over. "I made notes, if I want to make them again. Do you want them?"

"If you don't mind." I fit both pieces together, making the clam whole. As Shom had said, it would be no use in finding Cor, but the idea of these two halves invisibly bound together, always able to turn toward each other as long as someone put in the effort…Well, I was in the mood to find encouraging signs wherever I could.

Shom showed me how to activate the skillwork by tracing my finger around the rim of the shell, starting and ending at the point where the two halves had originally been attached.

"It has a decent range, at least across the garrison."

I smiled, but the expression turned into a yawn. "Thanks. It's almost like a Kuyene compass."

"Almost," Shom agreed. She'd been fascinated with the Earth version of the gadget I'd given her as a kid. Of course, it didn't work reliably on Kuyen. "We'll find him, Kate."

I nodded, but I couldn't manage anything better at the moment.

"Come on," she said, standing. "Let me walk you back to your apartment so you know how to get here without worldwalking next time."

I followed her out of the workshop, which turned out to be in one of the many outbuildings in the peacekeeper compound. Shom turned down a narrow pathway between buildings, lifting a hand in acknowledgement of a Lan man who stepped out of the way to let us pass.

"What will you do with the rest of your day?" she asked me.

"Sleep, I hope." I stifled another yawn. The thought of sleeping in Cor's bed here made me miss him even more, but the wards around my apartment were crudely set at best. It would be safer for me here. "Unless you know of something else I can do to help find Cor."

"No, I think yours is a good idea." She shot me a sidelong glance. "You'll be better off staying out of sight while Pella works things out."

"Out of whose sight?"

We turned down another pathway and came out near the central stone keep of the outpost. Soldiers and other members of Pella's coalition bustled in and out of the tall doors. Others were visitors or clients by my guess, non-Lan people in fancier dress than I'd expect on garrison staff. Shom maneuvered us past them all.

"Anyone's," she said. "The Scholars fear that your skill is too powerful, so you need to be careful. Things like what you did today at the Hall…The Scholars won't stop as long as they think you're a threat to Kuyen."

I didn't feel any guilt at all over destroying that skillwork silencer. After all, Scholar Anderlis had used skillwork on me first. I'd just defended myself. My accidental destruction in the arena nagged at me, though. My skill *was* dangerous, and not always under my control.

"How am I supposed to make them think I'm not a threat?" I

frowned down at the stairs as we climbed up to the floor where Cor's apartment was.

"Just be careful and try not to attract anyone's attention while Pella handles things with the Hirach council." Shom stepped aside to let someone pass us in the hallway.

It was Greta, the Drammon woman who had helped search for Cor. I nodded to her, hoping the gesture conveyed my thanks for her assistance. She tilted her head in response as she walked past.

"When Cor's back," Shom continued, "I can only imagine it will help your cause, that you're the *dacha* of a peacekeeper instructor. You might consider a position with Pella yourself. Someone who's using her powerful skill in service to the city might seem a lot safer than a solitaire."

"A solitaire?" I echoed. Cor had used the term when referring to the ex-Scholar Issai, who'd taken up living in the wildlands after her colleagues had decided to hide what they knew about humans and our skill. But I wasn't in exile and neither was Cor, even if he'd been barred from his House.

"Someone without strong ties to a group," she clarified. "You and Cor aren't connected to a House or a community or even a people. Or even Kuyen, really. It's not surprising that the Scholars might fear you'll act out of your own best interests and Cor will follow you because you're his *dacha*. Changing that perception might make you less of a threat in the Scholars' eyes." She shrugged her fingers, a quick ripple in the Thurei style. "It would be a start, at least."

"Thanks, Shom." I nodded, pausing at the door to Cor's apartment. The idea of being a soldier didn't appeal to me—I felt like I'd already been through enough fighting—but I didn't want to be watching over my shoulder for Hunters for the rest of my life, either. I had a lot to think about.

"Get some sleep," she said. "Pella will let you know if there's news." Shom worldwalked out, fading away before my eyes, leaving me alone in the hallway.

Not quite alone. Greta scuffed the floor with her foot and bowed, as formal as Cor, when she caught my attention.

"Kjelgaard, may I speak with you?"

CHAPTER EIGHTEEN

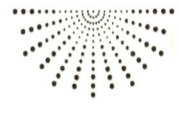

KATE

"Greta, of course." I offered my best, if awkward, Thurei bow of thanks. "I can't remember if I thanked you yesterday for helping look for Cor—um, Coraven. I really appreciate it."

She listened with a profound stillness that I found unsettling, although my thanks were sincere. The motionless intensity triggered some primal, subconscious corner of my brain. How had the Scholars put it? Hunters were true to their natures, no matter how many years they'd been under Truce. As if they were all just waiting to pounce.

I pushed their words out of my head.

She blinked slowly, and said, "I'm sorry I couldn't do more. *Tol* Pella is speaking for him at the Hirach council?"

"Yes," I said. "The Scholars said the Akevad kith has him, the same group that... Well, they've attacked us before."

"Come with me. Let's not speak about this in the hallway." Greta put a clawed hand on her doorknob.

She hadn't made it a question, as if she could just assume I would agree. She was right.

Where Cor's apartment had the same bare vibe as a just-rented studio, Greta had clearly lived in hers for some time. She'd left the space as one long, narrow room, with the bed in the far corner and a seating area closer to the door. Every surface was layered with subtly patterned textiles, from thick blankets on the bed to curtains hanging on the walls and overlapping rugs spread across the floor. Low, cushioned couches formed an L-shape in one corner. Greta pointed toward the shorter of the two couches.

"Please, sit."

I made some space for myself amongst the throw pillows. "I need to send a Summons first, unless this is going to be quick."

"I have paper." Greta reached for a long, flat box on the floor and unfolded it into a tidy, lap-sized writing desk. A tray in the front held a couple of metal-cased, Kuyene pencils. "Lift the panel there. You can use that paper."

I found a stack of blank sheets cut into squares for folding into Summons. It only took a minute to update Birasef.

"What was it you wanted to talk about?" I asked as soon as the message had disappeared.

Greta sat on the other couch. The pattern of the upholstery and pillows mimicked her own coloring. Drammons, I recalled, were ambush predators. At least, they had been back in the days before the Truce.

"Pella has gone to the Hirach council, but Coraven is still alive. You don't want to see this kith punished, do you? You want to have him returned."

I frowned. "Isn't that the same thing?"

"Hunter councils don't work like the Thurei council or the Lan's. The purpose of the Truce is to keep the rest of Kuyen from banding together to destroy our kind. Hunters who break the Truce threaten the safety of all of us. If the Hirach council finds this kith and they're holding one of Pella's peacekeepers captive, the council might kill them all. It would be better for the kith if Coraven isn't found. Better to argue they never had him."

"They'll kill him? You're saying that even if the council agrees to look for Cor, the group of Hiraches who have him will kill him instead of turn him over?" I bolted to my feet. "I have to stop Pella."

"She has no other way to find him." Greta relayed the information without any shift in her serious expression. "If Pella hunts the kith down and attacks them on her own in retribution, then she is breaking the Truce. The Hirach council may find him before the Akevad kith hears the rustle of the council's footsteps."

The layered rugs muffled my own footsteps as I paced, my mind spinning through my options.

It didn't take long. I had no options. The Scholars wouldn't answer any more of my questions. Pella had shut me out of negotiations with the Hiraches. Had Pella known that the Hiraches would kill him if the council went after him—and not said anything to me?

"Kjelgaard, sit down." For the first time, Greta had a sharpness to her tone. "Your pacing makes me nervous. I'll make you some tea."

"Will it help?" I asked rhetorically. It had been hours since I'd had dinner on Earth, though. While it was the middle of the night on my side, that didn't matter as far as my stomach was concerned.

"It might help you sit still." A Drammon joke? Greta went to rummage through a chest on the other side of the room.

I shook my head. It didn't matter. I knotted my cold hands together in my lap. "So you're saying there's nothing we can do."

She returned with a ceramic cup full of water, which she handed gently to me. "You could find him first. You said you knew the name of this kith."

I nearly dropped the cup, stung to have my uselessness shoved in my face. "I can't find him! I'd have done it already if I could."

"Not by yourself." She regarded me calmly with her moon-wide eyes.

I bit my tongue instead of blurting out something this time, trying to regain some calm of my own. Greta wasn't mocking me. But why would she take an outworlder aside and tell her to go hunt a pack of predators? Unconsciously, I lifted the cup for a sip of tea, then pulled back when I found it cold.

"It's a brewing cup." Greta blinked. "Do you know how to use one?"

I didn't care if it was the Holy Grail. I set the cup aside on the floor. "Can you help me find Cor?"

"Have tea, Kjelgaard. You are too…busy. It will help you focus. We can still talk."

Despite that promise, she didn't say anything further until I picked the tea back up. I swallowed my impatience and did what she wanted. The cup was unglazed on the outside, except for some asymmetrical, abstract lines that looked like decoration. Dried herbs or leaves of some sort floated in cold water inside.

"Cover as many skillwork lines as you need, depending on how hot you want it," Greta explained.

I curled my hands around the cup and activated the skillwork, my mind scarcely on the *jeira* it required. The rest of my attention was focused on whether or not Greta could help me get Cor back. She must have had some tracking abilities, since Shom had brought her to inspect the site where Cor had gone missing.

"If you can help me now, why didn't you help find him the night they took him?" I narrowed my eyes. "Back on my world, you said you couldn't tell who'd taken him, or where they'd gone."

"I couldn't," she said. "But if you know who it was, there are other ways to find them."

Suddenly, I wanted to throw the teacup across the room. "Then why haven't we done it already?"

Greta looked away. "They are not peacekeeper ways."

Hunter ways, then. Ones she didn't want to share with her peacekeeper employer.

The cup had finally heated. I tried a sip, only to find it bitter. Greta didn't argue this time when I set it aside. "You asked me here to talk in private. What is it you want to say?"

"My sister is sick."

"The garrison has healers."

"For peacekeepers," Greta agreed. "My sister, Erzi, lives on her own. She owes service to no one."

A solitaire. I opened my mouth to ask why that mattered, but of course it did. If Pella hadn't taken service from Cor, I would never have gotten to speak to the Shevern council in the first place. Not that it had done much good. Instead, I said, "I don't have any money for a market healer."

"You have influence. Shom led the search for your Thurei and Pella is bringing his cause to councils, though he has served her a scarce handful of days."

"That's Coraven's influence," I said. "None of that is me."

It was probably only seconds that the silence stretched, but under her unblinking gaze, time ran very slowly.

"Got it." I cleared my throat and tried something more politic. I had no influence with the healers themselves, but I could try. "I'll ask the garrison's healers. Is your sister—Erzi, is she injured? Sick? Why does she need healing? How bad is it?"

"It's the fade."

"Fade?" Of course, I wouldn't recognize it. Cor's House had a healer. He'd never talked about Kuyene illnesses and he'd worried over all my childhood colds and flus growing up. More than once, he'd made his opinion known. *What do human doctors do, anyway? You might as well be a Lan.*

"That's what they're calling it. She's sick, with fever and weakness. She's tried the usual tinctures and poultices, but nothing helps. People with the fade…they die."

"Then healers can't treat it?"

"If she saw a healer, I think she would live." Greta's expression darkened to a glower.

I shook my head. I was letting myself get distracted and I couldn't afford that. I'd get Greta a healer and she could handle the rest of it. I stood up. "All right, I'll ask around. As soon as I know anything, I'll send you a Summons."

"Thank you." The Hunter bowed her head.

Thank you. Like she'd given me a choice.

CHAPTER NINETEEN

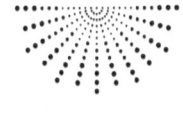

KATE

In the corridor, Birasef stood glaring at Cor's door. When he turned and saw me, relief flashed across his face. He dipped a bow as I approached.

"Bir, what is it?" I said, swallowing another spike of alarm.

"I got your note about the councils." He fished in the pocket of his short, brown jacket and pulled out a folded page, as if he needed proof. "If there's anything you need, just tell me. But if you'd rather I go..."

"Of course. I mean, of course you're welcome to stay." I rubbed at my temples. "Sorry. I've been distracted."

Distracted enough to apologize to a Thurei, but Bir took it in stride. "Naturally. Perhaps you'd like to go in and sit down? Or lunch—"

A sharp flick of my fingers cut him off. "I need to get a healer."

He lifted his green eyebrows and looked me over more carefully. "Are you well, Kate?"

"I'm fine," I muttered, barely listening. "But Greta's sister is sick. I'm going to see if Pella—no, I should ask Shom. Healers don't heal Hunters, right?"

Bir had both hands up, palms out. "Grant me patience, Kate, but I am utterly lost."

"All right." I took a deep breath. I hadn't really slept since Cor had gotten taken. I was so, so tired. "Pella has gone to meet with the Hirach council, since the Scholars said one of the Hirach kiths has Cor. But Greta—you remember Greta from last night—says that the kith will probably just kill Cor rather than be found with him. Apparently, Hunter councils kill Trucebreakers regardless of the crime. Greta said she'd help me track the kith down and get Cor back myself if I found a healer for her sick sister." I stopped and took a deep breath, trying to rein in my words. "So. I'm hoping Shom will help me talk one of the healers here into doing it."

At this point, I didn't know if Bir's eyebrows would ever come back down.

"Let me get this straight," he said slowly. "Pella tol dav Ferrum, commander of the peacekeepers—the *Truce keepers*—of Aubello, has taken grievance on behalf of Coraven No House to the Hirach council. Now you're going to ask the *tol*'s kin to talk the *tol*'s healers into treating a Hunter. Then you'll follow this Drammon into the wildlands, to the nest of the kith who tried—almost succeeded—to kill you and Cor. I will add, this kith has already managed to capture Cor, the one they call 'Hunterslayer.' When you get there, what's to stop them from killing both of you?"

"Me," I said, squaring my shoulders. "You've seen my skill."

He tipped his hand in my direction to concede the point. "You're only one person, Kate, strong as your human skill is. You and me and a Drammon against a Hirach kith?"

Bir had seen me train in Temarel's courtyard, but he hadn't been there when Cor and I had fought Tharkesh and his pack. He hadn't seen the football field's worth of destruction the last human worldwalker had unleashed in the wildlands.

All the rest of it, though, listed out the way Bir had...yes. It sounded...reckless, though I hadn't missed him adding himself into the tale.

"Then what should I do?" I asked him. "What would you do, if it were your decision to make?"

He hesitated long enough that I thought he wouldn't answer. Then he said softly, "I would call upon the House, but..."

"Right." I sighed. Calling on Cor's House—full of blade-wielding kin—wasn't an option. My plan to go after him alone might lose us Pella's support as well. "Do you think Greta's right? That the Hirach kith will kill him, rather than be caught with him?"

"Cor's the one who studied Hunters." Bir shrugged his fingers, the gesture sharp with his own frustration. "The only dealings I've heard of with Hunter councils involved restitution for the victim's side, but I've never heard of a capture, either. If anyone would know, it would be another Hunter."

That was the only answer that mattered. "Then I can't afford to wait. I'm going to speak with Pella's healers." I wished I could go to Shom for advice or help, but as Bir had pointed out, the niece of a peacekeeper wasn't likely to support this plan. "You're welcome to come with me if you want, but I understand if you want to stay out of it."

Bir smiled wryly. "Well, I do happen to have the rest of the day free."

Despite everything, I chuckled. I'd missed his humor. "Come on, then."

We headed downstairs to see the healers.

Fortunately, the garrison's senior Lewrit healer was available when we entered.

To my human eyes, Lewrit faces seemed predisposed to

kindness. Their round cheeks, large, hazel eyes, and flat noses, along with their short, soft-looking fur, reminded me powerfully of a rabbit, but I tried to suppress the comparison. We weren't on Earth.

Stolla looked us over with a professional eye. Apparently satisfied that we weren't injured, she offered a gentle greeting and added, "Coraven has not come to us, Kjelgaard. I will send for you if he does."

"Thank you," I said. "I was hoping to ask for a favor, actually."

"If I can be of assistance…" She trailed off, leaving the offer open-ended.

"I just spoke with Greta upstairs. Her sister, Erzi, is ill, and she was hoping—" I cut myself off when I saw the Stolla's welcoming expression snap closed. I supposed I should have expected it, but it took me by surprise anyway. "She's Greta's sister. This is her kin."

She straightened her healer's robes, her coal-black fur a dramatic contrast to the white fabric. "Greta is one of the *tol*'s peacekeepers. She has sworn to do no harm. If her sister has done the same, let her seek help from the one who holds her oath."

"Erzi lives alone."

Stolla sniffed, her velvety, tan fur wrinkling around her flat nose. "Then she still hunts."

Was that what Greta had avoided saying? I hesitated. I didn't want to put a Hunter back into condition to find new victims.

But this was for *Cor*.

"Are you sure?" I asked. "Are you certain that living alone must mean she hunts people?"

"She's a Hunter." Stolla waved her hand, sweeping any other possibility away. "She's avoiding lands under the Truce. Greta sent *you* to ask—there's no point in hiding a hand behind your back."

It took me a moment to unravel that idiom. "I'm not trying to hide anything from you. I just think maybe if we asked her—"

"Kjelgaard, please. Seeing this question brought by the two of you and not Greta herself makes me wonder how it's tied to your missing...friend."

"Well." It had sounded like a chancy enough plan when Bir had summed it up for me, and Bir was something of a risk-taker. I stuck to the basics, hoping to sound reasonable. "If I can find a healer for her sister, Greta will help me find the Hunters who are holding Coraven."

I didn't mention Pella's plan to speak with the Hirach council. If Stolla hadn't heard about it, I didn't want to be the one to tell her I was trying something in a different direction.

"I see," Stolla said, her voice quiet. "I regret to tell you—though I'm sure you're well aware, Temarel—but we do not heal Hunters, Kjelgaard. Lewrits, especially those of us who are full healers, want nothing to do with people who prey upon others. Are you aware that healing a person involves the mind as well as the body?"

"Yes," I said. When Tharkesh had attacked me, the Lewrit healer who worked for Cor's House had healed both physical slash and the corruption the Hirach had left with his skill. I was deeply grateful for Havro's help, but I'd found the experience unsettling. I had felt the healer in my mind, somehow, and it reminded me uncomfortably of the delusions ascribed to schizophrenia. I'd spent long enough thinking I was crazy. I didn't need reasons to doubt myself.

"Then you know that it brings the healer and the healed close together. Few Lewrits wish to undertake that intimacy with those who focus on killing."

"Forgive me. I hadn't considered that," I said. Maybe I should have left it there. "But if you spoke with her first, you'll find Erzi might not be as bad as you think. Right this moment, Coraven is the prisoner of Hiraches—"

"And who knows what cruelties Hunters are capable of," Stolla finished for me. "We see too much of Hunters' work here."

Bir swept the healer a bow, impeccably respectful. "Thank you for your time, Healer Stolla. We appreciate your kindness in offering an explanation, even if the answer wasn't what we'd hoped."

Not quite as obvious as an elbow in my ribs, but close. I closed my eyes and inclined my head, trying to recapture some calm. "Yes. Thank you."

I made it as far as the hallway outside before whirling around to ask Bir, "Do you think Havro would help?"

When he hesitated, I added, "It's for Coran."

"I'll ask," he said, then spread his hands wide. "He cares for Cor, certainly, but Cor is no longer a Temarel and—if the *tol*'s healers have seen the work of Hunters, so has Havro."

"Got it," I muttered, staring down at my shoes. My 'good shoes,' a cute pair of black ankle boots to go with my best dress. How ridiculous that I'd thought what I wore might make a difference. I shook my head and pointed down the hall toward the exit. "There's still the merchant healers. I can ask them, but I don't have any Kuyen money."

"If you can convince a merchant healer to treat a Hunter, then money won't be an issue." Bir's lips quirked into a smile as he fell in beside me, his long strides betraying a tension that he managed to keep off his face.

I raised my eyebrows. "Won't it?"

"Let me worry about that part," he said firmly. "You worry about convincing a Lewrit to heal a Hunter."

"Thank you, Bir. I'm glad you came."

He flicked his fingers, making the gesture of denial theatrical. "I'll be insufferable if you keep that up. No thanks are necessary."

I chuckled along, but I was distracted by some half-remembered thing I'd heard about Aubello's merchant healers. They were expensive? Hard to find?

"Wait." I grabbed Bir's sleeve, surprising us both. Pulling my hand back, I explained, "House Leratom offered Cor and me the services of their healer. I mean, I don't think this was what they had in mind, but it might be worth asking."

"House Leratom?" Bir echoed. "I'll accompany you if you wish. I can take the offworld leg."

"You just worldwalked here. Will you be all right?"

"It's been long enough." He bobbed a slight bow. "Plus, I'm sturdier than I look."

"You're welcome to come with me, then. Do you know the Leratoms?" I didn't know how many Thurei Houses there were, but they'd been strangers to Cor.

"To my knowledge, Temarel and Leratom have had few dealings with each other." He shrugged his fingers again. His expression was pensive a moment before he transformed it into a cocky smile. "If they are going to meet a Temarel, who better than I?"

CHAPTER TWENTY

KATE

Bir brought us to a slip anchor on some other world. The colorful, abstract mosaics underfoot made the waystation memorable for worldwalkers. Torchlight flickered over us and illuminated a pair of other travelers wrapped head to foot in striped robes, but I didn't pause for questions this time. I visualized the plaza in front of House Leratom, focused my *jeira*, and pulled us back across to Kuyen.

Today wasn't one of the House's public gathering days like Cor and I had attended, but the square out front still held a handful of Aubello's inhabitants. One of the large draft beasts I'd spotted earlier, which resembled a long-legged boar, stood munching at a bucket of feed. It was still harnessed to a cart filled with flowers and green, leafy branches. A Lan merchant held out a bouquet when he noticed our arrival.

"No, thank you," I said as I dropped Bir's hand.

On the same beat, Bir bowed to the man. "What a fortuitous opportunity at such a critical juncture and, I must add, those starblooms are exquisite."

The transaction was over in a moment, leaving Bir cradling the bouquet of silvery flowers. Fatigue shadowed the sharp angles of his face—maybe from two worldwalking trips, too close together—but he made no complaint.

I raised my brows. "Those flowers are exquisite, I have to agree with you."

"They'll make a tolerable guesting gift."

Right. I should have remembered that. I gave him a rueful smile. "This is why you bring a native."

He offered a slight bow, but he seemed pleased. As we walked toward the doors, Bir asked, "Why did the Leratoms offer their healer, anyway? The garrison has its own and you and Cor are under *Tol* Pella's care."

"The *denet* was trying to talk us into joining."

"Cor can't join another House," Bir said, his voice sharp. He stopped walking in the middle of the square, under the glare of the sun.

"She wanted Cor to come work for them as an armsmaster. Not...Not *adoption*. Sorry, I don't know the word in Kuyene. Not to be family, just to work. But I think his reaction was about the same as yours." I rippled my fingers, shrugging Thurei-style. "Cor turned it down, obviously, but the *denet* did encourage us to view her as an ally."

"An ally," Bir repeated.

"Cor wasn't comfortable with that, either. What's the problem?" Sweat prickled between my shoulder blades. I wanted to get out of this heat, find a healer and get Cor back. But I needed to know what I was getting into here.

"A House would have no use for a solitary *dacha* pair as allies. I wouldn't be surprised if Cor was skeptical about what they wanted on their side of the bargain."

Cor and I weren't even a *dacha* pair yet since I hadn't sworn my vow. Everything had moved too fast. I took a deep, steadying breath. I could handle that after I got Cor back. "Should we just find a merchant healer, then?"

Bir flicked his fingers in disagreement. "If you want my advice, I'll say be careful. If Leratom wants something, you should find out what it is. If you can afford it and it helps you get Cor back..." He left the rest unsaid. "But don't open negotiations looking needy, or the *denet* will know she already has you in hand."

"Not too needy, got it," I said. I straightened my dress, lifting my chin. "Right. Let's go."

We headed for Leratom's tall, wooden doors, dark planks and polished metal fittings sturdy enough to withstand a siege. A bell with a long pull hung on the wall to one side.

Whatever it takes to get Cor back, I told myself, then I tugged the bell pull.

One of the doors swung open to reveal Nabel Leratom. His formal clothing—an embroidered purple tunic, slim charcoal trousers and soft leather indoor shoes—underscored his assignment as greeter. His eyes slid over me to Bir.

Bir bowed, something low and precise, with a flourish I associated with greetings. Or was it introductions?

"I'm Birasef Temarel," he said, straightening as he offered the bouquet. "Katherine Kjelgaard has done me the grace of offering an introduction to your House. I hope your *denet* will indulge my haste. I fear I neglected to send word ahead."

"Nabel Leratom." The man introduced himself, giving us an equally precise bow. "Please, come inside and enjoy our hospitality while you wait. I will carry your greetings." Nabel took the flowers and stepped aside to let us in.

And I'd thought *Cor* was formal.

The building's foyer had vaulted ceilings, reaching two stories high, with a wide, sweeping staircase in dark wood leading to a balcony. The air was blissfully cool after the heat of the square. Nabel ushered us to a small salon off to one side of the entry, a room of graceful furniture, bright with lamps and midday sunlight filtered through gauzy curtains over high windows. Then he left, closing the door softly behind him.

I settled in a loveseat upholstered in a fuzzy, lime-green fabric. Bir chose a chair beside mine, sitting in a composed manner that said he could wait all day if necessary.

"I should have written ahead." I sighed.

Bir rippled his fingers in a shrug. "If Leratom offered you anything like alliance, you are welcome to call on her whenever you like. This is just… I wish to give you more options in case you need them." He spread his arms wide.

I considered that for a moment, closing my tired eyes. "So that I don't need to ask for a healer immediately."

"You don't know what she's after yet," he said. A rustling sound made me open my eyes. Bir was pulling off his coat.

Before Bir could offer more pointers, the salon door opened back up and Misora Leratom walked in. While she wore a slightly less formal outfit of loose, flowing trousers and a light, embroidered tunic, her hair in a casual, French-style braid, there was no mistaking her status as *denet*-heir.

"Welcome, Kjelgaard, Temarel," she said, with a bow. It was on the shallow side, which wasn't that surprising from the House's heir. She sat across from me, an intimate, conversational arrangement that this small salon favored. "I regret my *denet* isn't available, but I offer hospitality in her stead."

"Thank you." I decided to draw on Bir's opening gambit instead of jumping directly to the matter on my mind. "My friend Temarel has never visited Aubello before and I'm delighted to introduce him to your House."

Bir added a seated bow as I spoke, deeper than the one Misora had given us, but then she did outrank him.

"The increased interest from your House is a flattery, Temarel." Misora inclined her head graciously.

"Who wouldn't wish to flatter Leratom?" he mused aloud.

"All the world, I'm sure," Misora said. "It's merely luck that you're doing it right now. I rather think that breeze doesn't blow through House windows without carrying gossip."

Bir chuckled. "Don't I know it. Try to sneak a *morsai* into the kitchens just the once and you'll be hearing about it at every gathering you go to for years, I assure you."

A *morsai*? I pictured one of those riding mounts, like a horse-sized German shepherd, charging around a mansion's kitchen. Had he really? At the same time, I thought, how long did we have to talk about teenage pranks?

"I believe you," Misora said, her tone sardonic. "But you're not here to talk about stolen roasts and spoiled banquets."

"No," he returned, dropping his jokester façade. He shot me a look.

Misora spoke up before I could frame a non-needy request to meet their healer. "I'm permitted to renew my *denet*'s offer of hospitality on a more permanent basis, Kjelgaard. I know Coraven had a place he valued with *Tol* Pella's garrison and he turned down our offer of employment. You are still welcome, on your own merits, if you have need."

Me, alone? If I said yes, would that improve my chances with the healer? Even then, I couldn't bear to say it. Had they already assumed he'd never make it back? I inclined my head, hoping it looked at least a little like a bow. "I will consider it, thank you, but it's a subject I would prefer to discuss with Coraven."

How I would have loved to call him my *dacha* then. *Soon. As soon as I get him back.*

"Understood." Misora returned the little courtesy. "It's unfortunate that there's little we can do formally to help, without any formal ties between us. I do hope that *Tol* Pella is able to find a swift resolution with the Hirach council."

Gossip traveled fast, indeed. I couldn't tell if she was sincere beneath her practiced, polite mask.

"Thank you. I hope to see Coraven home safe as soon as possible, too." I laced my fingers together in my lap so I wouldn't curl them into impatient fists. How long would it take Pella to meet with the council? How long before they began searching for the kith? "When we visited last, your *denet* offered the services of your healer. I'm curious whether or not that offer still stands."

"It might." Misora crossed her legs, as elegant as royalty. "Maybe you can satisfy a curiosity of mine. I've never seen your skill in action."

"What, right now?" The abrupt change of topic threw me off. I looked around the tastefully appointed salon. Bir twitched his fingers on his knee, a subtle gesture of negation as if he feared I might suddenly dissolve the furniture.

"Not here." Misora waved a hand with breezy dismissal. "Your skill merits more space, doesn't it? We can arrange another time and then we can see about arranging an introduction to Nalya."

So, it wasn't a change of topic at all. It was an offer to trade. All Misora wanted was to see what I could do with my skill? I shared a glance with Bir.

"There's no need to delay," Bir said. "I'm sure Kjelgaard could accommodate you now."

"Of course." I started to dig in my purse for something I could spare dissolving, but Misora flicked the offer away.

"We have a gathering planned for tomorrow. You could give a demonstration there. I'm sure my *denet* would appreciate the chance to see for herself."

A demonstration in front of a crowd? If it got me the healer, got me one step closer to finding Cor, fine. "Sure, I can do that, if I can speak with your healer."

"At present," Bir put in quickly, "Kjelgaard has many demands on her time. As much as I'm sure she wishes to please your *denet*, I hope you won't be too disappointed if she's needed elsewhere tomorrow."

"He's right." I put on what I hoped was a contrite expression. He'd given me an out, just in case. *Thank you, Bir.* "There is a lot going on right now, so I may need to reschedule."

Misora pursed her lips a moment but tilted her head in acknowledgement. "Provisionally, then, you'll be here tomorrow around midday for a demonstration of your skill." She stood, apparently satisfied with the arrangement. "It would be pleasure to introduce you to Nalya, the House's healer. If you would both follow me…"

Finally.

The healer, Nalya, was younger than I'd expected. I didn't know much about Lewrits, but if I'd had to guess, she was barely out of her teens. Her fur, a rich brown, was longer than the velvety-smooth fur of the garrison's healers or any of the other Lewrits I'd met. Nalya also, if I were being honest, looked a little rumpled—her fur a bit mussed, her white robe wrinkled—not in the manner of someone who didn't care about her appearance, more like someone who got distracted easily.

"Please, please, come in." Nalya held the door wide. The walls bore shelves from floor to ceiling, supporting a cascade of plants rioting out of their pots. Gauzy curtains let in light that brightened the white walls.

"Nalya," Misora said. "Meet our guests, Katherine Kjelgaard and Birasef Temarel. I believe Kjelgaard has a question for you."

"I was hoping you'd be able to help me, Nalya," I began, but Nalya spoke up while I searched for the right way to frame my request.

Nalya tipped her head, curiosity brightening her hazel eyes. "It would be my honor to serve a guest of the House. You both look well." She let the last word hang like a question.

"It's not for me," I said. "Not directly. One of the peacekeepers for your city came to me with a concern for her sister, a Drammon." I watched her as I spoke, waiting for the walls to come up at the mention of one of Kuyen's Hunter peoples.

Instead, the corners of Nalya's mouth twitched. "Just the sister is a Drammon, or the peacekeeper is, too?"

"Both," I answered, confused. The lack of objection was throwing me off. "Um, yes, they're both Drammons."

"Please excuse my levity." Nalya offered a shallow, seated bow. "I didn't mean to make light of the peacekeeper's concern. I'm rather new in service to the House and I know nothing at all of human customs."

New to Thurei Houses. I definitely read that as *I'm not very formal.*

Misora spoke up. "You've served us admirably since Sanzo retired."

The healer looked pleased.

"Humans are fairly relaxed," I said. "But it's true the reason I'm here is a serious one. The peacekeeper, Greta, has agreed to help me find Coraven, my...my partner, if I can find a healer willing to treat her sister." I quickly explained what Greta had told me about her sister, both the illness and the fact that she lived in the wildlands, and the reason I wasn't going to the garrison's healers for help. I wrapped it up with, "Hiraches kidnapped Coraven and I fear that time is running out for him. Please, Healer Nalya, will you help me?"

"As a general rule, we don't heal Hunters." Nalya smoothed wrinkles from the front of her robe. "But I'm intrigued...by all of this, really. I've never even healed a Hunter who kept to the Truce, much less a...well, a feral. I'm curious about this Drammon peacekeeper who would seek a human's aid to heal her sister." She pressed her palms together. "And I've heard a little about you and Coraven. A young Thurei warrior determined to protect his heart-love and an outworlder with such a powerful, mysterious skill, who in turn has resolved to rescue him..."

My cheeks flamed with embarrassment. Who was telling these kinds of stories?

Nalya stopped abruptly and cleared her throat. Her next sentence came out less dreamy, much more businesslike. "I'm willing to meet this woman, Kjelgaard. I can't promise I'll heal her, but I'm willing to see."

Thank goodness for a Lewrit romantic.

"Thank you," I said. "Thank you so much."

Bir bowed properly and added his own thanks. "We will send for you as soon as the visit is arranged. Hopefully by the end of the day."

Please, please, before Kuyen's sunset, before the way between worlds closed and I was locked on Earth again with no way to push forward on this. I dreaded all those daylight hours.

We took our leave of the healer and Misora, back out into the afternoon heat and humidity of Aubello's streets.

"I need to write to Greta," I said, wiping perspiration from my forehead already. "But other than that, it's just waiting."

Bir held up his hand. "May I escort you back to your rooms at the garrison? Are you rested enough to worldwalk again?"

"Please," I said, setting my hand in his. "Let's get out of this heat."

Bir brought us to another place I didn't recognize.

A lacy-leaved canopy spread above us, and tiny lights looped and spun in the warm night air, creating a dome shape above us. They looked almost like fireflies but were a little too mechanical in their movements to be natural bugs. Similar domes marked the grove around us, some occupied by worldwalkers. This was a place of slip anchors, like the pond. Above, two moons cast silvery light through the filigree of leaves, though my eyes couldn't pick out much more detail in the dimness.

"Where is this?" I asked.

"Ah. It's Ervaine." Bir looked around us like he was just as startled as I was, despite the fact he'd worldwalked us both here.

Being Thurei, he could probably see fine in the low light where my human sight failed. *Cat eyes*, I'd always teased Cor. The memory made my heart hurt.

Someone giggled, under one of the other domes, startling me out of my distress. I turned and gravel crunched under my shoes. This time, I noticed that most of the other travelers were couples.

"Is this..." I tried to inject some levity to my voice but stalled as I realized I didn't even know the right words in Kuyene. I reached for them in English, "A *date night* kind of place?"

Bir didn't know any words from any Earth language, but he was clever and a master of innuendo, besides. He cleared his throat. "We can return to the garrison. No need to linger."

Bir was embarrassed? I hadn't even known that was possible.

"Of course," I murmured. "Wait, hold on."

I knelt quickly and scooped up a small handful of gravel, then straightened to take Bir's hand. "All right. Close your eyes."

I pulled us back to Kuyen.

As soon as we stood back in Cor's rooms at the garrison, Bir looked down at my handful of little stones, an eyebrow raised.

"Why did you take rocks with you?"

"For practice." I went over to the table and tipped the gravel onto the dark wood, then grabbed a sheet of paper so I could let Greta know about Nalya's offer. "One of the instructors asked me if my skill worked only on material from Kuyen or if it worked on things from other worlds besides Earth as well. It made me curious. I'd only tried with stuff from Kuyen."

After taking a seat across from me, Bir waited for me to write and send the note to Greta.

"Well, are you a fierce defender against all gravel, or just ours?" he asked, once the paper had vanished.

"The moment of truth is at hand," I said, trying to match his humor. A headache from pulling myself and Bir from world to world had built behind my eyes, but I had enough energy to take care of a pea-sized stone. I nudged one of the pebbles away from the pile. A moment of concentration, a touch of *jeria*, and it disappeared. "Looks like it works. Anything beyond Earth. *Zap*."

"Or at least," Bir pointed out diplomatically, "anything you've tried so far from Kuyen and rocks from Ervaine."

I tilted my hand toward him in acknowledgement. Then I had to ask, "Was that really a…a place to take your *nochel*?"

"Ah." His smooth cheeks darkened with a blush. "I wasn't thinking, Kate. I didn't mean anything by it."

"I wasn't assuming anything by it. I was just curious." And not about Bir, necessarily. About Cor. I didn't know anything about the way Thureis typically dated. Cor and I were…practically, kind of…married. Even if dinner at the taqueria hadn't ended horribly, I wasn't sure if that would have counted as a romantic evening.

Neither of us had ever dated anyone else, either. He'd been fourteen when he'd sworn his vow, and I'd lived in a mental ward during my teen years.

"That particular spot on Evaine is lovely," Bir said. "Away from the slip anchors, there are pathways through the woods, some stalls with finger foods and quite lovely wine, bowers where..." He cleared his throat. "I've been there a time or two."

Often enough that he could slip there with his mind halfway focused on something else. Despite everything, it made me laugh. Another Thurei might have been offended, but Bir joined me.

When the room was quiet again, Bir stirred the pile of gravel with his finger. "You should ask Leratom to gather some more materials for your demonstration. See whether your skill works on all of it or not. You might find some material from some world that is immune to your skill, like the Lan te Kos are. It would be better to find that out in practice, rather than discover it in crisis."

Now that I had a second chance to think about it, the possibility that I might turn House Leratom into Swiss cheese by accident worried me. I told him about how things had gone when I'd practiced with Eld this morning. "At least here, the arena is designed for it. And most of the soldiers are Lan. They have some idea of what they're dealing with. Maybe not me in particular, but they're prepared to handle dangerous skills."

"Don't try anything complicated or fast like you did with Eld," Bir suggested, shrugging his fingers. "Do something boring and easy. Just make sure that it's impressive and no one has to know if it's simple or not."

"You think I need to impress *Denet* Leratom?"

Bir had only been paying half a mind to our conversation, but I didn't realize it until now, when he focused his undivided attention on me. "You need to impress their guests. Show off your skill, as the Leratoms' ally, to whomever they chose as the audience. That was their half of the deal. I'm telling you since you look confused."

"Well, sure." If the added nuance was that House Leratom wanted me to show off for people, I would still have made the trade. I'd entertain as many guests as they wanted if it saved Cor's life. "Who do you think they'll invite?"

A ripple of Bir's fingers told me he didn't know. "I imagine we'll find out—"

He cut himself off when a Summons appeared beside me.

I caught the paper as it tumbled out of the air, the skillwork task of delivering itself completed.

"It's from Greta," I said, scanning over the short message, then I set the page down on the table. "Let's go meet her sister."

CHAPTER TWENTY-ONE

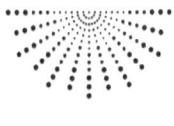

KATE

Arranging everything took another flurry of messages, but eventually Nalya and Greta joined us in Cor's rooms.

When Greta saw Nalya, she brought her fists up to her chest in a solemn gesture and bowed her head. Even I saw the respect there, no cultural translation required. "Healer, my thanks."

"I agreed to meet her," Nalya said, her soft voice serious. "I might do no more than that."

"I know," Greta said.

That seemed to satisfy them both. After that, Bir slipped us all to a utilitarian anchor point—nothing remarkable this time—and Greta pulled us back to the wildlands of Kuyen.

Sunlight hammered down onto a landscape of packed earth and twisted, dusty shapes that might have been either plants or rocks. A desert of some kind, but not like any I'd seen on Earth. Maybe it had a charming time of day, but the late afternoon turned it into an oven. Even though I still wore my dress, which came just past my knees, sweat already prickled on my skin.

"Let me go first," Greta said, then she moved with careful grace in among the lumpy, jagged shapes around us. With the mottled coloring of her fur, her drab uniform and the muted tans, grays and dusty greens of our surroundings, she soon disappeared.

I glanced at Bir, then did a doubletake when I caught the slight shimmer of his *zaret*. He held the transparent blade almost casually, but something in the careful way he held himself reminded me of his sparring match with Cor. Bir hadn't put in anywhere near the hours training that Cor had, but he was far from unskilled.

Beside me, Nalya held her white robes tightly around her, still and vigilant, panning her gaze on the rocks and Kuyene versions of cactus.

I would never have guessed that a place could seem both barren and also so full of places for something to hide. We were in the wildlands, looking for a Hunter, so I probably shouldn't have been surprised. I reached for my *jeira*, just in case.

Greta reappeared again as suddenly as if she'd worldwalked a few yards away from us, stepping out from among the rocky outcrops and plants. "Follow me. Try not to touch anything."

I went next, with Nalya following. Still holding his *zaret*, Bir took up the rear. I wouldn't have called the route Greta led us on a path, but there were gaps enough to ease between the pillar-like rocks and bulbous, twisted flora. When the hem of my skirt snagged on a stubby limb, I learned that at least some of them had wicked, barbed spines, so small, I hadn't noticed them before. Other ones might have had something worse. No wonder Greta warned us not to touch them.

Greta stopped after a short trek, gradually uphill from where we'd started, and crouched down next to what looked like an aggressively thorny small shrub. She reached down into it—not just between the maze of branches but *through* them—grabbed something, then pulled up. It wasn't a shrub at all but a domed cover, concealed by a skillwork illusion. Greta set it aside, revealing a vertical tunnel and the top of a ladder.

Oh. I wasn't claustrophobic, but I still had to steel myself to step onto the ladder after she climbed her way down into the underground lair of another Hunter. *It's her sister. We'll be fine.*

The shaft was longer than I'd expected, several feet down, darker and cooler as soon as I'd moved out of the direct sun. Then the room opened up below and my feet finally reached the floor. Nalya's shoes scuffed on the ladder rungs above me.

The smell hit first. Dirt and dust, yes, but a thick sour stink overwhelmed those milder scents.

The underground chamber was small, a little smaller than the bedroom of my modest apartment. Niches in the wall held stacks of small boxes and jars, a metal pot, a half-full cloth sack, a skillwork lamp that shone faint light, adding to the glow from the open entry shaft. The ceiling bristled with bundles of drying leaves and flowers. A tangle of bedding took up the far end.

Crouching down next to it, Greta murmured words I didn't recognize.

The blankets exploded in a burst of movement. A figure lunged at Greta and a pulse, deeper than sound, thrummed through me, vaguely familiar. Rattled, I tried to focus on my *jeira*, but I didn't know what I was defending against.

Greta tumbled backward and cried out in pain and frustration. Then I got a good look at her attacker. Another Drammon, in a long, tunic-like nightshirt. She'd collapsed, halfway in her sister's lap, like the attack had exhausted her.

I took a deep breath, trying to ignore the smell of sickness, and tried to slow my heart rate back down.

"Erzi, Erzi." Greta murmured other words I didn't recognize as she gathered her sister up, helping her back into her bed.

Above me on the ladder, Nalya had frozen. She started down, moving quickly. Bir followed.

"Erzi," Greta said, then she continued in the common tongue. "I brought you a healer. Remember?"

The Drammon lay still against her blankets, her round face gaunt, her eyes sunken and closed. Finally, she blinked them open and whispered some reply before closing them again.

"Come, healer." Greta turned to Nalya, who stood near the ladder still, with Bir and me. "She didn't know it was me and her skill is very weak. She won't harm you. I promise."

I'm not sure I would have found that convincing, but Nalya squared her slight shoulders and walked over to the bedside, settling herself on the ground beside the Hunters. She rested a hand on Erzi's forehead. The Drammon didn't so much as twitch.

Silence crowded around us, full of Erzi's rasping breaths.

A shudder ran through Nalya, shaking her petite frame. She raised her head and looked around at us before settling on Greta. "This is…not quite like anything I've seen before. I can heal her, but we need to take her back to Leratom."

Weakly, Erzi muttered something. Greta asked, "Can't you do it here?"

"You have asked for much." Nalya's soft voice suddenly had an edge to it. "I won't heal her of whatever…this…is in the middle of the wilds."

This time, I caught a couple of Erzi's muttered Kuyene words. "I claimed."

"If you wish to maintain your lands, you're free to stay here." Nalya stood, brushing dust from her palms.

"Wait." Greta hadn't moved beyond tilting her head to keep Nalya in sight. She looked back down at her sister and spoke in quick, quiet Drammon. Their conversation consisted of a few mysterious, intense exchanges.

To Bir, I whispered, "What's the big deal? What will happen if she leaves?"

He shrugged, a ripple of his fingers in the dimness, and whispered back, "She holds this place on her own, her will and *jeira* preventing it from shifting and changing like the rest of the wildlands. If she leaves, that hold will weaken. It's none too strong, now. If she's gone too long, she may have nothing to come back to."

The sisters' conversation ended with Greta lunging forward and scooping her sister up out of the bedding with almost surgical precision.

Erzi moved fitfully for a few moments before curling against Greta's chest and going still. I thought she might have been shorter than Greta if they stood shoulder to shoulder, but Greta carried her as if she no longer had any weight at all. She'd worn down to little more than matted, filthy fur over prominent bone.

I didn't know any of the Drammon language, but I would have guessed that their argument had not ended with any agreement on Erzi's part. Just as clearly, Erzi didn't have the strength to fight her.

"I'm ready, healer," Greta said, as calm as ever. She could have been carrying a load of groceries for all I could tell by her expression.

Nalya lifted her chin. "Then we'll return to my chambers."

I exchanged a glance with Bir, but he just gave a little shrug of his fingers against his leg and then stepped forward to offer transport to another slip anchor on our way back.

Erzi took the trip in silence, barely stirring as we all worldwalked across the gap and then back to House Leratom's atrium. Greta carried her gently but never looked down, and both Drammons kept their wide, sharp-toothed mouths pressed closed.

Nalya looked around at her domain briskly as soon as the world was solid around us. After a deep breath, she said, "Greta, please take Erzi into that room there. Yes. Get her settled in the bed and wait with her. I'll be in as soon as I'm ready."

"Thank you, healer." Greta disappeared to where she'd been sent.

As soon as the door closed behind the Hunters, Nalya turned to Bir and me, her eyes wide as if stricken.

"Are you all right?" I asked, my heartbeat kicking up into another gear.

"I... Yes." All the confidence she'd shown in the desert evaporated. "She's so... It's not easy. And the illness...I've never seen anything like it! I'm not sure I can heal it." Nalya clutched her white robe around herself like armor.

Nalya wasn't the only one with her confidence stolen away.

"I thought you said you could," I said, grasping at straws. Would Greta keep our deal, if her sister couldn't be healed? Nalya had to at least try. "Please, Nalya. You could save more than one life here."

The Lewrit glanced over at the closed door, like Greta might return at any time. "I'll see what I can do, but this isn't something I was going to try in the wildlands, in the den of a Hunter." She laughed, a high, almost breathless sound. "Foolish, I know, but the healing exhausts the healer as well as the patient and it would have left me vulnerable there. Only she knows where to find me now. These are my own rooms. She could come back at any time."

Bir flicked his fingers, *no, no, no*. "Greta is a peacekeeper, Nalya. I will swear to your safety, whether you're able to heal Erzi or not."

Nalya took another deep, shuddering breath. "Yes. Yes, of course. No need to take liability, Temarel. Hunters are...dark, even if they don't hunt people." She trailed off for a moment, then shook herself. "Perhaps... Perhaps I can unravel this illness. I'll do my best."

"Thank you," I said, trying not to show how much I'd been shaken, too.

Nalya turned, like she was facing a firing squad, marched straight for the door to her patient, and strode inside.

In the empty atrium, I looked over at Bir and I saw my own raised-eyebrow shock reflected back at me.

Then the patient room door opened, and Greta stalked out, her movements as smooth as a panther's.

In the scant moments Greta and Nalya had been in the patient room together, I assumed the healer hadn't updated the Hunter on Erzi's chances of being healed.

Greta came to us and swept in a deep, Thurei-style bow. When she straightened, she added, "I owe you a great debt, honored ones."

Bir bowed in return, a much shallower affair, with its own little gesture I didn't recognize.

I couldn't accept her thanks, though, not like that. "Greta, it may not work. You heard her. This is something she doesn't recognize."

"The fade, yes." It didn't disturb Greta's calm. "Erzi has a chance now. She had no chance before."

"Greta," Bir began, his voice a level of serious beyond even sick sisters, "Kjelgaard told me you would help her find Coraven if she found a healer for your sister. Will you do so now?"

Greta turned her round face back to me. "Kate, there is no way of searching for your Thurei if Erzi dies. I don't know the things she knows. If we need to use Hunter ways to find him, we need Erzi."

"Well, Nalya said she would do her best." I swallowed on a throat suddenly gone dry. "Hopefully, we'll have good news soon."

Greta had drawn the distinction between herself as a peacekeeper and her sister the Hunter. Now I knew what she'd meant.

CHAPTER TWENTY-TWO

COR

I woke from nightmares when someone dropped me on the ground. I curled on my side, aching everywhere, and rubbed my blurry eyes.

My hands. I needed to...*what* wasn't clear. My head pounded like it had been split open. *Zaret* first, remember the rest later. The world spun around me in tree shadows and—Hiraches.

I held out my hand for the hilt and reached with my mind for my *jeira*.

Claws closed around my throat and hauled me up to my knees. I gasped for breath, my thin focus shattered.

"Stop it," the Hirach hissed, her long face close enough to mine that even my blurry eyes could see her. Serkot. She gave orders in her language and more Hiraches closed in, reaching for my hands.

It wasn't a fight. Too quickly, I was bound again. Palms together, fingers laced, everything wound around and tied together. A tail of rope snaked away, as if they intended to tie me to something. Not a pole this time, as far as I could tell, but no closer to wielding a blade.

Serkot kept talking to the others—in their language rather than the common tongue, not something I could follow. I did my best to ignore the nausea and pounding in my head and focus on my surroundings. Although my vision still tended to double and blur, I could tell I wasn't among the huts any longer. It was night again, with no hope that I could worldwalk my way out of this. The dark shapes of Hiraches milled about, arguing with each other, moving between the taller columns of trees.

There weren't many of the Hiraches. Where had the other members of the kith gone?

Kate. My breath caught beneath my ribs. What had happened earlier today, when the way between worlds had been open? Was she alive? Even if she had written to me, the note would have come while I'd been unconscious.

Was that what they'd waited for? Kate might have led them right to her in trying to tell me where to find her.

Perhaps they'd tried, and Kate's powerful skill was why there were so few of them left.

Whether the kith had succeeded or failed in their plan, I didn't know why they hadn't killed me.

Serkot leaned down, holding out a travel jug. "Here. It's water."

As soon as she mentioned it, thirst burned down my throat, spread through me like fire. Whatever the jug held could have been laced with more of the sleeping draught, but in that moment, I didn't care. I leaned forward and guzzled down as much as I could.

Water, just as Serkot had said. After a couple of swallows, she pulled the jug back. "Don't throw it up this time."

My stomach cramped around the water, but I refused to give in to the queasiness.

"Why keep me alive?" I croaked. If Kate had found them yesterday and leveled the village, they couldn't want to draw her to them again.

The Hiraches around us started to move away, all heading off in the same direction.

"I think you're still useful," Serkot said.

"For what?"

She growled in answer before picking up the rope and tugging it, pulling at my hands. "To walk. Now."

"I don't think I can stand," I said, not much of an exaggeration.

She lifted her voice to one of her companions, who turned around and started back toward us. To me, she said, "We're not carrying you any farther. If you won't walk, we'll drag you."

I made it to my feet, though my muscles ached and my legs threatened to buckle. Whatever they'd given me to keep me unconscious had worked its claws in deeper than simple sleep. For a while, each step took all my energy. The Hiraches pushed forward into the wildlands without any road or path. The direction they chose sloped gradually uphill. Rocks and roots swam in and out of focus whenever my vision blurred. Pain gnawed at the area over my ribs where I'd been clawed. Serkot snarled at me, clear impatience with my pace, but she grabbed my arm to hold me up when I would have fallen.

Serkot carried a pack over her shoulder. As my vision cleared, I saw that most of the other thirty or so Hiraches did as well. A handful of children followed alongside their parents. Grathki might be among them. At first, I thought they had dragged their pace down to match mine, but more than half of them struggled, either limping or simply frail, not much better off physically than I was.

Kate's skill was strong enough to destroy their village. She'd never used it over an area that wide, but I'd seen evidence of what a human was capable of. Was that what had happened and now… they fled?

When Serkot let me stop long enough to catch my breath, I only had one question.

"What happened with Kjelgaard?" I leaned against a tree on my uninjured side. Even in the chill, night air and through the thin, human-style shirt, sweat dampened my skin.

"Corruption on your human!" Serkot cursed. More to herself than to me, she muttered, "Calling on the council like bleating *kittu*."

"The council?" I asked. My sluggish thoughts rearranged themselves. "Your council?"

How had Kate gotten a hearing with the Hirach council? Whatever this kith had tried, Kate hadn't fallen into their trap. Relief coursed through me and I leaned my throbbing head against the rough tree bark.

Serkot jerked on the rope, nearly pulling me off my feet. "Come on. Let's go."

"I need more water." That was true, but something was nagging at the corner of my mind and I wanted a moment of stillness to track it down. Walking over the rough terrain demanded all of my attention.

"You wasted your time talking." She moved off, along with the rest of her kith, and I had no choice but to follow. The uphill route the Hiraches traveled wound its way through a broadleaf forest. Fortunately, the canopy was thin enough to let in shafts of moonlight, making it easier to see protruding roots and fallen branches, though it was still a struggle to avoid them, bound and leashed as I was. Soon, I didn't have the breath for any more questions.

At least the way grew easier as we struck across a broad clearing on the hillside. The nausea that roiled in my stomach had subsided, replaced with the sharp edge of hunger. Weakness gnawed at my muscles. I pushed all of it to the back of my mind, the same way I'd handled fatigue or pain in the training circle while I'd been learning my skill.

Kate went to the Hirach council. The thought of her facing down a pack of Hiraches tangled up with the nightmares I'd had while Serkot's concoction had held me beneath the surface of sleep. I picked out truths like stones from mud. The real danger to Kate came from the Scholars. They feared her power. That was why they'd set Tharkesh on our trail and sent us on a route full of Hunters to Issai. That was why Tharkesh had hunted Kate to begin with, to pay his debt to the Scholars.

Tharkesh was dead.

His debt had died with him. The Akevad kith owed the Scholars nothing after Tharkesh had died, even though he hadn't killed us to satisfy the debt. He had been the one to ask the question; the price for the answer belonged to him alone.

"Serkot, I need water." My voice rasped like sand through my throat. How long had we been walking? I couldn't see the stars above clearly enough to tell.

"Shut up," she hissed, without turning around, her voice barely loud enough to hear.

The group of Hiraches had slowed, their footsteps barely stirring the brush and grasses as they moved. The scant moonlight outlined their long profiles as they scanned the hillside.

We were in the wildlands, with all its dangers. I could hope that this time the Hiraches were prey.

The next step I took, I set my feet firmly and hauled back on the rope as hard as I could. The end of the rope slipped through Serkot's fingers and she spun around, teeth bared.

"You burrow-dwelling—"

Someone ahead of us screamed and I looked up to see a flickering shape among the trees. Hiraches started yelling.

Serkot snarled at me but turned away, toward the threat.

I took a couple of steps to the side, close to a cluster of bushes, and ducked into a crouch, staying just high enough to keep an eye on what was happening. More shouts rang out from up ahead, from the direction of the scream. Serkot and I had been walking near the back of the group. A Hirach limped up the slope behind me, pulling one of the children along toward the cluster of their kith. I froze, suppressing the instinct to drop to the ground for fear of the movement catching their attention.

The Hirach voices cut off in silence. A faint string of clicks sounded through the area around the clearing, almost drowned out by the rustling of breeze through the leaves. Two shapes flew out of the tree canopy toward the group of Hiraches. The high-pitched whistles of Mokklas pierced the air.

Lesser Hunters, Mokklas were nocturnal predators with a skill for immobilizing their prey so they could make quick work of it with their slashing teeth and claws. They would kill their prey if they could, but a quick meal of blood served them almost as well.

Caught out in the open clearing, we would all make easy prey.

CHAPTER TWENTY-THREE

COR

Perhaps the Hiraches would be too busy with the Mokklas to bother with me.

I ducked out from beneath the bushes, heading away from the Hiraches. The rope caught in the brush behind me and I cursed under my breath. I hauled against the snag, which gave way all at once, tipping me off-balance. Unable to break my fall, I slammed into the ground. Pain lanced through me from my injured side. It took me a second to catch my breath as I rolled onto my back.

The bat-like silhouette of another Mokkla blotted out the stars above me. *How many are there?* As nocturnal Hunters, Mokklas saw in the dark even better than I did. Instinctively, I shielded my face with my arms, tensed against the threat of teeth—but the Mokkla kept going. It tucked its leathery wings a beat later and plummeted toward one of the Hiraches. Another scream, higher-pitched.

A child.

Don't, Cor. This is your chance. Run! I squeezed my eyes shut for a moment, but that only forced me to focus on the shouting and cries, the growing sounds of the fight. *You shatter-brained fool.*

I rolled over and rose to a crouch, keeping to the scant shelter of a wiry shrub. I had no way to gather up the trailing rope, not with my hands bound. One small Hirach curled against the ground, and a larger Hirach knelt low, shielding the child. The Mokkla sailed past—whether it had missed or been deflected, I hadn't seen, but it banked to make another run at them. Beyond them, three more of the winged Hunters harried the rest of the kith. Shouts and cries rang out, adding to the chaos.

The nearby Hirach man froze in the act of helping the child up, his gaze locked on the Mokkla—paralyzed by its skill. The Mokkla tucked its wings for another dive. Keeping low, I ran in their direction, spurred on by the heat of the fight. As I closed in, I swung my arms up in an overhand motion. The child screamed as I plowed into her protector, bringing all of us crashing down. The trailing rope lashed up like a whip into the Mokkla's flight path and it dodged away with a flare of its wings.

Released from the Mokkla's skill, the Hirach man struggled beneath me. I rolled free, not eager to meet with those claws, either.

"I'm *helping*," I snapped. I held up my hands. "Untie me so I can fight."

The Hirach—Vercho; I finally dredged up his name from yesterday—growled something in his language. I thought he would refuse, but as the rustle of leathery wings grew closer, he grabbed the rope, hooked his formidable claws beneath the knot, and yanked. His sharp claws severed it with a snap. Then he turned away, scooping up the little girl.

I wrenched my abused hands free of the remaining rope and flexed my stiff fingers. When I summoned my *zaret* and the familiar hilt settled in my palm, relief blotted out the worst of the pain and fatigue.

A long, wailing scream rose over the rest of the noise.

I spun around, staying low.

A Hirach stood in a patch of low brush up the slope from me, screaming but unable to move. A Mokkla clung to their back, teeth slicing into their shoulder to feed from the blood. Another one of the Mokklas dove out of the sky to latch on to the victim as well.

The closest Hiraches moved to defend their kin, but that left others vulnerable to the remaining two fliers, who swooped in. Lesser Hunters weren't as smart as the Greater ones, but in situations like this, they were smart enough.

This wasn't a defenseless child. These Hunters had intended death to me and mine.

But I didn't like my chances wandering around the wilds on my own until dawn came, either, and my chances of eluding their tracking ability for even that long were slim. They hadn't killed me yet. Perhaps I could make another way out of this mess.

I bolted for the feeding Hunters and their victim, my blade held ready. The feeding Mokklas lifted their heads as I approached, short muzzles dripping. One gave a whistling hiss. The other fixed its gaze on me.

No! I launched myself at them, but an instant later, my muscles locked in place, paralyzed by their skill. I banished the *zaret* right before I crashed to the ground at the Hirach's feet. I got a face-full of dirt before tumbling like a kicked ragdoll into the legs of the Hirach, who collapsed. The Mokklas sprang aloft, filling the air with frantic wingbeats, too startled to maintain their skill.

I could move, but the bulk of the Hirach across my back pinned me to the ground. The injured man groaned and stirred weakly, perhaps too faint with blood loss or shock.

I was wrestling my way out from underneath him when one of his kin reached us and lifted the downed man's shoulders so I could pull the rest of the way free.

"Get everyone back into the trees," I whispered, trying to catch my breath. "They won't be able to maneuver as well among the trunks."

"What do you think we're trying to do, prey?" Serkot growled back, fierce, though she kept her voice low. She lifted her injured companion, draping his arm over her shoulders, and dragged him in the direction of the rest of the kith as well as she could, remaining crouched down herself.

The rest of her kin were, as she'd mentioned, moving toward the closest trees, but that took them up the slope and more of their number needed defending. All four Mokklas circled above the gathered Hiraches, making diving attempts to separate someone far enough from the others to give them a chance feed.

One of the flying Hunters broke off and headed toward us.

I scrambled to catch up to Serkot and hissed, "Stand up! I'll get it as it moves in to feed."

"What? No." She lowered her kin back to the ground and turned toward the oncoming attacker, poised to strike with her claws.

"It will distract—" I started, but we ran out of time for strategy.

The Mokkla dipped lower, but not low enough. Serkot launched herself from her crouch, but it flicked its wings and swerved aside. Her claws found only air. The Mokkla circled around for another pass, whistling to its flock.

Another one turned to make a run at us.

My simple plan to bait a Mokkla out of the air might have worked with one, but not two. Especially not with someone incapacitated on the ground. They could paralyze the two of us and finish off the injured Hirach before anyone could come to his rescue.

I brought my *zaret* back to my hand. In the darkness, the transparent blade almost disappeared from sight. I stood, balancing the hilt in my hand. As soon as one of the two approaching Hunters trained its gaze on me, I flung the *zaret* like a spear. The Mokkla froze me in midmotion, paralyzed with my arm outstretched.

Too late, windbag.

The blade wasn't weighted properly to fly true, but when the Mokkla collided with it, the edge caught its wing and sliced through the membrane. The Mokkla shrieked and tumbled from the sky. Serkot darted toward it, perhaps to finish it off.

I still couldn't move. Paralysis locked the muscles in my jaw closed. I couldn't even call to her to help, if she would have given it. Weight dropped onto my back, claws gouging my skin through the thin fabric of my shirt. Skerot looked up from over a tangle of shrubs, but she was too far to stop a bite.

A snarl warned me a moment before something slammed into my waist. The Mokkla sprang back into the air as I was knocked off my feet and I could move again. I called my *zaret* to my hand and lashed out as I fell. The Mokkla shrieked a whistle and I thumped to the ground beneath a little Hirach.

"Grathki?" I asked, keeping my voice down as I tried to sort us both out and get us back on our feet.

The Hirach boy crouched next to me. "You're not supposed to be untied."

"Thanks," I whispered. "Let's get you to your kin."

"His *kin* is here." Serkot reached us, waving me over to the injured Hirach man who lay on the ground, unmoving. "Help me turn him over."

A quick glance over my shoulder showed me that the two remaining Mokklas had little chance of isolating any one of the remaining members of the kith. They struggled uphill toward the nearest trees, the flying Hunters circling above. I set my attention on helping Serkot.

The man groaned as we wrestled him onto his stomach, exposing the shredded muscle of his shoulder. Blood glistened in the moonlight. Serkot fumbled in her pack, producing a wad of cloth that she pressed over the wound.

"Grathki, get the little bottle out." She nodded toward her pack. "The glass one."

I sat back on my heels. Now that the fight had ended, a cold, shaky exhaustion drained away the temporary strength of the battle. I shifted around to sit properly on the ground before my legs cramped from crouching. A breeze picked up over the hillside, rustling through the nearby forest, and I suppressed a shiver.

"Is there water?" I asked.

Serkot glanced up, then started to bolt to her feet. She froze.

I ducked.

Grathki didn't.

The Mokkla passed over my head close enough to rake claws across my scalp, barreling straight for the boy. I swiped upward, overextended, and the edge of my *zaret* took the winged Hunter from below. The Mokkla's own inertia gave force to the desperate blow and the body fell, cleaved nearly in two, and rolled against Grathki's shins.

Serkot stumbled out of her frozen stance and whipped around to gather the boy against her.

"He's very fast," Grathki whispered.

More rustling behind me had me scrambling to my feet, legs shaky.

Ten of the remaining Hirach adults approached across the clearing.

A deep voice among them growled, "What's he doing loose?"

"I was saving you from the Mokklas," I snapped, my *zaret* still in hand, though I kept the point angled down. Blood dripped off the blade. I sidestepped, carefully, easing myself out from between Serkot and the others. "I could have left you to them."

Half the night remained until dawn would come and allow me

to worldwalk out of the wildlands, and in the meantime, I would be alone and injured, without food or water.

Bravado was all I had.

At the edge of the forest, the shapes of the rest of the kith were visible, resting or tending to each other's wounds. They couldn't afford to chase after me any more than I could afford to run.

"All you've done is slow us down, prey." The Hirach man gestured to the others, and they moved to cut off my escape route.

"He was useful, Gozmal," Serkot said from behind me. "We should keep him. There's still a chance that they'll listen."

They? The Scholars?

I brought my blade up, trying to ignore the way it wobbled with my fatigue. "If Kjelgaard has brought word of my capture to the council, let me go and the matter is done. Tharkesh is dead and his bargain with the Scholars is over. She is too strong for you to hunt. She'd be the end of your kith. We aren't of any further use to you. I promise you we will not pursue revenge on your kith if we part ways here and never meet again."

"What do you know of the Scholars and their bargains?" Gozmal snarled. The Hiraches drew closer around me, tightening the circle. Few of them were in the peak of health, but they were in better shape than I was. And there were eleven of them. I tried to push the pain and chill and thirst out of my mind.

"Wait," Serkot said. "Thurei, what *do* you know of Scholars?"

"Tharkesh brought a question to them and owed a debt to them for their answer." I tried to remember the details Shom had told me, gained from a friend of hers who was working off her own debt to the Scholars. "They set him to hunt Kjelgaard and me as payment for his answer. But the debt ends on his death. They have no hold on you."

Gozmal laughed, a harsh sound echoed with low growls from

the others. "They held their answer hostage and now they refuse to tell us in exchange for either of you."

Hiraches closed in from every side and I stood there as stunned as a fool. "They don't want us dead?"

"I'm sure they'll take you dead," said another Hirach, an older man who hobbled forward more eagerly than his companions. "That was the agreement. If we bring his body, they'll have to find us a cure, whatever they're saying now."

I brought my *zaret* up to orient it on him, shifting my feet and nearly tripping as my heel came down in the mouth of some animal's burrow. I sidestepped to firmer ground, short of breath.

"We'd lose our chance to bargain, then," Serkot protested. She moved closer, though not quite past me, her clawed hands spread wide as if to ward against the man.

If they attacked, there were too many to fight. I might account for a few before the rest tore me apart. No matter how depleted this kith was, it was more than enough to deal with one lone Thurei at the end of his endurance. Maybe if I'd been in better condition…

"You asked them about an illness," I said, my memory sluggish. That was why there were so few of them, and so many of them ill. It hadn't been a clash with Kate that had depleted their numbers. She would have had the sense to go to someone for help, not charge off into the wildlands after a nest of Hunters.

At least, I hoped.

I released my *zaret*, all but useless now anyway, and held up empty hands. "There are other ways to bargain with the Scholars."

"If we had both of them…" one of the Hiraches murmured. They were just out of reach of my blade now and creeping closer.

"No, don't!" Grathki's voice spun me around.

Serkot stopped in the middle of her lunge at the same time that I brought my *zaret* back to my hand, holding it at guard.

Pain exploded in the back of my head, plunging me into darkness.

I woke a short time later, by the angle of the moonlight, lying on my back in the shadows of the forest. My hands were tied together again. Several Hiraches sat or lay on the ground around me in various stages of injury or illness. My head pounded, but my vision was clear enough and at least I didn't have the bitter tang of their brutal sleeping draught in my mouth.

Low voices sounded in the near distance, perhaps the argument continuing among the kith.

Even I wasn't confident enough with my skill to summon my *zaret* in hopes of dropping down and slicing through the rope on my hands while they were resting on my chest. I sat up as quietly as I could, wincing from the fiery burn of the claw slashes in my side. It didn't take a healer to tell me the wound had become infected. My hair and the back of my neck felt sticky—perhaps from the blow to my head. The Mokkla's claws were a likely second candidate. The lines of pain down my back and shoulder reminded me I'd suffered deep scratches there as well. The cold, damp air beneath the trees chilled my skin, but the rest of me felt warm enough.

"Good, Gozmal didn't kill you." Grathki stood beyond the ring of ill and wounded.

Ah, good. I have a watcher. Whether he'd been assigned or had volunteered at this point didn't matter much.

"Not yet," I agreed wearily. "But he wants to, doesn't he?"

Grathki didn't offer his interpretation of events on that one, but another Hirach growled something in their own language.

The boy answered in the common tongue. "He fought the Mokklas."

"To save his own blood," the older Hirach said and then he coughed, a heavy, wet sound.

The two of them could argue it out. They wouldn't be the ones untying me. I got to my feet, careful of my uncertain balance, and picked my way between the invalids toward the voices of the rest of the kith. A shiver surprised me, almost knocking me off my feet, but the chill dissipated a moment later.

"Hey, wait," Grathki said, racing around the edge of the group to cut me off. "Where are you going?"

The cluster of Hiraches up ahead fell silent and a couple of them broke away to head in my direction. I held up my bound hands. Hopefully that would be enough of an indication of my intentions.

"Tie him to something. Or dose him again. I told you he's more trouble than he's worth." Gozmal, though I was sure there were others in the kith who would have agreed with him. Perhaps not all of them.

"I'm worth more than you realize," I said, forcing confidence into my voice. "You want a cure from the Scholars. I can help."

If I could keep them talking instead of hitting me over the head or dosing me into delirium, maybe I could think up a way to bargain my way out of here.

"You're no healer," Gozmal said, as if I might have turned Lewrit since the last time he'd knocked me out.

"You didn't go to the Scholars for a healer. You went for a cure." I had no hope of getting a healer to treat Hunters. I looked around at the group of them, one by one. "The Scholars broke the Truce by asking you to kill Kjelgaard and me. Evidence of their treason will prove a better bargaining point than promising them my life."

"We can't call them up before council for Truce-breaking," Serkot said. "Who will listen to Hiraches against the Shevern

Scholars? They already refuse to see us or give us the cure they promised Tharkesh."

"Between your council, myself, and Kjelgaard, they must listen." I wanted to spread my hands for emphasis and couldn't, finding a new reason to curse the bindings. What a foolish reason to be frustrated. Perhaps my thinking wasn't as clear as I'd imagined.

"Our council?" Gozmal asked. "Our council will see us all left for scavengers if they catch up with us."

"They—" My voice caught, and I cleared my throat. Death for kidnapping? Among Hunters, it followed a brutal logic. If I had still had a House, there might have been hundreds of *zarets* eager for Hirach blood over this. Perhaps they judged it safer to simply be rid of a kith who hunted unwisely. If that was the case, the kith couldn't afford to let either Kate or their own people find them. "I will clear the accusation against you with your council myself. Only release me."

"You can't trust a word out of a Thurei's mouth," one of the Hiraches said. Vercho. "Especially the Hunterslayer."

I glared at him. "I fought for you. I could have escaped when you cut me free, but I stayed and fought. I have no love for Hunters, it's true, but the Scholars were the ones who set you on my trail. It wasn't even the choice of your own Finder. I built a reputation to *avoid* fights, not encourage them."

Tharkesh, the kith's Finder, might have chosen Kate as prey if he'd crossed paths with us on his own, but we hadn't met by chance. The Scholars had used the Hiraches in an attempt to neutralize what they saw as a threat: a human, and the person who was her protector.

Great job on that last part, Cor.

Gozmal switched to the Hirach language, moving the conversation out of my reach. Several others joined in. Serkot stepped aside, rummaging through her pack. She found her stoppered water jug.

"We'll go no farther tonight, not until we know who can keep going," Gozmal said, switching back to Kuyene. "If he wants water, let him drink it with the *yusmeir*. That will shut him up."

Yusmeir? *Yusmeir* was a poison. I took a step back.

"I'll take care of him, don't worry." Serkot lunged forward and caught my wrist.

I resisted the urge to yank back. Hands bound, and within reach of the rest of the kith, there would be no escape. I'd had my chance to run and had used that freedom to fight Mokklas instead.

"Come on," she said, tugging me back in the direction of the wounded. The trailing rope was much shorter this time, since Vercho had sliced it more or less in half, but it was still long enough for Serkot to tie it firmly to a sapling. With little other choice, I sat down.

She caught the eye of one of her kin, a young man barely past stripling age sitting against a tree trunk. He looked more lucid than the others, without any visible blood or bandages. Ill, perhaps. "Yell, if you see him trying to escape."

"I will," he whispered, then he shivered, though he was wrapped tightly in his thick, shadow-gray cloak. Fevered, then.

Serkot pulled the stopper from the jug, then held the vessel out for me to drink. "Here. It's plain water. Don't make a fuss and you'll get to spend the rest of the night awake."

"But if I fuss, you'll poison me?"

"The *yusmeir*? It's a small enough dose to make you sleep and keep you from slipping out of here."

A single dose, perhaps. But dosed to a stupor, day after day? I took the water. My empty stomach twisted around it, but at least it didn't turn queasy.

"Is there any food?" I hadn't eaten anything since...since the dinner with Katen's friends.

"Not much and it's for us. Unless you can justify it. Think up a way to get the cure from the Scholars." Serkot turned away from me to bring the jug to the fevered boy and let him drink the rest of it.

"Serkot, if we speak with one voice, the council will listen to us. Yours and the Scholars' council both."

"You would stir up your House to stand shoulder to shoulder with a Hirach kith? One that sent a pack after you?"

"My House." *Ah*. Hiraches had no reason to keep an ear pricked for Thurei gossip. Perhaps it would always hurt to say aloud, no matter who was the audience. "I have no House. Temarel closed its doors against me. I serve as a peacekeeper now. My commander will add her voice to mine." The Hiraches could provide proof of the Scholars' attempts to kill us. *Tol* Pella wouldn't be able to brush it off as 'the assumptions of a hotheaded boy' any longer.

Not that I planned to say who my commander was. If they didn't know where Kate and I lived now, I wouldn't be the one to tell them. Although that pressed another question to the fore.

"And you think your peacekeeper commander would support you, to speak for Hunters?" Serkot's lips curled in a silent snarl.

"To speak against lies and assassination by those who hold our trust." I drew my knees up toward my chest, shuddering so hard, it rattled my teeth. When had it gotten so cold?

"The Scholars, you mean. No one trusts us."

"It could only help your cause to set me loose." I tried to smile, but it felt more like a grimace. "A show of goodwill."

"Goodwill." The word fell like a stone from Serkot's lips. She stood, brushing forest detritus from her knees. "Use your time wisely, Thurei, and give me a solid reason to keep Gozmal from leaving you behind when we leave."

She didn't need to explain what being left behind would entail.

CHAPTER TWENTY-FOUR

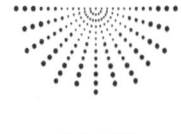

KATE

Pella's note came while Bir, Greta, and I were waiting in Nalya's antechamber. It had been a couple of hours since Nalya had started treating Erzi.

Greta had sunk down in one of the delicate-looking wooden chairs and sat staring at the door her sister had disappeared behind. Her head snapped around at the crinkle of paper as I caught the Summons.

"The Hirach council agreed to look for Coraven," I paraphrased as I read. "Even though he was taken on Earth, outside of the Truce. She convinced them that the hunt started at Scholars Hall. Just by chance, though. It doesn't look like she pushed the Scholars' role in it at all. She does say...it may be difficult to get him back."

"Erzi will know." Greta's voice startled me. She had been so quiet and still this whole time.

"Erzi had dealings with Hiraches?" I asked.

"She *has* dealings with many people." The way Greta emphasized the verb reminded me of the way that using the present tense had become so important to me since Cor had been taken. "She forages and trades her findings at the Wild Market."

"Where is that?" Bir asked.

Greta stared at him a moment, or maybe that was just her default expression. "In the wildlands. Hunters aren't always welcome in city markets."

A market full of Hunters, held somewhere beyond even the theoretical protection of Truce. I shot a worried glance at Bir.

"You're saying she might have traded with the Hiraches, then," Bir said.

"I'll ask her when she's well." Greta returned to staring at the closed door, apparently done with the conversation.

I dropped my volume a little to continue talking with Bir. "She didn't sound mad."

"The *tol* likely hasn't heard about your change of plans yet," Bir pointed out.

The paper crinkled as I folded it into a smaller square. I sharpened the creases, too fidgety to keep my hands still. "Should I tell her? So that she doesn't find out from... It would be Stolla, I guess."

"I'm sure Nalya has paper and pencil around here somewhere. I can look if you want me to." He lifted an eyebrow. I could hear the *but* in his voice. I waited it out. He shrugged his fingers and continued. "There is a saying in Thurei: 'You can always bow lower.'"

"We have one like it in English, too. 'Better to ask for forgiveness than permission.'"

He smiled. "That's a good one. I'm stealing that one."

I couldn't muster up an answering smile, not under these circumstances. Too much hung in the balance and more crises were lining up to pile on top.

Eventually, Nalya pushed the door open and came out.

Exhaustion made her move like a much older woman.

"Is she well?" Greta asked.

"Well?" Nalya echoed, her voice thin. She closed the door softly behind her. "She's…better. Greta. There's something there I couldn't heal. She's better than she was—the fever and physical deterioration are mended, though she will still need food and rest to recover more fully. I've done everything a healer can for her, but she's not… I don't think I can call her 'well.'"

Greta bolted to her feet. Nalya flinched back, but the Hunter only said, "Thank you, healer. May I see her?"

Nalya stepped aside and waved a limp hand in the direction of Erzi's room. As Greta hurried inside, Nalya drifted over toward me. Bir vacated the chair beside me immediately and offered it to her. She wilted into it.

"Are *you* well?" I asked her, worried. What had I done, asking her to do this?

"Worn out," she murmured. "That was more difficult than I expected."

"Would you like refreshment?" Bir asked, as polite and attentive as a five-star waiter, as if there were no other concern in the world than Nalya's appetite.

"Please. And something hearty but plain for the House's guest." She sighed as Bir disappeared into the hall. "When they're not tedious, Thurei manners are quite nice."

"Agreed." That made me chuckle, though the humor quickly dissolved. "Healer Nalya, is Erzi still sick?"

"There's something in her that feels…strange. Wrong." The fur over Nalya's scalp rippled, like a shiver. "Unlike any illness I've ever experienced, and my training was extensive. I have never healed a Hunter before, but I don't think that is the difference I felt. Other differences, yes." The healer closed her eyes for a moment and shivered, then brought her gaze up to mine again. "But there is something about this illness that I can't eradicate from her. I can only hope that it does her no further harm."

As long as she can help me find Cor. I bit my lip. No. I hoped she'd be okay. Of course I did. It just seemed that every minute that ticked away made it less and less likely that I'd get Cor back and every step forward I took just brought new complications.

Bir returned, trailed by a Thurei boy carrying a tray in his hands. It held a soup tureen, cheese rolls, and a couple of stacked bowls. It took some juggling, but the pair served a bowl up for the healer, who declined a roll, and proceeded to the patient's room. I followed.

The room's white-paneled walls and crisp, white sheets made Erzi's mottled, camouflage fur appear even more ragged and dusty in contrast. Her gaze held a lucidity that had been missing when I'd first seen her. A bath and a good night's sleep would have her well on her way to normal, though she still looked gaunt compared to her sister. The bones stood out sharply in her round face and her large, wide-set eyes seemed sunken.

The Leratom boy ladled up a bowl of soup for her, bowed with some sort of hospitality inflection, and saw himself out.

Greta touched her sister's shoulder. "Erzi, this is Kjelgaard, the one who is searching for her mate."

Erzi studied me a moment, though she kept hold of her spoon like someone might take it from her. "Tell me while I eat."

I gave her what little information I had—a little of our history with Tharkesh, the name of his kith, and the Scholars' assertion that they were the ones who held him. When I finished, Erzi scraped up the last of the soup broth with her spoon, then set spoon and bowl aside in favor of one of the rolls.

"And he calls himself 'the Hunterslayer'?" she asked, neatly tearing the roll in two with her long, clawed fingers.

Not a single twitch of her mouth, her eyebrows, or anything else gave her emotions away. I found the lack of expression unnerving.

"I'm from a world without a Truce. Coraven protected me for years while I couldn't protect myself. I didn't even know how to hide my *jeira*. That's why he ended up with that reputation."

Erzi swallowed a mouthful. "But he's *called* 'Hunterslayer,' yes? People will remember something like that. Good to know for when I ask around."

"Are you familiar with the Akevad kith?" I asked. "That's the group Tharkesh belonged to."

"Not personally," Erzi said.

"Can you ask at the next market?" Greta asked.

Erzi tilted her head and give her sister a look. Greta blinked back.

"What?" I asked, trying not to snap at them. I didn't need any other problems to crop up.

"The next Wild Market on Kuyen is five days from now." Erzi brushed crumbs off the front of her shift. Another glance at Greta. "But there's one on Erramire tomorrow."

"There's no Truce on Erramire," Bir said, his arms folded across his chest.

Erzi grinned, baring an impossibly wide mouthful of sharp teeth. "It's the Wild Market. There's never a Truce where it's held."

Bir turned to me. "It would be my pleasure to accompany you, if you go to this market."

I raised my brows. It didn't escape my notice that the offer was borderline pushy, compared with his recent manners, but I didn't have any objection to him coming along. "Sure."

"Tomorrow, then," Erzi said. "Third hour of the morning, at my home. That early in the evening, the market will still be quiet, but the people I'll need to speak with should be there. We don't need to alarm your Thurei guard."

With a jolt, I realized she meant Bir. When I glanced over at him, he did look severe, his dark-green brows set at a grim angle, the good-natured jokester entirely gone.

Then he inclined his head in a little bow and said, "It keeps the blood pumping. Don't hold back on my account."

Erzi coughed a laugh.

"Then I'll see you tomorrow." I stopped at the door and turned back. "Erzi...I hope the healing works."

"I have a chance, which is more than I had before." Erzi blinked slowly, an expression I didn't know how to read.

Bir followed me out into the main, carpeted hall of House Leratom. Nalya had retired somewhere while we'd talked with the Drammons. Fatigue and a deeper pull tugged at me, but I still had bargains to fulfill. I rubbed the heel of my palms over my eyes.

"Sunset is getting closer," I said. "I still need to arrange this demonstration for Misora."

"A letter will serve just as well for that. Saves you interrupting the heir at her business." He rolled his shoulders, like he couldn't quite get the tension to release. "I'll write it, if you like. A selection of materials from various origin worlds. Nothing related to combat training. Is that the roof and walls of the matter?"

"That would be wonderful," I said, sighing. One thing taken care of. One thing at a time.

"Until tomorrow, Kate."

CHAPTER TWENTY-FIVE

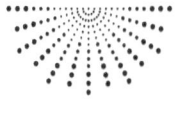

KATE

As the sun crept the last few degrees toward the horizon back in San Jose, I killed time picking out an outfit appropriate for the demonstration of my skill for the Leratoms. This wouldn't be a simple practice session in the arena with Eld. The Leratoms wanted a show, whether I was a showman or not.

I went with my floral print dress, as formal as I could get. I could change for the Wild Market after the demonstration.

I'd written a handful of Summons addressed to Cor and ready to go. As soon as the sun dipped out of sight, I sent one. Seeing it flap away and disappear filled me with relief. At this point, I doubted he'd get the message—I'd simply written *see you soon* on all of them—but at least I knew he was still alive.

Birasef's note arrived at almost the same time that mine disappeared, true to his promise. I unfolded it and scanned the text.

The Leratoms had accommodated my request for a collection of items from different worlds. Plants, which seemed easy enough. Despite the short notice and early hour, they'd also made a guest list that impressed Bir, at least, including some of the city leaders.

Breakfast and a show. I dropped the note on the table. Good, I'd be unlikely to repeat my mistakes from yesterday when Eld had lobbed stones at me. With just plants and a few spectators, I could remain calm and in control.

Tucking the extra notes to Cor in my bag, I slung the strap over my shoulder but stopped before I worldwalked out of my living room. I sent Shom a quick note not to expect me at the garrison, just in case she worried.

Closing my eyes, I imagined the imposing wooden doors of House Leratom, the tall, plastered walls, and the smooth, dark gray paving stones in the square in front. Focusing my *jeira*, I reached for the mental snapshot and pulled myself across the gap.

Dawn light washed the Kuyene sky above the square. This early in the day, the air remained cool, but the streets of Aubello already bustled with carts and foot traffic. I rang the bell hanging beside the door and it swung open moments later.

A young man pulled it open. Nabel, I thought, the greeter from the first time I'd been here. He bowed deeply. "Kjelgaard, good morning to you. I believe the *denet*-heir is upstairs, preparing for the demonstration. And Temarel is here as well. Allow me to escort you."

"Thank you," I murmured, forcing down a surge of hope. *Birasef* Temarel, not Cor. The worry and grief settled back over me even worse than before. I followed him through hallways and up several flights of stairs, finally stepping out onto the building's flat roof. Several of his kin busied themselves moving potted plants and outdoor furniture around. I spotted Misora's aqua hair where she stood surrounded by a handful of guests from a range of Kuyen's peoples. The small group included Bir, decked out in his formalwear, though he carried his black leather House coat folded over his arm.

"Kjelgaard, good morning." Misora offered a shallow bow, echoed more deeply by Bir.

"Or evening," said a guest, one of the chameleon-like lizard people Cor and I had met at the market. She had a triangular face that reminded me of a gecko, and her skin was bright blue, but I had no idea what mood that signified. "Earth is a night world, isn't it?"

"Um, yes," I said, assuming she meant worldwalkers could only travel to Earth at night, unlike Kuyen, a day world. But I needn't have worried about coming up with a reply, since someone else spoke up before I could add anything else.

"And a world without Truce, as well," said an elderly Lan man whose dark hair had gone almost entirely white. "I paid my fair share of sweat in the training yard as a young man, but I don't mind telling you that I don't envy you the perils of your world. I've heard the tales."

"It's not..." *That dangerous*, I'd almost said. Sure, I'd had Hunters after me on Earth and needed Cor's protection, but Kuyen hadn't proved to be much safer, Truce or no Truce. Had that fact made it into the tales, too?

Bir spoke up. "Kjelgaard is more than capable of meeting any challenge."

But they didn't want to hear from him, either.

"No wonder your defensive skills are so powerful, if the stories we've heard are true." The lizard woman tipped her head in acknowledgement to Misora.

"You'll be able to see for yourselves shortly," Misora said, adding a gracious smile. She waved to a few more guests approaching us. "Katherine Kjelgaard, I'm pleased to present you to some of the Selectors of Aubello."

She continued with introductions, but I missed them, distracted by the sight of a Shevern. In place of a Scholar's austere robes, this woman wore patterned cloth arranged like a toga. Misora hadn't mentioned a Scholar's title, either, but the sight of the Shevern still made all the muscles in my shoulders tense up. The Leratoms wanted to show off how powerful my skill was, but I didn't want to be flaunting that in front of someone who might report back to the Scholars.

"I was fascinated when I heard a human would be here, Kjelgaard," the Shevern said as soon as the introductions were over. "I have never seen a worldwalker from Earth before, so my curiosity was piqued."

That's awfully careful wording. She didn't say she hadn't known about human worldwalkers before, only that she hadn't seen one herself. I wiped a hand over my face and attempted a smile. Maybe I was just becoming paranoid. "We're rare here, but there are almost eight billion of us on Earth, so it would be wise not to discount us."

I hadn't intended for my tone to sound so aggressive, but it had slipped out before I could edit myself. Even Bir shot me a startled glance.

The Shevern widened her large eyes, her coppery skin wrinkling at the corners. "I didn't have the impression that Earth ought to be considered hostile, Kjelgaard. I imagine you're speaking theatrically."

My face flushed with embarrassment, but Misora interjected before I could think of the right thing to say. Of course, Earth wasn't *hostile*—no one else even believed Kuyen or the other worlds existed—but I would defend myself and the people important to me if anyone threatened us.

"I believe the display is ready, honored ones." She gestured to the arrangement of potted plants.

When I'd last been on the roof, the impressive collection of potted plants and trees had been arranged to divide the flat space into smaller, room-like areas for mingling and conversation. Now, most of them had been pushed to the side, out of the way. About thirty of the plants were loosely scattered across a long, open stretch of the roof with plenty of room to move between them.

The specimens ranged from a tree with sinuous limbs like a Californian manzanita to a low, wide container of trailing vines with tiny, blue, heart-shaped leaves and spikes of peach flowers. A collection like this must have taken time and effort to gather and skillful tending to keep them alive and healthy.

I wondered what my father, who owned his own landscaping business back in Oregon, would think of the exotic collection, then shook the thought from my mind. I had a debt to repay to the Leratoms and I intended to do it well.

"Thank you, *denet*-heir," I said, slipping into Thurei formality as best I could. "It's my honor to demonstrate the human skill for your guests." I considered explaining what I could do but decided that it would be more dramatic to simply do it. I inclined my head to the group and strode out into the center of the arrangement of plants.

A short, stout teal-leaved plant in a glazed, ceramic pot sat in front of me, innocent as any other plant. I spread my arms wide, trying to be dramatic—*just like Cor, when he tried to get the Hiraches to attack him instead of me. No, stop thinking about that.*

I glared at the plant. *You don't exist.*

The potted plant dissolved, like a CG vampire struck by sunlight in a low-budget movie. Some of the observers gasped as it disappeared. The soil and pot all dissolved—

I managed to rein my skill in before I did structural damage to the roof. Some of the ceramic pot remained, maybe a wobbly half-inch of the very base.

Concentrate, Kate, I told myself, turning to the next plant. A fern of some sort, with deep-green fronds that waved in the light, warm breeze of the morning. I imagined that I was the eraser tool of a graphics program, and I unmade the feathery leaves from the top of the plant all the way to the potting soil at the base of its stems.

I let out the breath I'd been holding, a slow sigh of relief. *It's going fine. Just don't put any holes in the roof.*

"She's sending those things across the gap." The hesitant voice of the lizard-woman behind me almost made me flinch. "She's transporting them without worldwalking herself, that's all."

"No, the human ability allows her to destroy the plants entirely." That was Misora's voice. *Destroy.* She'd said it matter-of-factly, but it still made my skin crawl.

"It's simple elimination of material."

Shom? What was Shom doing here? Did she have news?

I glanced over to find Shom standing near the edge of Misora's group of guests, her expression as warm as bare stone. She wore what I thought of as her working clothes, a stark contrast to the finery of the other guests. She simply stared at me, with no hint of either delight at good news or the shock of bad. She just looked angry, and I couldn't ask about that in front of an audience.

Misora gave me a *keep going* wave of her hand. To her guests, she added, "We shouldn't distract Kjelgaard. She needs to concentrate."

"For the safety of us all," muttered the Shevern.

I took a deep breath and let it out. *Just get this done and I can take care of the rest in a minute.* I skipped any theatrics this time and simply walked a few steps over to the next plant, a small tree with spiky leaves that reminded me of a bonsai. It had that same, meticulously manicured look.

The people watching me were still chatting, though they'd lowered their voices enough that I couldn't catch the words.

What are they saying?

I concentrated on the plant and destroyed it, following the thin trunk down into the potting soil to erase the main roots as well. I moved on to the next one and tried not to think about anything but the job I had to do.

As I worked my way through the display, though, it brought me closer to the crowd around the edges of the roof. Not too close. It didn't escape my notice that the audience members pulled back anytime I walked too near to them.

But I could hear them speaking to each other.

Look at the human killing all these plants was what this seemed to boil down to. Look at what I could destroy with my skill.

I stood before my next target, a potted tree tall enough to wave its leaves above my head. Maybe I didn't have to destroy them all. I'd learned a little about pruning and the like from watching my father work while I'd been growing up. He'd deadheaded flowers, trimmed hedges, and trimmed back perennials, each in their season. Not to kill them, but to allow them to come back stronger.

The tree in front of me was immaculately tended, not a leaf out of place. It didn't need pruning.

But I had a demonstration to give.

I walked around the tree, considering it from all angles, and selected three branches that it could afford to lose and still look balanced. I concentrated more closely, reached for my *jeira*, and began to unmake the first branch.

It wasn't the most professional tree pruning job in all the worlds, but the tree survived it. I moved on to the next, a long, wooden planter filled with tall, flowering plants with long leaves, like irises. I could thin them, I decided. Remove the spent blooms and any plants that crowded their neighbors.

People still murmured to each other, but I'd made up my mind to ignore them.

The work went more slowly this way, and it took more concentration, but at the same time, it gave me more time to pay attention to what I was doing. The plant I was working on—trimming some of the wayward tendrils from a trellised vine with heart-shaped leaves—felt familiar. Something about it, about the way it resonated somehow with my skill, nagged at my mind. But when I looked back over the plants I'd 'pruned,' there was nothing quite like it. Maybe it was the same as one of the early ones that I'd destroyed?

It surprised me to see that I only had eight plants left.

The detail work I'd been doing sapped my strength faster than regular, broader use of my skill. The climbing sun had brought the familiar Aubello heat to bear. I wiped perspiration from my brow and got back to the task at hand.

A wide bowl planted with long, flowering grasses caught my attention a couple of plants later, something similar to the familiarity I'd felt with the vine plant. I stopped my work, halfway through thinning the individual, tiny bulbs in the pot. Among the thin, grass-like growth of the main plant, there was a little seedling of the heart-leaf vine. At some point, the two pots must have sat next to each other and a seed from the vine had dropped into this pot.

Intrigued, I bent down to get a closer look.

Something flew over my head, close enough to ruffle my hair. *What was that, a hummingbird?*

A gasp from the crowd and a faint clatter in the opposite direction brought me upright to see what was going on.

A second arrow arced toward me, too close to miss this time.

No! I reached for my *jeira*, my focus sluggish after the intense work for the demonstration. The arrow blurred in my sight, the metal searingly bright in the strong sunlight—then it shattered apart as my skill shredded it. A cloudlike puff of whatever it had been made of splashed across my chest before disappearing completely.

One second more and I would have been too late.

I looked back along the arrow's path. Like many others, the roof across the street held a cluster of potted trees, a miniature forest. A shadow moved among the leaves. People screamed. Someone started to bark commands.

With a flare of my skill, the vegetation dissolved like mist, revealing a shape I knew too well. A Hirach crouched among the half-destroyed pots and remaining saplings, a crossbow in their hand. The Hunter moved, lifting the weapon.

"An assassin," someone cried.

I reached out for the figure with my skill... *No, wait.* I unmade the crossbow, the metal and wood flowing apart like dust in a breeze. Then the Hirach faded away, too. For a moment, my breath caught in my chest. I'd wanted to...but I hadn't used my skill on the assassin directly. The Hunter had worldwalked away.

A hand closed over my shoulder and I screamed. Shom pulled me around toward the door leading downstairs.

"Get inside!" she ordered, pulling me in that direction.

All around me, guests were headed for the door, led by *Denet* Leratom. Bir lingered close by, his *zaret* drawn and ready. Misora stood beside him, also armed with her blade, scanning the surrounding rooftops with narrowed eyes.

"Right." I hurried back inside along with the others.

A couple of members of House Leratom ushered guests down the hallway to the stairs, but Shom pulled me aside.

"Kate, what are you doing here?" She kept her voice low, but the frustration in it was plain.

"I...I owed the Leratoms a favor," I said, taken aback by the question. *Giving a demonstration* seemed obvious enough, but I didn't really want to explain any further. My voice wavered from the adrenaline still coursing through my system. "What are *you* doing here?"

"You didn't come back to the garrison and your note didn't say why, so I went to check on you at your apartment. I was worried about you." Shom narrowed her eyes. "And now you're flaunting your skill in public and drawing assassins? That's what you're doing instead of staying safe?"

"I'm trying to get Cor back," I said. Bir and Misora finally came inside from the roof, their *zarets* banished. Misora took a quick look at the two of us and hurried past to take care of the rest of the guests with her *denet*. Bir stayed, though he stood back far enough to offer us the semblance of privacy.

"Pella is the one trying to get Cor back." Shom crossed her arms. "What is it you're trying to do over here? What kind of favor?"

"I'm trying to find Cor before the Hirach council does." I took a deep breath, trying to steady my voice. "Did you know the kith might kill him instead of letting themselves be caught with him? Going to the council might have been a death sentence."

"Going to the council is in line with the Truce, and the council has sworn to uphold the terms," Shom said, her words clipped and precise. "This kith is a group of feral Hunters, living in the wildlands. Predators. They don't make a practice of taking captives, much less releasing them. If there's any way to convince them to give Cor up, Pella will see it done."

She flicked her finger in a Thurei gesture of negation, as if she were throwing something away, and continued. "When Cor had nowhere else to go, Pella took him in because I asked her to give him a chance. I spoke up for both of you. And now you're trying to go behind her back? Is that what you're doing?"

Her statement had teeth in it and cut the way she'd meant it to, but I couldn't argue her points. "I'm just trying to find Cor as fast as possible. Erzi needed a healer and she promised to help us out if she could."

"And this Erzi couldn't find her own healer?"

"Most healers won't treat a Drammon," I said. "I told her I'd look around."

"Where did you...? A Drammon needed healing. Greta's involved in this, isn't she?" Shom's tone made me bite my tongue. I didn't want to get Greta into trouble, but Shom didn't wait for my confirmation. "What do you think is going to happen to her when she betrays her *tol* and helps you break the Truce? That's *if* the both of you don't get killed doing whatever it is you've got planned." She indicated Bir with a shrug of her shoulder. "Oh, and him. Are you going to take this Temarel pretty boy out into the wildlands with you, to save an exile from his House? What's his *denet* going to think of that? Or are you going to use them both and then walk away?"

I stepped back like I'd been slapped. "That's not what's happening. I'm not using them."

The sound of someone clearing his throat spun us both around. Bir bowed slightly to Shom, and though he kept his expression polite, it seemed clear that he didn't consider 'pretty boy' a compliment. "I've been honored to assist Katherine in whatever manner she requires. Coraven is her *dacha*, after all, and I defer to her concerns for his safety."

"What about your own?" she asked. She made a sharp motion toward his empty hands. "If you're headed out on a hunt, how's your bladework, Temarel?"

"Good enough, I hope," he said firmly. "Whatever skill I have, this is what it's for."

"Cor did whatever he could to keep me safe," I said. "I won't do any less for him."

"Pella's the one who's trying to get him out safe." Shom shook her head, using the human gesture so there would be no mistaking her meaning. "Kate! Be smart for once. Running yourself and everyone around you headlong into danger for the sake of your whim isn't noble. You haven't changed at all."

She faded away almost before she'd finished speaking, slipping across the gap to get away from me, just like the assassin had.

I squeezed my eyes shut and took a shuddering breath.

Bir touched my shoulder. "She's wrong, Kate. It's an honor to help you, and Greta made you that offer freely as well. You're not putting anyone unwitting into danger."

I did my best to smile. "Thanks. I do think we're Cor's best chance." Even if it did put us at risk. Shom wasn't wrong about that part.

But I didn't see any option that was certain or safe.

With a more genuine smile than I'd managed, Bir steered me toward the stairs. "Let's take leave of our hosts and continue with the plan, then. What do you think?"

The guests, including the Shevern, had left by the time we found Misora. She renewed her offers of hospitality, embarrassed that such an attempt had been made during an event she'd arranged. The peacekeepers, she said, were working even now to determine what they could from whatever slipwake the Hunter might have left as he'd fled, but it wasn't likely to give me any clues to Cor's current whereabouts.

For that, I needed the Wild Market.

Bir and I made our goodbyes as quickly as we could and slipped back across the gap to Earth.

CHAPTER TWENTY-SIX

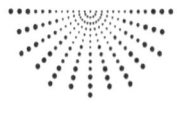

KATE

While Bir waited in my living room, I dressed as best I could guess was appropriate for a Wild Market. Jeans and sneakers would work for running if I needed to, and a long-sleeved shirt and a hooded sweatshirt in case it was cold. I still hadn't replaced my coat since Tharkesh had slashed the back of it—and the back of me—open with his claws.

Unfortunately, I didn't have anything that would make me look fierce, either.

I always have my skill, I reminded myself as I went back out to the living room to join Bir, who took us to Erzi's desert.

The cactus-equivalents and odd rock formations shimmered in the heat rising from the baked soil and the dark entry shaft to Erzi's home yawned before me.

She only attacked last time because she was delirious, I reminded myself.

Well, given a choice between venturing down there or staying up in the oppressive heat, I started down the ladder into the earth. Bir followed.

We found Greta and Erzi waiting for us. Greta had abandoned her peacekeeper uniform in favor of a patchwork jacket in browns and tans buttoned up to her neck and subtly striped trousers over brown boots. Camouflage, head to toe.

Erzi had similar clothes, plus a knapsack slung over one shoulder. The bones of her face and hands remained too prominent, and fatigue shaded her eyes. Nevertheless, she waved us closer when we entered.

"Prompt. Good. I like that." Erzi looked us over. "Many at the market will be Hunters, but not all. Stick close to us. Kjelgaard, try not to show off your skill."

"Why not?" The point of the Wild Market, as I understood it, was to hold it outside of the Truce, where using one's skill to threaten or harm another was forbidden. Hunters would be free to use their abilities if they wanted. How was I supposed to defend myself?

"Hunters out for status like rarity and a challenge," Greta explained. "As a human worldwalker, you're already rare."

"I don't expect trouble," Erzi added. "We tend to act as council for ourselves, but try not to draw more attention to yourself than necessary."

"All right," I said. If I had to use it, my skill would still be an option. Drawing attention to myself only counted for so much. In any case, Greta, Erzi, and Bir would all be with me, and they were each threats on their own merits.

"Good," Erzi said, passing something to Greta. "Here, Scruff. You take us to Erramire. Ready, everyone?"

Bir's eyes narrowed at the exchange, but then he grinned, broad and guileless. "'Scruff'? Aren't children's nicknames the worst? If you never hear what my cousins called me in the training circle when I was but knee-high, I'll die happy. Greta, do you happen to know where, exactly, the market is that you're taking us to?"

Erzi answered with a flash of teeth that didn't look much like a smile, pointing to the small object in Greta's hand. It looked a lot like a shark tooth, only made of stone. "It's a token to Osembri. She's the anchor for this market."

"I'd expected *you* would take us, as we agreed," Bir said, his shoulders still tense. Not curiosity, then, but distrust.

Erzi huffed a breath and grimaced. "Worldwalking...is yet beyond me. The fade worked on my *jeira* as it did my strength and I'm not yet recovered. Satisfied?"

Nalya had said that something remained from Erzi's fever. That must have been it.

Never short on bows, Bir offered a polite one. "Thank you for the explanation, Erzi. I admit freely, I'm jumpy."

Erzi blinked her large eyes and when she opened them again, she stared at me, not him. "Don't be jumpy. We don't need a brawl."

"Of course," I murmured, though it seemed we weren't the only ones on edge.

Token in hand, Greta worldwalked us all to Erramire.

I'd been to a local craft fair or two when I'd been little, when my family used to do those kinds of normal things together. Some part of me had expected an event like that—rows of stalls, tables of merchandise, the smell of fried foods served on sticks. Maybe further along the horror scale since most of the attendees would have sharp teeth and lethal skills.

Even before I opened my eyes, I registered the roar in the air. Next, a chilly dampness that prickled against my skin. I shivered, dropping Bir's and Greta's hands so I could wrap my arms around myself.

Then I opened my eyes.

About ten feet in front of us coiled a creature that my human mind immediately labeled as a dragon: long, wingless, serpentine body as big around as a saltwater crocodile with maroon scales that gleamed in the moonlight, three sets of lizard-like legs and a head like an iguana, but sharper and more predatory. Or maybe that was just my personal bias since the head was bigger than a draft horse's and could probably bite me in half.

Erzi walked boldly up to the dragon and folded both of her hands together over her own chest in a formal gesture. In Kuyen's common tongue, she said, "Osembri, good evening."

The creature, Osembri, brought her head forward like she intended to sniff Erzi. When she opened her mouth, she displayed rows of triangular, serrated teeth and a slender, red tongue.

"Erzi. You've been missed," she said, her accent slipping over the consonants in a way that made it difficult for me to catch all the words, especially above the ever-present, low roar in the background.

"I'm back now." The Drammon hitched the pack over her shoulder. "Hopefully, people still need what they need."

"Perhaps even more so," Osembri answered. "Some of your ingredients have been in short supply."

The dragon didn't speak to the rest of us directly, though I saw her hooded eyes make note of each of us in turn. It didn't seem like she was about to eat us. I relaxed, just enough to look around.

Mist billowed in shredded curtains around us, making details harder to pick out in the moonlight, but I saw enough to tell that the roar came from waterfalls, a broad cascade above and below us. We stood on an island of mossy stone big enough to park a couple of semi-trucks side by side. It was one of many, part of a massive, naturally terraced cliff face, as if a giant's stone stairway had crumbled and someone had dumped Niagara Falls' waterflow over it.

This seemed like a terrible place for a market. Everything must have been dripping wet and ruined.

Nevertheless, points of light flickered across the islands like constellations of candle flames. The nearest, on the other end of the island we stood on, came from a wide bowl filled with fire. Silhouettes gathered around it.

Judging by the lights, the market spread across many of these islands. The visitors clustered around these bowl lamps, farther than the mist and darkness would allow me to see.

Erzi ended her chat with the dragon and came back to us and beckoned us to follow her to the dark edge of the island, where water thundered past. I watched my footing carefully, keeping to patches of a tough, grassy plant that seemed to grow straight up from the stone. I did not want to slip.

"Don't speak of the Hunterslayer here," Erzi said, looking at each of us, even her sister, a fellow Hunter. "Or councils. Let me ask. Be quiet, as much as you can be."

When Erzi had our agreement, she led us to the lip of rock at the end of the island. The gap between this one and the next spanned a good ten feet across, almost as wide as a lane on the freeway. There were steppingstones, of sorts—rough blocks of stone like molars in a rotting jaw. Water surged between them, pouring over the edge of the waterfall to crash into the roiling depths two stories below.

Erzi walked out onto the steppingstones, as nimble as a hopscotch player. She was halfway across by the time Greta nudged Bir and me.

"Who's next?" she asked.

Bir stepped forward as his answer, moving from stone to stone a good deal more slowly and carefully than Erzi had.

All three of us—Bir, Greta, and I—had taken turns worldwalking scant minutes ago. If we missed our footing, we could try escaping across the gap to save ourselves the fall, but making two trips close together could be brutal. Pushing the time a little could cause headaches and muscle pain. Pushing too far…I wasn't sure what it would do. My friends had never told me.

I hoped I wouldn't get to find out.

Taking a deep breath, I stepped out onto the first rock, grateful for the grippy rubber soles of my tennis shoes.

The broad first stone gave me a bit of reassurance, but I could tell these weren't deliberately placed stones, but natural high points in the rocky bed of the watercourse. They ranged in shape and size, spaced irregularly apart. Drifting spray made them all slick with water and my foot slid just a little on the next stone. My heartbeat skyrocketed.

Bir and the others at least had good eyesight in the dark, unlike me.

As I hesitated, Greta spoke up from behind me. "Take courage. You've someone waiting at the end."

Without thinking, I looked to the far side, where Erzi and Bir stood, but I didn't think she meant them. Greta had gotten involved in this to save her sister. She meant this would get me closer to saving Cor.

The next stone was a close one and I made it with no problem. The one after that would require a jump and it was almost as flat as a floor tile. With all the dampness , it would be slick. I hopped as conservatively as I could, trying to come down with my foot solidly planted. I slid a little, unable to catch my balance, and flung myself forward to the next stone. The tread on my shoe caught firmly, but the small stone couldn't support both feet. I jumped to the next, pushed forward by the same momentum, and then Bir's hand was reaching for mine.

When I caught his hand, he yanked me the last few feet across, steadying us both on the solid stone of the next island.

I squeezed his wrist, a little shaky. "Thanks."

"It's purely self-interest," he murmured, offering half a smile. "I'd rather not be left here alone, if you please."

Greta managed the crossing with no drama and far more grace, then her sister led us over to the closest fire.

Of the four figures clustered around it, the only one I would have pegged immediately as a Hunter had a long muzzle like a hunting dog and a tall, rangy build emphasized by the long, brown duster coat he wore. Another person looked nearly human, except for their all-black eyes and pale blue skin, barely visible beneath the layers of fur they wore wrapped around them. The smallest two people, so similar they could be twins, stood scarcely four feet tall. They wore loose green robes and had stockier proportions similar to a human child's, but with incongruously large, blocky heads.

Before the twins lay a collection of whistles, spread out on a black cloth—wood, metal, and other materials I couldn't identify. They ranged from the size of my littlest finger to one the twins could use as a walking stick. The blue person leaned down to examine them as one twin compared two brass models side by side.

The other twin smiled at us as we moved into the fire's surprisingly wide radius of warmth.

The grin opened the man's mouth like a snake's, as if he might be able to unhinge his whole jaw and swallow something larger than himself.

"Erzi!" He greeted her in a light, almost singing voice. "Tell me you have some blazebird bones! Worthless as lures, but I have a concert piper on Aliopay who would sell his molars for a flashing flageolet."

"Not today, Mabran," Erzi said, padding over to crouch next to him. "But if you want to buy some next time, I'll keep an eye out for them."

The hound-faced man moved aside to make room for her beside the merchant without looking up from the wares. Greta, Bir, and I remained as out of the way as we could and still be within the fire's warmth. The pervasive mist didn't seem to reach us there, as if the bubble of light created a barrier around us.

"Here to buy, then?" the small man asked, running nimble fingers over a row of tiny whistles. "I do have a bird flute or two, if you need the help."

"Not tonight. I'm on a different trail." Erzi kept talking, but I tuned her out. Her voice got in the way of the music that tickled at my ear. I cocked my head, trying to hear the melody.

Bir made it two steps before I noticed, a third before I put things together and grabbed his arm. He blinked at me, his amber eyes unfocused.

Greta glared past me. "Knock it off."

The other merchant, standing next to the blue man, pulled the whistle from his lips and held it up. It had the same creamy white color as bone. He nudged his customer and said something in a language I didn't understand. He added, in Kuyene, "I told him there's a tune for everything."

Bir shook his head sharply, his expression still dazed.

"Is that for hunting Thureis?" I suppressed a shiver, though the skillwork fire had banished much of the clamminess from my clothes.

"Not especially." The merchant smiled his unsettling smile. "It appeals to more than just Houselings."

The blue man murmured a comment in the same liquid-sounding language, then added his own heavily accented Kuyene, "Too distant of home."

Before I could puzzle out that translation, the merchant steered the conversation back to me. "Say rather that I just have an ear for what people want to hear. I bet I have a whistle that can play a song you'll never forget. Might be handy."

"No, thanks," I said. Bir didn't seem inclined to wander off any longer, so I let his arm go. "Wait, can you lure anyone to you with something like that?"

If I had that whistle, could I make the Hiraches come to me? Or even Cor?

"You have to be good at it, as with any instrument." That impossible smile grew even wider. The little man had needle-like teeth no as thin and curving as eyelashes, thousands of them. "I do offer my services if you have someone in mind."

"Not tonight," Erzi said firmly, yanking our attention back to her. The twin with whom she'd been speaking held a handful of bamboo-like plant stems and beckoned his counterpart over to inspect them. Erzi pointed to another fire in the middle distance, two or three islands away. The mist made it hard to tell. "This way."

As soon as we stepped out of the firelight, the damp chill closed back in.

Bir walked beside me, following the Drammon sisters.

"Thank you," he murmured.

"I'd prefer it if you don't get eaten," I said, trying to keep an eye on my footing over the uneven stone, moss, and clumps of leafier vegetation.

"Me, too."

We reached the edge of the island, where the lip of rock dipped into a stretch of rushing water the width of a city street. It continued immediately over the edge, the plunging drop masked by drifting spray. I wiped beads of water off my brow.

The next island held more fires, more silhouettes.

"How do we get over there?" I asked.

"We walk." Erzi stepped onto the water. Onto rock, just an inch or two beneath the shining surface. "Careful, there are deeper places. And it's slippery."

We crossed in a close single file, as careful as Erzi had suggested.

My shoes were soaked in seconds, numbing my feet, but the waterfall spray was well on its way to soaking the rest of me by this point.

On the opposite side, Erzi paused as a hard shudder ran through her. The shaggy, camouflage fur on her head and neck dripped water down the collar of her wet patchwork coat.

"Who puts a market somewhere like this?" I muttered, balling my hands in my sweatshirt pockets.

"The wildlands aren't for the weak, human." Erzi growled. Greta reached out to touch her shoulder, but her sister struck out across the island again, pulling us along with her like a tour guide. I kept my comments to myself.

We passed the next few fires, the merchants and customers clustered around them glancing our way as we hurried along. People passed us in the misty darkness between the fires as well, on their own routes from merchant to merchant. Eyes gleamed in the dark and sometimes I spotted the flash of fangs or the profile of a predatory muzzle.

A narrow, deep channel of water separated this island from the next, a short enough distance for a nerve-wracking leap. Greta caught my outflung hand to steady me on the opposite side.

"This one," Erzi said, starting toward the nearest circle of firelight. It held a small crowd, large enough that the outer ring of customers stood out in the cold.

Some of these Hunters were types I recognized. Two of the small, lizard-like Viseni, bundled in layers of thick-spun robes and necklaces made of large, dull white carved beads. Another resembled the short, brown-furred individual who had stolen Cor's money in the market, though this one had the pale frost of age around his muzzle, and he was nearly as tall as I was. One I recognized from the *Hunter Survey* book Cor had shown me, a tall person with broad shoulders but a clearly feminine form under her long, belted coat. Mist droplets dappled her smooth, greenish skin and her breath rasped in her throat.

"What kind of merchant is this?" I had to ask Greta as Erzi pushed forward into the crowd and the rest of us hung back on the edges, heedless of the wet.

"The apothecary," Greta whispered back. "She trades with Hiraches, on and off."

With a second, closer look, I could pick out a handful of those gathered around who might have had illnesses they'd come to treat. I started to shuffle around to the other side of the group, upwind. Just in case. I'd seen enough of the fade to be leery. Fortunately, the crowd was thinner there, since it was colder. Greta and Bir followed.

The apothecary herself stood near the fire bowl, a tall woman with a mop of curly, black hair and thin, stick-like limbs, flanked by two wooden cabinets, each the size of a shallow mini fridge. When she opened them, I saw they were gridded into small compartments. Glass bottles inside caught the flickers of firelight.

She carried out most of her conversation in Kuyene, doling out cough oils and fever syrups, memory cures and strength powders. Erzi slipped through the crowd toward the front.

"One of my finest suppliers and a satisfied customer!" The apothecary beckoned Erzi closer. "Erzi can tell you how successful my wares are."

"I'm back, Betts," Erzi said diplomatically. Perhaps she had tried some of Betts' cures before seeing Nalya. "That speaks for itself. I brought you more ingredients." She swung the bag off her shoulder and pulled open the flap to display the contents. When Betts' eyes widened, Erzi tucked the bag next to the apothecary's cabinets. Erzi nudged the door open and plucked out a slender, cork-stoppered bottle of sparkling, purple fluid and held it up before the crowd.

"This helped with the chills. And Betts' cough remedy is among the best."

Several customers pushed forward.

"Do they even work?" I muttered, mostly to myself.

"They work," Greta replied, equally quiet. "Betts is very good. They just weren't enough to cure the fade."

"But are we here to sell things, or…"

"Patience," Greta said simply.

As I stood there and shivered, customers drifted away with their purchases. The crowd thinned until the three of us could edge our way into the welcome warmth of the skillwork fire.

Betts spread her skinny arms out in a questioning gesture. "Are you giving up your solo practice, Erzi? Who have you brought?"

Erzi tapped the cabinet door shut with her foot. "I'm here to pay a favor. I'm looking for some Hiraches, the Akevad kith. Have they brought you any supplies lately?"

"Haven't been here to sell for some time," Betts said. My heart sank. "Buying, on the other hand… They've been doing that for a while, but I haven't seen any of them in the last couple of days. I heard they ran into trouble on a hunt."

"Do you know where to find them?" I asked.

The apothecary turned to look at me. She had a triangular face, with a broad brow, narrow lips, and a sharp chin. She frowned, the expression dramatic on her winkled face. "Who are you?"

"I'm the one Erzi owes a favor to," I said, reluctant to share my name here. "The Hiraches kidnapped someone important to me and I need to get him back. Do you know where to find them?"

"I might," she said, giving me an appraising look. "You four? Against a nest of Greater Hunters? I might be doing you a favor if I *don't* tell you." She held up a twig-fingered hand when I would have objected. "Even if it's not a favor, if I start pointing revenge parties after my customers and suppliers, I won't have a place at the Wild Market much longer."

"Please," I said, my hands clenched into fists so tightly that my fingernails dug into my palms. "I grew up on a world with no Truce and Coraven protected me for years. I'm stronger than I look and I'm not going to turn my back on him just because it's dangerous. Please. He made a vow that placed his life in my hands and I will honor it, whether you help me or not." I cleared my throat. "It would be easier with your help, though."

Betts pointed at Bir. "Your Coraven is a Thurei, like this one? That's the vow you're talking about?"

"I'm his *dacha*, yes," I said, surprised at myself.

"You might have said," she muttered, like I should have known exactly which snippets of Kuyene culture she knew. "I'll bring you to the edge of the Akevad kith's claimed land, but I have no intent on helping set up an ambush. Fair's fair. I do business with them."

"That's a deal," I said.

The apothecary waved her hands at the few customers hanging around at the edge of her firelight. "Market's over for me, fellows. Look for me at the next one if you have need or write if it can't wait and we'll work something out." She pointed at Erzi. "Douse the fire, would you?"

Erzi crouched down next to the ceramic bowl of fire and picked it up. Despite the fact that it warmed a wide area, the bowl didn't seem to be hot. When Erzi traced the fingers of one hand over the surface, the flames flickered and dimmed. She narrowed her eyes and repeated the movement to no effect. Greta took it from her and after a moment, the fire finally died.

The air cooled immediately and mist rolled in around us.

Bir lowered his voice to ask me, "What do you plan do to once we get there?"

"Hopefully they'll be smart and give him back," I whispered.

"And if not?" he pressed.

I shrugged shivering fingers. "Then you should get yourself back to somewhere safe. But I'm bringing Cor home."

Bir grinned, though I knew him well enough to see the worry underneath. "You keep trying to get rid of me, Kjelgaard. I'm considering taking offense."

Meanwhile, Betts bent her long body down to reach a set of latches along the doors of her potion cabinets and snapped them closed. Then she tugged out a pair of leather straps on each one that I hadn't noticed. She slung one cabinet over her shoulders like a backpack, to the subtle sound of many small bottles rattling in their individual compartments. The cabinet sat on her back like a deck of cards on a pencil. Then she hoisted the other cabinet and shouldered the straps so that it sat against her thin chest, balancing the weight on her back.

She held out her hands. "Well?"

We gathered quickly and Betts pulled us back to Kuyen.

CHAPTER TWENTY-SEVEN

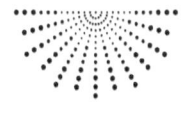

KATE

The ground softened beneath my feet and the chilly air carried a resinous scent like pines. I opened my eyes to find us in the middle of a forest, with both broadleaf and coniferous trees arching above to filter the sunlight into green-tinted shadows.

In front of us stretched a high wall of close-packed, thorny branches, broken only by a gate made of rough-hewn planks.

The gate stood open.

Erzi and Greta both lifted their heads and sniffed the air, their senses apparently keener than mine.

"That shouldn't be ajar." Betts frowned at the open gate. She thumped a bony hand on the cabinet she carried, raising a racket.

The Drammon sisters flinched at the noise. A flicker of movement to my left drew my attention to Bir and the nearly transparent *zaret* he held ready. I focused my attention on my own *jeira*, ready to unleash my skill.

But nothing around us stirred. No one came to the gate.

Dread crept down my spine. Had the council beaten us here?

Was Cor already dead?

I reached into my purse, digging out one of my Summons. When I sent it, the Summons traveled the typical couple of feet away and then disappeared, slipping away to its destination. Just inside the gates, or on another world, I couldn't tell, but at least Cor was alive.

Betts drummed her fingers on the cabinet strapped in front of her, an idle motion like she might as well have been standing at a bus stop. "Hmph. If I have to wait around before I worldwalk again, I'd rather wait inside."

She strode past us all on long legs and disappeared through the gate. The Drammons followed, as stealthy and alert as prowling cats. Bir and I took up the rear.

Inside the wall, we found a village. A couple dozen small, thatched houses crouched among the trees. It didn't look as if any of the residents had cleared the forest of anything but undergrowth when they'd made their settlement.

There were no residents, though. Nothing stirred, though it seemed to me that we all remained on alert, except maybe Betts. The stick-and-mud huts had no windows. Some of the doors hung open, revealing nothing but shadows.

"Was this the Hirach council's work? Is that why they're gone?" My voice sounded too loud in my ears. I whirled to Bir, startling him. He was as twitchy as I was. "Cor could be home already."

"You sent a Summons," he said. "If Cor gets it and can send a reply—or someone can reply for him—we'll know soon. Until then, I think we should see what we can find out here."

He didn't mention that we had no other leads. The kith could have slipped anywhere from here.

"I'm only here as a guide," Betts said, unloading her cabinets onto the ground so she could use one as a seat, folding her long, thin body to perch atop it. "I'll holler if I see anything move."

"Split up, then," Erzi said, dividing the group with a gesture. Bir and me, Erzi and Greta.

Arranged around a central fire pit, the huts were small and simple, a single chamber with stick-and-mud walls and roofs thatched with conifer branches. They were bare, some in better repair than others.

"This isn't what I imagined," I murmured, though what I'd pictured made little sense now. I'd envisioned Cor held in something more like a castle dungeon somewhere. Stone walls and iron bars, a place he had no chance of escaping. In comparison, these structures seemed flimsy.

Then again, even the strongest stone walls wouldn't have held a worldwalker. The Hiraches had used something else to keep Cor from slipping away.

"I'm not the student of Hunters Cor is, but I believe Hiraches move every so often." Bir spoke calmly enough, but he lashed a foot out to knock a hole in one of the walls. I wondered if he was imagining the same escape scenarios I was. "Most Hunters who live outside the Truce do, I think. Either they claim portions of land lightly, like this village, and change their location as they need to, or they pick a single, small spot and claim it more thoroughly, like Erzi and her underground home. Claiming a larger space takes a larger group. A larger group pushes naturally toward cooperation, toward relying on others, toward the Truce." He stopped and flashed me a sardonic grin, our surroundings ignored for a moment. "Not that you asked for a lecture in Kuyene social history."

"Mostly, I'm trying to concentrate on the fact that Cor's still alive," I admitted.

We completed our share of the sweep in silence.

When we gathered back at the central ring of ashes, Greta gave us a short rundown on what they'd discovered.

"They left their dead. Fresh graves, but no old ones. And this place feels…strange." Greta looked to her sister for confirmation.

Erzi curled her lips back in a silent, frustrated snarl. "The Hiraches moved on. Not a battle, I think. No sign of violence, but some of the homes smelled like illness." She turned her round face to me. "A Thurei was among them as well. I caught a hint of that."

My heart kicked against my ribs and I couldn't help but glance around the village, even though I knew it was empty. *He must be close.*

"I agree with Greta." Betts hopped off the cabinet she'd been using as a perch and began the awkward, animated-scarecrow process of loading her burdens back up. "There's something strange here that makes me uncomfortable. Grates on my senses, as it were. It's time for me to go. Good luck."

With that brusque goodbye, she faded away.

"Now what do we do?" I asked, around a growing feeling of hopelessness.

"We see if there's way to follow." Greta took the question seriously. She returned to the gate, the rest of us trailing behind her.

Crouching down beside the path on the way out of the village, the two Drammons examined the ground. I glanced at Bir and he just moved his hand in a slight shrug.

The sisters stood, regarding me with their unnervingly steady stares. Greta said, "I think they went out on foot instead of worldwalking. The scent on the path is the freshest. Many Hiraches came this way."

"Why would they travel on foot?" Bir asked, a frown on his narrow face. "If they fled, why not slip away?"

"They left few belongings behind," Greta pointed out. "If they fled, they had time to pack. Maybe time enough to walk their way to a new hiding place."

That made sense. Worldwalking with more than a handful of

people together took a great deal of effort and going to an anchor point would have drawn the attention of other travelers. Not a safe choice for a kith being hunted by other Hunters. But slipping from world to world without a carefully chosen landing place could have landed them in even more dangerous territory, maybe even scattered the group across the wilds.

As arrogant as Tharkesh had been, I could imagine that a large group of Hiraches rarely needed to flee en masse.

"These are the wildlands," Erzi said. "The only way to travel them reliably is on foot."

"As they get farther away from their claimed land, the wilds will continue to shift," Greta added. "It will be harder to track them the longer they're gone."

"Then we should go now," I said, hoping that saying so would make it happen. Greta barely knew Cor and Erzi had never met him. The fear that they would simply call their end of the bargain finished and walk away filled me with dread. I would have to return to the garrison with my tail tucked between my legs and hope that the council found Cor alive.

Bir cleared his throat. "We're going to track a Hirach kith through the wilds? Just the four of us?"

Greta narrowed her dark eyes. "Would you like to Summon your House?"

Bir took a deep breath and released it, folding forward into a bow as he did so, as if formal manners were armor he'd only just remembered to don. Straightening, he said, "They wouldn't come, unfortunately. We'd best simply move forward with all speed."

"I heard they teach Houselings to fight under your roof." Erzi bared her sharp teeth, but somehow, it managed to look more like a laugh than a snarl.

"There's light left in the day," Greta said. "Kjelgaard, they have been gone a full day, maybe more. We can't afford to let them get any more of a head start on us. I make no promise that we can find them as the trail lies now, but without knowing where they were headed, all we can do is follow."

"Isn't the Hirach council looking for him, too? Are we just following on their heels?" If we were tagging along behind the council, then our effort was wasted. The council would find the Akevad kith first and Cor could be dead before we reached him.

"There are different ways to search. I think they were not at this place long." She lifted her hand and shrugged her fingers like a Thurei, the gesture over-careful. "This is where they last contacted Betts. If we're lucky, the council started at an even earlier camp and must catch up to us."

"Right," I said. If we weren't lucky… "Then let's do this. We'd better go."

"And quickly." Erzi flashed another grin.

I agreed. It still surprised me when Greta and Erzi set off at a trot. Bir was startled, too, and both of us hurried to catch up.

The pathway out of the gate faded into what, to me, looked like trackless forest almost immediately. We didn't jog far, as the sisters had to slow down to double-check their sense of the trail.

But after that momentary lull, I gathered that Greta was making a point. She pushed us relentlessly, jogging for short stretches and walking as quickly as we could across the rough terrain when the faster pace wasn't possible. She glared at Bir and me for any extra chat between the two of us and soon I needed my breath for travel, anyway.

Back on Earth, I didn't have a car—I used my bike and the bus to get around San Jose—so I was a little surprised to find that I ranked on the lower end of stamina for the group. None of us could keep up with Greta, but Bir came close. Erzi managed it for a while, but as the afternoon dragged on, her breath began to rasp in her throat and it reminded me that *healing* and *recovery* weren't the same. I doubted Erzi had had enough time and rest to be back to full strength, if that were even possible with the aftereffects of the fade.

I did what little I could to help, using my skill to carve a way through thick brush and downed trees as we followed the Hiraches' track, but I couldn't banish any miles.

Between the two of them, the sisters assured us they could still detect a trail, though at times we had to stop and wait while they cast back and forth across the landscape to pick it up again. We left the forest behind after the first hour or so, passing into a marshy valley, and eventually crossed a stream, burying our feet to the ankles in mud. Bir, still in his formal House attire, didn't utter a word of complaint, though he did shuck out of his leather coat and bundle it under his arm.

Then we headed back up the other side of the valley, as quick as we could manage.

The sun inched its way down toward the horizon, stretching our shadows out behind us as we reached a ridge. When we got to the crest, Greta stopped us.

"Wait here," she said, then she continued over the rocky ground. Erzi sank into a crouch, every line of her betraying fatigue. Bir settled next to her, cross-legged on the ground, though he was barely winded. I paced, even though I was sure I had a blister forming on my left heel.

I had about another hour and then I needed to be back on Earth. The Hiraches of the council had no such limitations.

"Erzi, what happens when the sun goes down?" I asked, keeping my voice down.

She'd caught her breath somewhat, though she still had a haggard quality about her. "We stay so we will not shift away from their trail. The space between us and the kith will keep changing, but the only way to stop that is to catch up." She turned to Bir. "It's more dangerous after dark, Houseling. Will you stay?"

Bir scrubbed a hand over his face, smearing dust and sweat. "There may be a few cousins of mine who would come, if they knew we faced a fight next."

"Fighting Thureis." She gave him a quick flash of her snarl-laugh.

"How will we find you?" I asked. "Do you have a token we can use?"

I wouldn't be able to worldwalk back to this exact spot. That was the difference between claimed lands and the wilds. The landmarks here would shift and change. If I pictured this ridge when the sun set on San Jose tomorrow, it might be miles away from the sisters, or gone entirely, and I would end up who-knew-where. Only claimed land was stable enough to count on.

With a personal token, on the other hand, I could slip across to the exact spot of the person who'd made it, just like the one Cor had given me before we'd set out into the wilds last time. If I hadn't lost it, finding Cor would never have been a problem.

"Personal token?" Erzi wrinkled her nose. "No chance."

"Oh, wait! Here." I dug in my purse for Shom's compass and handed half of the silvered shell to Bir. It wasn't quite as good as a personal token, but it would help us find each other if we were separated.

I explained how to activate the skillwork, but my demonstration was cut short by Greta's return.

She pointed back over the ridge. "The Hiraches are camped on the other side, about halfway down the slope."

"They're here?" I whispered, adrenaline kicking my heartbeat into a higher gear. Bir and Erzi both climbed to their feet.

Erzi, though, reached her hand out to her sister. She blinked at me, her red-rimmed eyes kind. "All honor to your hunt, Kjelgaard."

"Wait, what?" I asked, too puzzled to make sense of it for a moment.

Then the sisters slipped away, dissolving into the waning afternoon air.

Bir and I looked at each other, stunned.

"They just left," I said because I needed to hear it out loud. "She said…Greta said she'd help me find him." But no more than that. She hadn't promised to fight for him. I added, reluctantly, "But not that she'd help me get him back."

Bir dusted off his hands, shook out his coat, and put it on.

"I'm here to help you get him back," he said. "Cor is my kin, no matter what anyone says, and if I'd paid that debt properly growing up, maybe it wouldn't have come to this."

We found an outcropping of stone to shelter behind as we peered over the edge of the ridge. The other side of the slope, like the one we'd just climbed, was a steep but walkable jumble of rocks and dirt, punctuated by the occasional twisted conifer holding on by sheer tenacity. There was no trail. From here, I couldn't see any sign of the Hiraches.

It would be a long hike down.

"Halfway," I whispered.

"It looks like there's decent amount of cover."

Bir pointed to a route that would get us at least a hundred feet or so from our current spot. In other words, as far as we could see from here. We could creep as close as possible, figure out where Cor was, hopefully get him free before too many Hunters converged on us.

I straightened up and leaned back against the boulder, trying to draw some psychological strength from its steadiness.

"We don't want cover. We want them to see us." The wide eyes of the audience at the demonstration wouldn't leave my mind.

"I know your skill is powerful, but I'm not a master with the *zaret*," Bir said. "There is a whole kith of Hunters down there and they have Cor. We can't fight them all."

He had his blade in hand already. The fingers of his free hand flicked over and over, a constant stream of refusal. "What's to stop them from killing him when they see us coming? Him, and then us?"

I had answered this one already.

"*I'm* what's going to stop them from killing Cor." I took a deep breath, then let it out. "I'm not their council, here to punish them. They can walk away from this alive for all I care. But if they kill Cor, I'll wipe this place down to bare dirt. And I need to make sure they know it."

Bir set his jaw, the line of his mouth as sharp as a sword's edge. I thought he would continue to argue with me, but he just stepped back and spun his blade, one-handed, in a circle. The transparent weapon glinted in the golden light of late afternoon. He tilted his free hand in the direction of the slope.

I thought he would follow me. If he didn't, there was nothing I could do about it, like the Drammon sisters.

I started to step out from around the outcropping of rock, then checked myself.

If you're going to do this, Kate, then do it. I concentrated on the boulders in front of me and dissolved them. The stone cleaved apart, the gap growing until it was wide enough for us to walk through. Rock crumbled to sand and then dust before disappearing entirely. I strode past and down the slope, Bir at my back.

I focused on the boulders, picking my way down the incline, clearing an area in front of and around us that would prevent any Hiraches from attacking us out of hiding.

I didn't know where Cor was, so I went slowly. It made sense that the Hiraches would hold a prisoner near the middle of the group, but I couldn't be sure. I couldn't simply strip everything to bare dirt as I'd so confidently told Bir. Instead, I had to select stones one by one and concentrate on them precisely. Anything else, I left alone. It looked as if I were clearing a wide roadway down the rocky slope.

What I hadn't taken into account was how exhausting it would be. Adrenaline thrummed under my skin, but that couldn't truly stand in for rest. This task matched the demonstration for painstaking accuracy, while stretching it over a greater volume than I'd ever exercised my skill on before.

When the first Hirach stepped out from cover up ahead of us, I had to bite back a sob of relief.

"The prey has arrived," he said, the common tongue rough in his deep voice. The Hirach was tall, even taller than Bir, broad-shouldered beneath his smoke-colored cloak. Somehow, he managed to loom, even when he stood downslope and twenty feet away. His snarl showed off the sharp, white teeth in his powerful jaws. He scanned the leveled area with hard eyes. "Do you think you can intimidate the Akevad kith?"

"Ask Tharkesh, who used to be your Finder, and the warriors who followed him," I said, proud of the courage in my voice. I destroyed the rock beside the Hirach, a boulder the size of a refrigerator. Another Hirach who was hiding behind it retreated farther back into cover. I trusted Bir, a couple of steps behind me, to keep an eye on my back. "I'm here for Coraven. Give him to me and I'll leave. Refuse and you will share his fate."

"You're not leaving," the Hirach said. He prowled forward, his pace deliberate. "You are going to fix everything for us."

So much for my courage. *We've got to be close—to Cor, or to whatever this Hunter cares about.*

Or they're close to us, closing in for an ambush among the rocks.

"Your own council is on your heels, sent by peacekeepers. Even if you worldwalked away right now, they'll hunt you until they find you." I pitched my voice to carry. *Someone, please listen.* "You broke the Truce. Don't make it worse now."

The irony didn't escape me, but what else could I do?

I took a gamble, reaching for my *jeira*. I left the advancing Hirach untouched but pushed back the boundary behind him. Too weary for the fine control I needed, I razed all of it down to bare soil. Five more feet. Then ten.

"You'd better know what you're doing," Bir growled from behind me.

"Enough, Kjelgaard," called another voice, higher in pitch. Hearing my name blew my hold on my skill. Another, slightly smaller Hirach leaped atop a boulder, visibly startled for a moment to find it sliced almost in half, right at the edge of the boundary I'd made. She recovered quickly and glanced at the first one. "Gozmal, enough. We'll do no better if they find us with her."

She turned to me. "Will you call off the Hunt if we let you take the Thurei?"

I caught a sharp breath at a hope so fierce, it hurt. The Hirach man, Gozmal, spoke before I could, looking past me, up toward the ridge.

"It's too late, Serkot."

Serkot, the one who'd tried to bargain with me, followed his gaze and snarled, then she ducked back down among the rocks.

"Nice try," I said, my voice unsteady. My heart had jumped into overdrive, but this was the oldest trick in the book.

"Kate," Bir said from behind me.

I whirled around to see more Hiraches pouring over the ridge, charging down the broad, straight path I'd left for them.

CHAPTER TWENTY-EIGHT

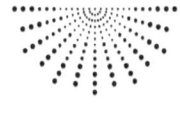

KATE

I started straight down the slope, but Bir caught my arm before I'd gone two steps.

"This way," he hissed, tugging me to the side, across the slope at a right angle to the path I'd carved. I sprinted beside him, and we made it to the shelter of the remaining boulders. Bir didn't stop when we were out of sight of the new group of Hiraches advancing downhill. Instead, he started heading downhill, too, parallel to the path.

"That's the council," Bir explained, keeping his voice down.

I'd guessed as much. I scrambled after him over a jumble of stone, trying to stay out of sight and not break an ankle at the same time.

"They don't want us," he continued, "but I think we're better off if we stay out of their way."

"The kith will kill him." *Not now. We were so close.*

"It's too late for that," Bir said. "Getting caught with a dead body isn't going to do them any good."

We were heading roughly in the direction Serkot had disappeared. She'd seemed willing to deal with us.

"What's to stop them all from worldwalking out of here?" I whispered back.

"Nothing. Don't slow down." He stepped sideways between a couple of boulders too tall to climb.

I followed, with difficulty. Thureis were *thin*.

Only now we were trapped in a ring of head-height rocks with no convenient gaps between them. Bir immediately leaned against one and laced his hands together in a stirrup. "Up and over. Give me a hand when you get up there."

"I can just—" I started, reaching for my *jeira*, even though I was tired.

"No, Hunters can sense that. If we go over, they'll only see us if they happen to glance this way. Trust me. Come on."

Bir boosted me high enough to get a good handhold and I clambered to the top. Turning around to offer him a hand, I saw a chaos of dark shapes streaming down the roadway I'd made, fanning out to dart among the rocks. A group of Hiraches waited, bunched up farther down slope. The kith, and they weren't escaping across the gap to another world.

Bir grabbed my hand and as I helped him up, something else caught my eye. On the top of the ridge, right next to where I'd created the first gap in the boulders, the bright white of a Scholar's robe stood out against the dark gray rock.

"I think we need to stay out of the way of the council, too," I said.

As we dashed across the top of the wide boulder, someone shouted among the Hunters on the path. I couldn't understand the Hirach language, but it seemed a safe bet that we'd been spotted. Bir cursed as we dropped back out of sight over the other side of the rock.

Bir and I ran as fast as we could, dodging and slipping over loose and jagged stones. A scraping sound behind us pulled us both around. Beside me, Bir's blade gleamed in his hand.

A Hirach readied itself to leap from a boulder ten feet away.

We're breaking the Truce, some part of me noted, but I reached out with my *jeira* anyway, desperate.

I'd targeted so much of the stone on the way down the slope.

The boulder beneath the Hirach's feet dissolved just as he'd started to launch himself at us. He slipped, flailed, and went down among the smaller stones headfirst.

We didn't wait to see if he got up again.

The route around the next outcrop brought us right into the middle of three more Hiraches. Two of them spun to face us, and the third remained crouched at the base of an overhanging rock shard.

The closest one snarled, bringing up clawed hands. I recognized the one standing next to her: Serkot. She snapped something in a quick word of their language. The first woman lowered her claws. The one on the ground didn't stir. I wasn't sure they were alive.

I kept my *jeira* ready, just in case. "Where's Cor—the Thurei? Let us take him and leave so the council won't find any of us here."

I didn't mention the Scholar. At this point, I had no idea if that would make things better or worse, but the growls and yells were growing in volume behind us.

Another Hirach appeared over the top of a nearby boulder. They'd come from the direction of the fighting. Judging by the instant defensive postures from the two Hirach women, I gathered that the newcomer was not one of their friends. This time, I'd had time to think about my options. Before the Hunter could jump down from the rock, I used my skill to bore straight down into the rock as deeply as I could quickly go. The Hirach plummeted like I'd stolen a manhole cover out from under him.

Serkot looked at me and hissed what I guessed was a curse and then pointed farther downhill and off to the right. "Back there. Tell him it's for the Mokklas. Prey would have run."

I didn't know what that meant, but I didn't stay to ask. Bir and I ran in the direction she'd sent us, past the Hirach who remained huddled on the ground.

Past the next pile of boulders, we found another group of Hunters. Five Hiraches, all sitting or lying down, though one struggled to his feet when he saw us, his posture weak and unsteady.

Cor lay curled on his side just beyond them, his hands tied together so thoroughly that I couldn't see his skin. Dried blood streaked his face and clothes. The sight stabbed straight through me as piercing as any *zaret* and I grabbed for Bir's arm before my knees could buckle.

Coran can't be dead.

"Kate!" Bir snapped.

My grasp was dragging down his sword arm and pulling him off-balance.

I forced myself to straighten up. Glaring at the Hirach blocking our way, I pointed at Cor. "We're just here for him. Let us pass."

I hadn't doubted our ability to finish the feeble Hirach off, but I hoped to leave without more bloodshed. Either way, I wasn't leaving without Cor.

And fast.

"You owe a debt." Bir lifted his blade, more defensive than threatening. "For the Mokklas."

The Hirach grunted, then shuffled aside, smothering a cough.

Bir and I quickly picked our way past the remaining Hiraches, who barely seemed to notice us, and knelt next to Cor. Bir's *zaret* disappeared.

Cor wore the filthy remnants of the human-style T-shirt and

jeans I'd last seen him in. Stained bandages circled his abdomen beneath the ripped black shirt. Blood and dirt covered his bare skin and more of the same had turned his bright orange hair into a matted mess. His head lolled as Bir gathered him up off the dirt.

I curled my hand over Bir's where he held Cor's shoulders, placing my other palm on the curve of Cor's cheek—*warm, he's breathing and warm*—and pulled us all away from the chaos in the wildlands and back to House Leratom.

To a healer.

The white walls of Nalya's atrium formed around us, but the arrival of Bir, Cor, and myself startled a gray-furred Lewrit man from his perch on a chair. He set down a book he'd been reading and joined us as I helped Bir stagger to his feet, balancing Cor in his arms.

"Kjelgaard, I gather," the Lewrit healer said, with only a quick glance at me.

I couldn't have answered anyway, my throat too tight with relief and too much adrenaline.

The healer directed his attention to his patient, pressing a bare palm to Cor's forehead and briefly closing his eyes. Opening them again, he said, "Let's get him to a room."

He kept up a running line of chatter as he ushered us where he wanted us. "I'm Ferno, by the way. And you are...? Ah, Temarel. Thank you. Yes, lay him here..."

I followed along, barely attending what he was saying. Cor hadn't opened his eyes, even when Bir laid him on the narrow bed. I remembered someone saying it would take a lot to keep a worldwalker captive, to keep Cor from simply slipping away.

The approach of Kuyen's sunset tugged at my bones, a threat I wished I could ignore. I would have to leave soon or be torn back to Earth when the way between our worlds closed.

For now, I ignored it and started to work at the knots on Cor's bound hands. The Hiraches had laced his fingers together and then wrapped strips of leather around them, all the way to his wrists. I guessed they had, at some point, been wary of his *zaret*, though he was far from able to use it right now.

"Please fetch some water and towels, Temarel," Ferno ordered, though he kept his voice gentle. "Do you need scissors for that, Kjelgaard? No? Good. Permit me a moment to see what I can…" He fell silent, his hand resting on Cor's forehead.

I unpicked the knots and unwound the bindings as quickly as I could, uncovering Cor's beautiful hands. The skin beneath was grimy and raw, especially around the knuckles. I uncurled his long fingers carefully. The shallow cut across his palm from when he'd chased the pickpocket was an angry red, infected.

"Kjelgarrd, will you help me with his clothes?" Ferno's voice startled me back to attention.

As we eased him out of his clothing, Cor stirred again, his expression sliding between anger and distress. His golden eyes fluttered open for a moment, but the vertical pupils were blown wide and he didn't seem to see me.

I'd been wrong in the wilds—Cor's skin wasn't warm, it was hot.

"What's wrong with him?" I asked, my voice stretched thin over the words. "Why isn't he waking up?"

Bir returned with the water and a couple of towels and I moved a small table over from the corner of the room to the bedside to accommodate it all.

"A number of things," Ferno said calmly, deftly cutting through the ragged bandages with a small pair of scissors. He revealed four parallel slashes across Cor's side, claw marks from a Hirach. Caked with blood, the skin around them was puffy and red there, too. "This, for one. And they dosed him with something nasty to keep him under."

Ferno caught my gaze with his. "He will be well again, don't worry."

"Can I stay?" I asked. The last time, Cor had been too badly wounded and I'd been so terrified that Havro had insisted I wait elsewhere.

"Until sundown," Ferno said. He took one towel and offered me the other. "I'll see to his wound. Will you tend to the rest of him? Tell me if there is any more injury. Temarel, will you stay?"

"I need to get back to the House," Bir said. When I looked at him in surprise, he added, "There are those at home who will want to know he's been found and is recovering."

"Of course," I murmured. Even if they didn't call themselves kin, Cor's sisters and his former teacher, at least, would want to know he would be okay.

"I can send news to Pella as well," he offered. "Your hands are busy."

I nodded, wiping the dirt and blood from Cor's face. Underneath, his skin had the flushed-but-pale look of a fever. "Thank you, Bir."

When I looked up again, he had slipped away.

I wasn't able to stay much longer, enough to wash Cor's face and his precious, ill-treated hands, then fetch another clean bowl of water for the healer. I slipped out of the room with the image of Ferno leaning over Cor's bedside, his hand resting on Cor's forehead burned into my mind.

"He'll be fine, he'll be fine, he'll be fine," I repeated to myself in the predawn darkness of my empty bedroom. *Everything's okay. He's safe.*

I climbed into bed fully clothed and curled around my pillow, crying with exhaustion and relief.

CHAPTER TWENTY-NINE

COR

I drifted awake on the familiar euphoria of a major healing. Opening my eyes, I found the expected white ceiling, though I didn't recognize the particulars of the small room. Not House Temarel or the garrison. Too fine, I guessed, for a merchant healer's.

Light came from a lamp hanging over the bed. The shuttered window had nothing but darkness beyond it. It was late but still before midnight.

No Kate, then. The healer's recent work blunted the edges of missing her. She would come in the morning.

The Hunters hadn't gotten her.

The thought floated away, unable to gain purchase. I remembered the Mokkla attack and arguing with Serkot about the Scholars, about working together. I remembered they'd forced more of the sleeping concoction in me anyway.

I lifted my hands, relieved to find them whole and free. I flexed my fingers. Summoned my *zaret* and let it go again before I accidentally scratched the plasterwork.

Where am I and how did I get here? I sat up and discovered myself in need of some clothes and a bath, though someone had washed the worst of the grime away. *In a hurry, then. But where's the healer?*

Muffled voices beyond the door gave me a good guess. A moment later, I had my answer.

A weary Lewrit man wearing healer's whites carried in a covered bowl and a glass of water. I'd never met him, but Misora, the *denet*-heir of House Leratom, followed, dressed in full formals. And then Shom, who held a bundle of what looked like pajamas.

"I hope you'll excuse me if I don't bow," I said, bunching the sheets around my waist. A simple giddiness at being alive overlay everything. The knowledge that this was House Leratom woke some confusion, but it drifted away. I was sure I'd find out everything soon.

Misora's cheeks colored, and she looked away. Shom, her own skin laced with nearly as many scars as mine, just snorted.

"If it was bad enough to make you flippant, then I'll let the formality slide, just this once," Shom said, dumping the folded clothes beside me on the bed.

I pulled the top on over my scars. I had noticed new ones on my side, where the claw slashes had been. *Kate doesn't care about scars. She wants me as her* dacha, *no matter what I look like.* The thought gave me a truer comfort than the aftereffects of the healing.

"He's presentable again," Shom said. Misora stopped pretending to study the plasterwork.

"Shom, is Katherine well?" I asked, using the longer form of Kate's name for the sake of Misora's sensibilities. "She must have been distressed."

Terrified, I'd bet. Hunters had appeared on Earth and attacked me, a nightmare she'd already lived through herself.

Shom and Misora traded a look that sent worry scraping through me, recent healing or no.

The healer set aside the serving cover and handed me a bowl of buttered porridge. "Kjelgaard left in good health, reassured that she had gotten you away safe but distressed over the ordeal. Birasef Temarel felt the same, I believe."

Kate got me away from the kith? And Birasef *was here?* I stared up at him, the bowl almost forgotten in my hands.

"Eat that," he said, his voice firm. "Slowly. It's been a while since you've had food."

I took a spoonful of the bland stuff, which predictably tasted like the best thing I had ever eaten. Before I turned fully into a ravenous *morsai*, I asked, "What happened?"

"You were taken by Hiraches, correct?" Shom waited for my acknowledgement, then continued. "Here is the briefest possible version as I know it. Katherine returned to the garrison and asked Pella to bring the matter before the Shevern council. She thought the Scholars were responsible. They denied it and told her that the Akevad kith of Hiraches held you. Pella went to the Hirach council, who promised to find you and return you, if you still lived."

She had gotten you away safe, the healer said. I swallowed another spoonful of porridge. "They allowed Katherine to go with them?"

"No." Shom glared at me. We three had known each other long enough that I could tell I was merely a proxy. Kate wasn't here to glare at in person, so she gave it to me. "She befriended a Drammon at the garrison and put a group together to hunt for them herself."

I had a good imagination. My former *denet* had said it came from spending so much time offworld so young. But the picture of Kate leading a contingent of peacekeepers into the wildlands still surprised me.

I frowned. We weren't in the healer's rooms at the garrison. Shom had said *Tol* Pella had made an arrangement with the Hirach council, and the arrangement hadn't been for a troop of

Aubello's peacekeepers and a human to hunt down the offending kith. The Hiraches had intended to handle their own Trucebreakers.

"But my *dacha* found me first," I said, trying to put everything together in spite of the healing effects muddling my mind.

Shom's explanation put a different slant on the matter. She wasn't here as a friend—or not just as a friend. She was here as a niece, unofficial spokeswoman of her *tol*. And Birasef…Why had Birasef been here? I was at a loss. Maybe he had a *nochel* among the Leratoms at present and had just happened to stop by.

"What was Birasef doing?" I asked.

Shom raised her black brows in overdone surprise. "I got the distinct impression that Birasef was part of Katherine's mark."

For a moment, I thought Shom misunderstood the word. We were speaking in the common tongue, not in Thurei, and a mark was a distinctly Thurei concept. A mark meant kin, close by the bonds of affection in addition to the bonds of blood, the dear friends who remained that way from childhood throughout one's life. Members of a mark would have their blades in hand any time one of their number needed defending. It was a House term because who could fill that role outside a House, outside of kin? A mark was the true *all for one, one for all*.

Birasef had a mark of his own. I'd never had one—*denet*'s heir and then House rebel, neither role had lent itself to camaraderie with my kin. The closest I'd ever come was with Kate and Shom. Kate couldn't have one, either, not even a human version, after her parents had abandoned her far from home.

Shom knew all that.

"Katherine doesn't have a mark," I said, setting aside the empty bowl and trying to imagine Birasef throwing in with this bold and risky scheme.

At best, I could believe him sympathetic.

Misora spoke up. "I would say he's been taking kin duty, if it doesn't offend you."

"No offense taken," I assured her, too close to the healing and in too puzzling a situation to take issue with it. Birasef had meddled once or twice when Kate had first returned to Kuyen, but that was a world away from offering kin duty, and we weren't kin anymore. I'd just have to ask Kate about it when I spoke to her next.

The false calm of the healing had retreated far enough to leave me restless. "Perhaps I can have a moment to finish dressing?"

"Of course," Misora said. After all, I was a guest in her House.

I thought Shom would protest—she'd come here to say something and clearly would rather have it out, but in the end, she went, too.

The healer tarried, closing the door behind them.

"Coraven, I'm Ferno. Pleased to meet you while you're awake." He came to sit on the chair beside the bed.

"My thanks, Ferno." I remained seated. Though there was no point in being shy before a healer, especially one who'd already used his skill on my behalf, I waited for him to say what he needed to say.

"You were in bad shape when they brought you in. Trauma to your head, dehydration, infected wounds, fever, herbal soporifics and paralytic poison." Ferno fixed his large, hazel eyes on mine. "You are nearly recovered."

"I know I won't fully recuperate until I sleep," I said. I could already feel the weight of fatigue pressing on me. I gave him a wry smile. "I'm no stranger to healing from grave wounds."

Ferno folded his hands together. "I'm not sure that you will ever recover completely. It's slight, but whatever remains of the damage, I could not aid you in repairing it."

"What kind of damage?" I asked, though surely he would have said, if he'd known. I felt whole and well, if tired, with none of the dizziness, nausea, or blurred vision I'd experienced as aftereffects of the *yusmeir* poison.

"I'm not certain," Ferno admitted. "But the Leratom's previous healer, Nalya, spoke of something similar that has been affecting Hunters. I have heard it called 'the fade.' Fever, aches, weakness, coughing. It presents as a physical illness but ultimately, it seems to affect the use of *jeira* and eventually leads to death."

"Some of the Hiraches in the kith had a sickness like that," I said. Growing unease banished the last shreds of the healing calm. "How did Healer Nalya learn of it?"

"She treated a Drammon with those symptoms. In return, that Hunter led Katherine to you. As in your case, Nalya healed the woman of much, but there was an aspect to it that she could not reach with her skill. Neither of us has seen its like before."

Ferno had said that the impairment remaining within me was minor. He'd taken care of the rest of it. I held out a hand, away from the healer, and called my *zaret*. It came easily, its slight weight a familiar comfort in my grasp. The lamplight flashed off the transparent blade as I tilted it from side to side before releasing it again.

"I doubt you'll notice any effect," Healer Ferno hastened to say. "It's barely detectable. But I'd like to see you in, say, five days, just in case. Sooner, if you feel at all unwell."

"Perhaps I can follow up with the garrison's healers," I said.

"Ah." Ferno rose. "I believe Shom still wishes to speak with you. I'll excuse myself and allow you to dress."

After Ferno had left, I dressed quickly, the tranquility with which I'd woken well and truly dispelled.

Shom waited in the atrium, sprawled comfortably on one of the simple wooden chairs. "The *denet*-heir had to get back to her party, but she gave me directions to your guest room."

"Please do correct me if I'm wrong," I said, keeping my voice polite, "but I believe I have a room at the peacekeeper garrison, only a carriage ride away."

"Maybe I don't want to roll you out of the carriage when you swoon." Sighing, she stood and gestured for me to follow her out into the hallway. "Pella's upset. Leratom has agreed to let you rest here for a day or two. *Denet* Leratom, by the way, not just the heir. Give my aunt some time to find out what happened and think it over. She'll want to talk to Kate tomorrow, I'm sure."

"How bad is it?" I asked, trying to ignore the awkwardness of navigating a strange House in borrowed pajamas, parquet wooden floors cool under my bare feet.

"I don't know." Shom lifted her broad palms in a gesture of uncertainty. "Even if they managed to walk in and walk out without drawing blood, Kate broke an agreement made between Aubello's peacekeeper commander and the council of Hiraches, under the Truce. If she didn't break the Truce herself, she at minimum flouted it at the expense of someone who was trying to help her."

"But the Scholars are using Hiraches to attack us. That shifts the scope the conflict, doesn't it?" I'd studied Hunters and how to fight them, not the finer points of Truce law. "It makes the Hiraches weapons of a separate aggressor."

"It won't be an easy walk proving any of that." Shom looked at me sidelong. "In the meantime, Kate's running around as fickle as a child and a thousand times more dangerous."

"It wasn't a child's undertaking, to rescue one in her care from Hunters," I said, my voice sharp. Kate had taken her role as my *dacha* seriously, more seriously than I could have foreseen as a headstrong stripling myself. When I'd sworn my vow, I'd been focused on Thurei custom that gave her, as my *dacha*, the first call upon my service. At the time, she'd needed my protection whether she'd acknowledged me or not. But my oath also made her responsible for my life. I'd never imagined a time that Kate would be called upon to preserve it. So far as I understood events, she hadn't hesitated when the duty had presented itself.

"She was courageous and resourceful to have searched for me herself instead of waiting on others." I flicked my fingers in denial. "It's not fickle or childish to have done her best to see me safe and well. She's my *dacha*."

And wants me to be hers. It wasn't just the recent healing, or even my freedom, that gilded the edges of everything.

Thurei customs of duty might have mattered to a Thurei council, but I had no idea how they'd weigh before Hunters.

I added, "Kate doesn't know anything about the Truce. That doesn't make her decisions childish."

"She knows enough," Shom said darkly.

By which I surmised that Shom had told her what Shom had thought she'd needed to know.

We stopped finally, and Shom gestured at one of the doors in the long hallway. I opened it and asked, "Will you stay and talk, or do you have to return right away?"

The guest room matched Leratom's original offer: too fine for a guest but inappropriate for a son—because I wasn't a son of this House. It looked like a chamber for new *helons*, meant to welcome the spouse of an alliance marriage who would make the space their own for however long the marriage lasted.

While I tried to read entirely too much into the room, Shom simply found a chair with deep cushions and dropped into it. After a moment, I followed her. It was not as if I were going to protest the room and have them move me to another, for such a short stay.

"Kate will tell us all about it tomorrow," I said, drowsy already as I leaned back into the soft cushions. "Perhaps I can get a story out of Birasef as well."

She raised a brow at me. "He calls you by your close-name."

"If he does, that's new. He didn't when we were cousins." That wasn't precisely true. Birasef never took anything seriously, but I could say with confidence that he had never used my close-name in the spirit that such address was intended. At least not once we'd passed ten or so. Perhaps my sister Damen had sent him over to… My mind was too tired to supply what Birasef might be useful for in a crisis. To keep Damen informed? He could gossip, I knew that.

"I think Misora had it right. He stood as your kin to one you're indebted to. I imagine he helped with whatever Leratom arranged up here." Shom waved a hand at the room, then gave me a searching look. "You look like you're sliding off the far side of the healing cloud as we speak. Get some sleep. And, if you don't mind me saying, take a bath first."

I ran a hand through my hair. It crackled with what might have been dried blood, but at least the lacerations on my scalp were gone. "I can hardly mind when you make a good point."

"You'd be surprised at how often people do anyway." She rolled her eyes and levered herself up out of the chair. When I started to climb to my feet as well, she waved me back down. "No, don't. Take care of yourself. I'll see you tomorrow."

I sat there for a while after she'd left, trying to sort through all the pieces, but eventually, I gave up. I'd have to find out tomorrow.

CHAPTER THIRTY

COR

I let myself into Ferno's atrium a little before dawn, careful to move quietly, though all the interior doors were closed. I didn't wish to disturb the healer's slumber. The guest room's wardrobe had provided a set of formal clothes in the style Leratom favored. The loose, black trousers and lightweight tunic in pale blue fit tolerably well for something readymade and I fancied Kate would like the color on me.

I willed the lamps two ranks brighter, though my eyes didn't need the light. I studied the effects on the spare, white room, then adjusted them one step dimmer.

Humans found candlelight romantic, I recalled. Candles weren't overbright.

Kate appeared mere moments after dawn broke, as insubstantial as a dream in her flowery dress, as real as a promise a heartbeat later when she stood solidly on Kuyen. She broke into a smile so full of joy that my own lips answered it. The healing euphoria came in a far second to the best I'd felt since I'd woken up here.

"Coran!" A couple of quick strides brought her to me, and she flung her arms around my neck as I picked her up and swung her around in a circle, her dress fluttering around her knees.

"Shh, the House is sleeping," I murmured in her ear. My *dacha* wore her dark brown hair up in a simple twist, held in place by the hair comb I'd given her. I fought the temptation to pull the comb out and send her hair spilling across her shoulders. I didn't need to start heading in that direction in the middle of the healer's atrium.

"Oh, it wouldn't do to wake up the House," Kate whispered back, her voice teasing. She pressed her face against the curve of my neck and hugged me as tightly as she could. "Don't go missing again."

"I'll do my best," I promised, rubbing her back. "The *denet* gave us a guest room. Would you like to see it?"

She tilted her face up toward mine, smiling, though I saw tears in her eyes. "Save me from Thurei guest rooms, please. Besides, I need to speak with *Denet* Leratom first."

"If she's awake," I said, hiding a pang of disappointment. I'd been hoping to sneak in some private time with my *dacha* first, before all the questions I'd discussed with Shom last night insisted on taking precedence, but I was no stranger to bowing to duty.

"What's that face for?" Kate traced the line of my lips with a fingertip. The sensation etched itself into my memory. "On Earth, a wedding is considered a happy occasion."

I remembered not to shout and wake Healer Ferno, but I did pick Kate up and spin her around again.

It seemed Kate had made arrangements because the *denet* was ready for us, serene as if her days normally began with a formal hearing in her receiving rooms at dawn. I gave Leratom a deep bow, acknowledging a debt I couldn't repay—for myself and for my *dacha*, to find the two of us sheltered here—with a little flourish of irony at being outmaneuvered. I'd taken pains to stay out of her debt at our last meeting, yet here we were.

Denet Leratom offered a slight bow in return, gold pins winking amidst her intricate, pink braids. "Coraven, Katherine Kjelgaard."

Kate inclined her head in acknowledgement and perhaps it was my own bias, but it looked less as if Kate were unpracticed at bowing and more as if she and the *denet* were equals.

"*Denet* Leratom," Kate began, raising her chin slightly, "I wish to inform the House—all the Houses—of my vow to Coraven."

"The House hears," Leratom said, speaking for her kin. She departed from tradition, as Kate had, to add, "And what House Leratom hears, all Houses will hear."

Years ago, I'd rattled off the words of my vow as fast as I could, over orders to stop from my own *denet*, both of us intent on seeing our own will win out.

Kate turned to me and reached for my hands. She clasped them in hers and made no comment about my palms sweating. *This must be a human thing*, I thought, utterly transfixed by her gentle touch. *She ought to face the* denet.

That part didn't matter. What really mattered was the words. In Thurei.

Her warm, brown eyes held my gaze, as if she could read the history written on my heart, as she began to speak my language.

"Under the eyes of *Denet* Leratom, I pledge myself to Coraven." Her Thurei bore a heavy accent and the words ran in an unfamiliar cadence more reminiscent of English. "I walk in his steps through times of darkness and through light. Everything of mine and all that comes after is his, all that I am now and everything I will grow to become. He holds my love, my honor, and my loyalty above any other."

She leaned forward and went up on her toes to brush her lips against mine. My cheeks flamed with embarrassment at once, and I thought I caught Leratom looking away out of the corner of my eye, but I was rooted in place. Kate could have run me through with a blade and I wouldn't have moved.

Switching to the common tongue, Kate turned to *Denet* Leratom and said, "The kiss is a human tradition. I didn't mean to cause offense."

I took a breath—it felt like the first one in ages—and squeezed Kate's hand.

Leratom flicked her fingers in dismissal. "Not at all. It was my honor to bear witness. Now, I believe we all have business to attend to... Although, don't forget your message."

The *denet* pointed and Kate and I both looked at the floor. A Summons sat next to Kate's dainty sandals with bright yellow straps. I hadn't noticed either the Summons or the shoes. Kate scooped up the letter and we made quick, if proper, goodbyes to the *denet* and let ourselves out into the hallway.

Dachas. Both of us.

Kate pressed cool fingers against my cheek. "I embarrassed you with that kiss. Sorry. It really is a human custom. Sealed with a kiss, you know."

Her own cheeks were tinged charmingly with more than a little pink, her dark eyes so bright, they nearly sparkled.

Having spent an evening with Kate's friends, I could believe that kissing in public might have been a formal custom among humans.

I took her face in my hands and kissed her until I ran out of breath. She pulled back just enough to shake her head at me, leaning back against the wall outside the *denet*'s formal chambers and trying to catch her own breath.

"Coran, I'm a bad influence on you," she claimed, though she kept tracing the line of my jaw with her thumb.

"I'm honored," I said, then I switched to Thurei. "Lead me in your footsteps, *dacha*."

"Oh." Kate cleared her throat. In quiet Kuyene, she said, "That's the walking part, right? I didn't actually learn to speak Thurei. I just memorized the vow, really."

"I'm still impressed. Did one of the Leratoms teach it to you?"

She shook her head. "Bir sent me the words. I practiced until I knew them by heart."

Kate knew the vow in English. Whether she knew Thurei fluently or not made no difference—she'd known what she'd been promising.

"Well, I'll have to thank him the next time I see him." For more than just that, according to everyone, I supposed. "And my enduring thanks to you, *dacha*, for your vow."

I swept a bow, deep and formal, both sincere and symbolic—a Thurei offering, just as she had given me her vow with a kiss, according to the human custom. As I straightened up, she smiled as warmly as sunlight and held out her hand to me. The other one still held the Summons.

I'd already managed to forget about the Summons. Unsurprising. I felt I might forget the ground itself and simply float along by her side.

Instead, I took her hand and led her down the hallway to our suite. "We should see what that letter says."

"I doubt it's *congrats on your wedding*." She said the last phrase in English, unfolding it as we walked. "It's from Pella. She wants to hear how things went yesterday."

"How *did* things go?" I asked, at the limits of my own curiosity.

"Greta and Erzi helped Bir and me track down the kith and it turned out we were right ahead of the Hirach council. We found you during all the distraction."

"Wait, just the four of you?" I tried to keep the spike of alarm out of my voice.

There had been no group of peacekeepers along on the mission.

It took me a moment to place the name Greta, but then I remembered the practical Drammon from among the many new students and colleagues I'd met at the garrison. I didn't recognize the name Erzi at all.

And Birasef, of all people. Had he mocked the Hunters into submission?

"No, it was just Bir and me." She glanced at me as if to gauge my reaction. "Greta had promised to help me find you, that's it. They left when we located the kith."

"You and Birasef." My mental image revised itself again, my imagination sorely taxed. "What happened, exactly?"

Kate narrowed her eyes at me. "What's wrong with 'Bir'?"

"Bir, then, my mistake." I flicked my fingers in dismissal. My former cousin wasn't the issue at present. "Please?"

"The kith was hiding among a bunch of boulders and things on a slope. *Bir* and I"—she leaned on the short form of his name a little—"walked down and I got rid of the rocks around us so they couldn't set up an ambush. The Hirach council showed up and started fighting with the Tharkesh's Hiraches. One Hirach—Serkot, I think—pointed out where you were. She said it was for the Mokklas. Then we came back here."

Kate shrugged, human-style, as if it had been as easy as that.

I tried not to think of how it could have gone, striding boldly in among the desperate Hiraches I'd seen. "Your bravery terrifies me, *dacha.*"

We'd made it back to the room, pausing out in the hall until she'd finished her story. I held the door open and as soon as we'd both made it inside, I gathered her against me and held her close. I couldn't keep all danger away from her, no matter how much I wanted to—and she'd proved she could handle danger herself—but I *could* wrap my arms around her and soothe my heart for a moment.

She was no longer the Kate I'd protected for years, ignorant of Kuyen's dangers and unable to defend herself. She was dangerous now in her own right and rectifying her ignorance as fast as she could. Above all, I owed my *dacha* for that help, not some former cousin or chance-met stranger.

"Hardly brave." She shook her head, dropping her gaze to her feet. "The whole time, I was afraid I'd be too late to save you. I almost was. You were... It looked bad when we found you."

"Ah." I indulged my wish and pulled out the hair comb, freeing her dark tresses to uncoil over her shoulders. "They tied my hands together so I couldn't use my *zaret* and dosed me with a sleeping draught so I couldn't worldwalk. I mostly slept through it."

The less said about it, the better. I brushed the hair back from her temple and pressed a kiss there. "Thank you for not giving up."

"Don't disappear again, please, and thank you," she murmured into my shoulder.

"I'll do my best."

"*Dacha*," Kate said, tipping her head back to look at me. The look in her brown eyes was soft and as warm as velvet. "Should we read the letter first?"

"The letter can wait," I said, having grown impatient with waiting myself. "At least for a little while. Let me show you our rooms, *dacha*."

We had found each other in more ways than one and for now, the rest of the world could wait. We explored the newlywed suite and found it to our liking.

Perfect for a pair of new *dachas*.

GLOSSARY

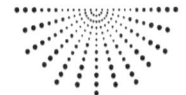

Akevad kith: the group of Hiraches for which Tharkesh served as Finder.

Anchor/slip anchor: a memorable landmark used as a destination when traveling between worlds, especially a public location specifically designed to be easily visualized for such a purpose.

Aubello: a city on Kuyen, home to and claimed by a heterogenous mix of Kuyen's peoples, led by a body of selectors.

Betts: an apothecary, not native to Earth or Kuyen.
Birasef Temarel: a member of House Temarel.

Bolgen: a solitary Lesser Hunter, not native to Kuyen.
Claimed land: land that has been settled by the combination of *jeira*, focus, and occupancy, typically by a group of people, and is no longer subject to the unpredictable changes of wildlands so long as the claim continues.

Coalition: an interdependent network of Lan te Kos social, economic, and familial groups, ruled by a consensus among the *tols* responsible for each group.

Dacha: by Thurei custom, a permanent spouse. One member of the couple severs ties with their natal House and joins their partner's House. As a protection and recompense for the "orphaned" spouse, needs of the *dacha* take precedence above other responsibilities.

Damoret Temarel: *denet*-heir of House Temarel, Cor's sister.
Day/night world: refers to the local time that a world is open for travel by worldwalkers.

Denet: head of a Thurei House; upon assuming leadership, they take the name of the House in place of their personal name.

Drammon: a Lesser Hunter native to Kuyen. They are solitary predators and use their unique species skill to send a debilitating pulse of energy into their prey at a touch, often from ambush.

Eld gar Tharsel: a member of the dav Ferrum coalition, serving as an instructor for Pella tol dav Ferrum's peacekeepers.

Erzi: a Drammon solitaire, Greta's sister.

Grathki: a member of the Akevad kith of Hiraches.

Greta: a Drammon serving as a peacekeeper under Pella tol dav Ferrum.

Havro: a Lewrit serving as the healer for House Temarel.

Helon: by Thurei custom, the spouse of a marriage arranged for political alliance. The marriage is understood to be temporary, with the duration negotiated between both parties. Upon completion, the "visiting" spouse returns to their natal House.

Hirach: a Greater Hunter native to Kuyen. They hunt in packs and live in social groups called kiths. Their unique species skill is to infect even slight wounds they inflict with corruption, weakening and slowing their prey.

House: an extended kin group of Thureis, led by a *denet* who takes the name of the House; also, the building in which most House members live.

Human: a people native to Earth, a night world. They are almost exclusively without *jeira* and blind to non-native worldwalkers.

Hunters: a sapient predatory species that currently chooses or historically chose prey capable of using *jeira*. Many worlds use the terms "Greater" or "Lesser" Hunters based on the perceived threat level.

Inner/Outer House: Thurei terms for relative closeness to the *denet* and influence within the House; also, can refer literally to where an individual Thurei lives.

Issai: a Shevern solitaire, formerly a Scholar, banned from Scholars Hall.

Jeira: the energy present within an individual that, with focus and training, can be used to worldwalk, use a unique species skill, or create and activate general skillwork items and effects.

Kith: a social or kin group of Hiraches.

Kuyen: one of many worlds accessible to worldwalkers. Cor's native world.

Lan te Kos: a people native to Kuyen. Their unique species' skill is immunity to the *jeira*-based skills of other species.

Leratom: a Thurei House based in the city of Aubello; also, the *denet* of that House.

Lewrit: a people native to Kuyen. Their unique species' skill is the ability to accelerate their own physical healing. Especially strong healers can boost the healing of others and offer their services to other species.

Mark: a unit of Kuyene currency; in Thurei, a close-knit group of cousins of similar age within a House.

Misora Leratom: the *denet*-heir of House Leratom.

Morsai: an animal native to Kuyen, domesticated and used for riding and draft purposes; has a dog-like build and is roughly the size of a horse, in Earth terms.

Nabel Leratom: a member of House Leratom.

Nalya: a Lewrit serving as the healer for House Leratom.

Netari Temarel: a member of House Temarel, daughter of the *denet*, Cor's younger sister.

Nochel: by Thurei custom, a casual romantic partner with whom one shares no permanent or legal ties.

Osembri: a Hunter, of a species not native to Kuyen.

Pareshol: a Thurei House allied with House Temarel; also, the *denet* of that House.

Pella tol dav Ferrum: commander of Aubello's peacekeepers and a *tol* of the dav Ferrum coalition of Lan te Kos; Shom's aunt.

Rose: a human, Kate's friend and co-worker at After Image.

Scholar: a member of the Shevern elite. Most serve at the Scholars Hall on Kuyen, where members of the public can ask questions in return for payment, usually in goods or services.

Seretun Temarel: armsmaster of House Temarel.

Serkot: a member of the Akevad kith of Hiraches.

Shevern: a people native to Kuyen. Their unique species' skill is perfect memory, which is passed on to their heirs.

Shom dav Ferrum: a member of the dav Ferrum coalition of Lan te Kos, employed as an inventor of skillwork, and childhood friend of Kate and Cor.

Solitaire: a person living outside of communally claimed land.

Summons: a letter that delivers itself using folded paper skillwork, the name of the recipient, and the *jeira* of the sender.

Temarel: the natal Thurei House of Coraven; also, the *denet* of that House.

Tharkesh os Chigaf: a Hirach, former Finder of the Akevad kith, responsible for selecting prey.

Thurei: a people native to Kuyen, with the unique species skill to materialize a transparent, sword-like blade.

Tirona: a wooden practice sword or staff.

Token: a skillwork item that guides a worldwalker to a specific person or location, with no previous knowledge required.

Tol: leader of a unit within a Lan te Kos coalition.

Vercho: a member of the Akevad kith of Hiraches.

Viseni: a Lesser Hunter native to Kuyen. They hunt in packs and save bones as trophies from their kills.

Wildlands: unclaimed territory on a world with *jeira*. These lands are subject to unpredictable shifts and changes in topography.

Worldwalker: a denizen from one of many worlds who has *jeira* and is capable of using it to travel across the gap between their world and others, so long as the gap is open. Worldwalkers must return to their native world before the gap closes. Each species with *jeira* has a unique skill that some Scholars theorize developed as protective mechanisms against predation by Hunters.

Ziddesh: a people native to Kuyen with the unique species skill that allows them to change the color of their scales.

www.ingramcontent.com/pod-product-compliance
Lightning Source LLC
LaVergne TN
LVHW091716070526
838199LV00050B/2420